ABLE TEAM

CALIFORNIA

Gadgets Schwarz found the second at the top of the stairs, sprawled facedown amid the litter of spent shells and broken glass. Although he thought he saw a sign of life, he quickly realized it was only a trick of light.

But the third one was still alive—huddled in a corner, clutching a sucking wound and gazing up at the gently swaying lanterns suspended from the peaked roofs. As Gadgets drew closer, the gaze fell to meet him . . . the frightened and imploring gaze of a twelve-year-old boy.

"Oh, my God," Gadgets whispered. "He's just a kid!"

He sank to a knee and gently lifted the boy's hand away in order to examine the wound. The boy responded with a shallow sigh, and a bubble of blood formed at his lips.

"Look, kid, you're going to be all right," Gadgets told him. "You just hang on." Then, looking over his shoulder, he yelled, "Ambulance! Somebody call an ambulance."

But all that the Able Team commando heard in response was a footstep and another cocking bolt.

Even as Gadgets Schwarz reached for his weapon he knew that he was too late, that behind him stood a fourth Desmondo, already squeezing a trigger.

ABLE TEAM

DICK STIVERS

MEAN STREETS

A GOLD EAGLE BOOK FROM
WORLDWIDE®

TORONTO • NEW YORK • LONDON • PARIS
AMSTERDAM • STOCKHOLM • HAMBURG
ATHENS • MILAN • TOKYO • SYDNEY

First edition September 1989

ISBN 0-373-65401-4

Special thanks and acknowledgment to
Ken Rose for his contribution to this work.

1

The girl's eyes flicked nervously as she spoke. Now and then she turned her head toward the open end of the alley. The fading light of dusk cast a blue-gray pallor over the barrio street that lay beyond.

"You don't understand," she pleaded in an urgent whisper. "I'm not talking about something different. I'm talking about something you've never even seen before."

Gabby Salinas leaned against the tenement wall, and reached into his shirt pocket for a cigarette. Then he remembered—he had quit smoking a week ago. He looked away from the girl, and out of the corner of his eye he caught a glimpse of a shadow snaking across the open mouth of the alley.

The girl sensed the tension in his muscles. Out of instinct more than anything else, she grabbed the front of his shirt and repeated her plea.

"You don't understand. These guys aren't just another gang. They got things like you wouldn't even believe. They even got stuff you guys don't have."

Her voice grew taut, cracked, as Salinas kept watch on the end of the alley. A cop's instinct told him something was going down, but there was nothing in sight. He clenched his teeth to face the girl again.

"Look," he said, trying to muster the calmest voice he could, "I do understand. I understand that these guys whacked your brother and I understand that you're scared. But there's nothing I can do without real evidence. And that's what *you've* got to understand. I've got to have evidence."

"Hey, you want evidence, man, I'll show you evidence. You come down to the morgue and take a look at Manuel. Then you'll see your evidence. I mean I could hardly even recognize him. That's how bad they cut him up. And for what? Because he wouldn't blow away some old man? Because he wanted out? Because he wanted to get off the streets? Forget what you know about the gangs, man. These guys are something else."

Salinas tried to comfort her by placing his hand over hers, but it didn't work. She just couldn't seem to stop shaking.

"All right, I'll tell you what I'll do," he finally said. "You come down to the station with me, and I'll have you look at some mug shots. You recognize any of the guys that killed your brother, I'll have them brought in for questioning. Now, how's that?"

She shut her eyes, then slowly shook her head.

"Listen to me, man. Forget about your mug shots. Forget about asking questions. These guys mean business. They've got machine guns. They've got grenades. Shit, they've even got rockets. You ready for that? Rockets?"

She glanced up again, and saw the cop's eyes flit toward the street. Then she froze, knowing without needing to look. The whole thing was coming down right now, right here.

Salinas squinted to get a better view of the three figures standing in the dim opening. But it was too dark. They had no features...only shape. He glanced inside his car and calculated the time it would take him to reach it, grab his shotgun, cock and fire. He was also conscious of the little things: the stench of garbage from an open Dumpster, the equally pungent stench of cheap cologne, the girl's slender body trembling in his arms, the soft tread of footsteps from the black alley.

Then at last, so faint that he hardly recognized it, a tiny red light fluttered on her cheek...the spotting beam of an electronic star scope.

Salinas shoved the girl to the pavement as the first shot slammed into the brick behind them. He caught another glimpse of the spotting beam on her shoulder and literally dragged her to the gutter. Finally, as the spotting dot settled on his own shoulder, he dived into the front seat of his Chevy. A third shot shattered the windshield, sending an explosion of glass flying into the air, and he didn't bother with the shotgun. He had the engine on and the car in reverse even before he had closed the door. In fact, it wouldn't close. She was hanging on to it, imploring him in Spanish to slow down long enough to allow her to get in.

"Hang on!" he shouted as he tromped down on the accelerator.

In his rearview mirror, he saw the three figures disappear behind the edges of the buildings. In a second, he blasted past them into the street. He didn't notice where the girl fell off. She would just have to take her chances for now.

Once in the street, he shoved the car into drive and floored it. Smoke and the smell of burning rubber filled the air. He was halfway down the street before he looked in the mirror.

And then he saw it.

A flash of light that was so bright he had to shield his eyes.

What the hell . . . he wondered.

Hell for Gabby Salinas was a Chinese-made Silk-worm missile, snaking through the barrio dusk, locked onto the heat from the engine of his beat-up Chevy. The Desmodo warrior who had released it stood up slowly and removed the launcher from his shoulder. He had a thin, smug grin on his lips. He made a point of not turning his head to see the admiring smiles of his companions.

The girl was hypnotized by her terror as she watched the rocket rip through the dusk. Impact was just a second or two later. The fireball of the explosion rose forty or fifty feet into the air, high above the sur-rounding tenements. White-hot scraps of the debris that had been Gabby Salinas and his unmarked pa-trol car sprayed out in every direction for hundreds of yards. There would not be a body to identify.

IT WAS AS IF EVERYTHING were moving in slow mo-tion: the settling debris, the rising smoke, the phan-tom forms of the three Desmodos approaching from the alley. There was something odd about the light, a lunar light that seemed to have washed the shadows away. Then, although she knew she had to run, she finally just let them take her.

They dragged her to a warehouse adjacent to the alley, a cavernous building littered with vegetable stalks, splintered packing crates and rat pellets. Although the light was bad and her vision still suffered from the missile flash, she was able to see her abductors clearly. The youngest could not have been more than twelve or thirteen. The oldest looked about twenty. The third was about sixteen, but his dead gaze and pinched features suggested a wizened dwarf that might have been at least a thousand years old.

The youngest approached first, moving cautiously out of the shadows with a deceptively innocent grin. Next came the oldest, dangling a Coke bottle and what looked like a hatchet. Finally the Dwarf stepped forward, nudging the girl's hip with the toe of his boot before asking the youngest, "Hey, little brother, you want her or what?"

They stripped her in stages, pressing her shoulders to the concrete, then yanking off her blue jeans and tearing her blouse away. Although initially the youngest seemed uneasy, he was actually the first to touch her, extending a hand to her breast and sliding a finger along her belly.

"Go on, man, take her," the Dwarf whispered. "You want her? Take her." Then casually slapping her flanks, "Go on, little brother. Let's see you do it."

She began to cry when the Dwarf kicked her thighs apart, and encouraged the boy to kneel between her legs. She winced as the Dwarf began to pull on her nipple, softly murmuring, "Hey, look at that, man. She wants it. She really wants it."

She shut her eyes and whispered a prayer as the boy dropped his weight on her. *Hail Mary, Mother of God. HailMaryMotherofGod.*

They rolled her on her belly as the oldest approached, and she felt what she thought was the hatchet blade gently tracing the curve of her spine. They pried her legs apart again, and she felt what must have been the Coke bottle gently nudging her. Then screaming with pain, she imagined herself splitting like cheap vinyl as they plunged the thing inside her.

They regarded her coolly for a moment, while she continued to shiver on the floor. Now and again the Dwarf would lift a few strands of her hair or touch her breasts, but for the most part they simply watched.

"So, bitch, you think we're bad?" The Dwarf smiled. "Because if you think we're bad, wait till you meet Falco."

The oldest suddenly squatted on her hips, the youngest held her shoulders as the Dwarf pressed her left hand flat against the concrete. She heard one of them mumble something, and then a sharp reply from the Dwarf, "Hey, brother, no one says you got to look." She caught a glimpse of the rising hatchet, and suddenly realized that they were going to take a finger; they were going to cut off her finger....

But although the pain seemed mainly concentrated in her thumb, they had actually taken the whole hand.

WHEN RESIDENTS of the neighborhood eventually found the girl, huddled on her side with the ends of a makeshift tourniquet clenched in her teeth, they were naturally surprised to find that she was still alive. Señora Romero even went so far as to call it a miracle, a sure sign from heaven that God would soon send them a savior. Of course, Señora Romero had been talking about saviors ever since the appearance of the Desmodos. The only savior they had seen thus far was death . . . a quick and painless death like the death of Gabby Salinas. Yet having found the girl alive, Señora Romero was now entirely convinced that someone or something would soon come from heaven to rid the east-side neighborhood of this plague from the depths of hell.

"I can feel it," she told her neighbors that night. "I can feel our savior coming. Very soon he will be here, and then you'll know that I was right."

"And what is this savior going to look like?" asked Señor Perez. "Huh, old lady? How are we to recognize this savior when he comes?"

"Well," she said, "he might not just be one person. He might be three. And for another thing, you won't have to recognize them. All you'll have to do is stand aside and let them work their magic."

"And what kind of magic can they possibly possess to stop the Desmodos? What kind of magic can any man possess that will possibly allow him to stop the Desmodos?"

"Very powerful magic," she said. "Very, very powerful."

Although they had all laughed at her, told her that she was just a crazy old woman with crazier ideas, eventually there came a point when they also began to pray for a savior . . . or saviors.

2

The Los Angeles Police Department spent about twenty-five hours collecting and examining the pieces of Officer Salinas and his Chevy. The results of the investigation were summarily passed on to the Homicide Division before finally reaching Captain Hector Florio's Urban Counterterrorist Unit. Then there were another five or six hours of meetings, at which Florio finally had to pass around photographs of the girl's hand in order to make his point. And even then he was told he would have to consult a certain Dr. Gerald North before he could send a team into the streets.

It was about half past noon on a Tuesday when Florio reached the UCLA campus and Dr. North's office. A bleak and rather foreboding structure, the Psychiatric Services Department stood at the far east end of the campus, presumably so that patients could enter and exit the facility without disturbing the so-called adjusted students. The security arrangements did not actually begin until one passed the foyer, and even then it seemed that the concern was not so much to keep people out but to keep them in.

In accordance with his surroundings, North was a large man—at least six feet, with the body of a lineman gone to seed. For that vaguely distracted academic look, however, he wore a full beard and kept his hair habitually shaggy. His office was also a mess, with all sorts of odd relics on the shelves: shards of Roman pottery, the fangs of a saber-toothed tiger, photographs of himself with various presidents of the United States, a couple of human skulls. There were also a number of framed citations, including one from the LAPD recognizing his work as a consultant in the area of criminal behavior and what was now fashionably called the "psychology of urban existence."

North was seated at his desk when Florio entered. Apart from a brief nod, however, the doctor barely acknowledged the captain's presence. Then finally laying aside a stack of papers, he leaned back in his chair and smirked.

"I suppose you're here to grill me about that Salinas business," he said.

Florio responded with a weary shrug. "Ever seen a Silkworm in action, Doctor? Thing will blow a goddamn tank apart."

"I'm afraid my expertise is limited to the brain behind the weapon, Captain."

"Fine, then let's talk about brains. Let's talk about what happened to Salinas's brain when that missile hit the back of his Chevy. And while we're at it, let's talk about the girl. I'm sure she had some interesting psychological insights as she watched those animals cut off her hand."

"Tell me something, Captain. Was Officer Salinas a friend of yours?"

"What's that got to do with anything?"

"Panic factor. We're discussing the death of one man. You've asked me to support your proposal for a tactical assault on the entire east side. I call that a panic response, and to be honest, it concerns me."

Florio shut his eyes in order to control his simmering rage. "I'm going to make this real simple, Doctor. The Desmodos aren't just a bunch of socially deprived kids. They're killers—plain and simple. Now, we can sit around and talk about how they never got enough love as little babies, or we can do something to stop them."

"And what exactly do you propose we do, Captain?"

"You know damn well what I'm proposing. I want a team on the streets, a team that isn't afraid to kick a little ass. Now I realize that this may not be standard psychiatric practice, but the fact is we've got a war on our hands and there's only one thing that's going to stop it—firepower."

"And how, may I ask, do you expect to keep that firepower from igniting the entire east side? Because regardless of your emotional state right now, we are still discussing an extremely complex problem, a problem that involves a wide range of socioeconomic factors that are beyond our immediate control."

Florio rose from his chair and moved to the window. On the broad lawns below sat at least a dozen psychology students, probably discussing the urban malaise...while less than fifteen miles to the east, the Desmodos were cutting people down for amusement.

"Don't tune me out," North said into the silence. "I'm very serious about this. Escalating our reaction to violence in the streets will only escalate the problem. Granted these people may be well armed, but that simply means we must find a new arena in which to meet them.''

"They're not in an arena, Doctor. They're in the streets. And as far as escalating the problem, maybe you'd like to see what's left of Gabby Salinas. It's no big deal to bring him in. In fact, he'd probably fit nicely in your ashtray.''

Florio pressed a tense hand to the cool glass of the windowpane, then said softly, "I can't hold out any longer, Doctor. I've got people dying out there every day. So I've got no choice. I'm sending the proposal this afternoon. I'd like your signature and your endorsement, but either way I'm sending out a formal request for help—hard-line help.''

"Are you giving me an ultimatum, Captain?''

"Maybe.''

"Then I have no alternative but to oppose you. Because regardless of your emotional state, professionally I cannot endorse a wholesale military response, not in the wake of last year's riots. Besides, you people have a tradition of formulative reaction syndrome.''

Florio shook his head, then briefly shut his eyes again. "What the hell is that supposed to mean?''

"Let's just say it means you've undoubtedly become a little too emotionally involved with your personnel... by which I mean both cops and robbers. Now, I don't mean that as a condemnation. I just think you should try to realize that there is a greater reality here... one that transcends individual crimes and incidents. Yes, of course, the loss of an officer can be a crushing blow, particularly inasmuch as it attacks any sense of security you might have on your job. But if we are ever going to truly understand and, what's more, be able to do something effective about the causes of such ... horrors ... we must temper our responses with informed restraint. Meeting force with force—exacting an eye for an eye—although temporarily satisfying, I know, will only continue to aggravate the situation...."

A full five or ten seconds passed before Florio was able to move, to lift his hand off the glass, to actually turn and face North again. Then he said only, "Doctor, are you going to help me or not?"

"And by help, you are specifically referring to—"

"Yes or no, Doctor?"

"No."

As he moved back through the white-tiled waiting room of North's office, Florio noticed a girl sitting on the sofa. Her hair was disheveled. Her miniskirt was rumpled. She looked as if she hadn't slept in days. Her face had a drawn, gaunt look that all but hid a certain natural beauty. Her eyes traced a rapid pattern back and forth on the carpet before her. As he exited the reception area into the hallway, he heard the receptionist at the desk tell the girl that she could go in now.

HECTOR FLORIO DID NOT return to his office that afternoon. Instead, he drove the neighborhoods—first along Sunset to the Strip, then south to the wastes of lower La Brea where the Desmodos were said to have whacked at least a dozen homeboys over the past six weeks. As always, there was a fair amount of action on the pavement: runners on skateboards with nickel bags of scag; dealers in the doorways with dime bags of crack; hookers on every corner.

Twenty, twenty-five years ago a unit could patrol these streets for hours without responding to anything more serious than a domestic squabble or a petty theft. Now there were shootings virtually every night. At least half were random, bullets sprayed through tenement windows or into milling crowds at a corner. Search and Destroy, the homeboys called it. Pile in a car, whack some fool for the fun of it, then go home and watch it on the six o'clock news.

We must temper our responses with informed restraint.

Then, as his car emerged from a cavernous alley adjacent to the Hyper-torque Video, he saw at least seven Desmodo warriors in black vinyl and distressed leather sitting on the front steps of the arcade. Florio eased to the curb, rolled down the window and withdrew a sawed-off shotgun from beneath the dashboard—not exactly standard department issue, but a handy piece in a pinch.

Tell me something, Captain. Was Officer Salinas a friend of yours?

The seven Desmodo warriors eyed Florio suspiciously from the steps of the video arcade, but still remained seated—whispering, laughing, passing a gram or two of crack. The oldest must have been about eighteen, the youngest about twelve. The others could have been any age—sixteen going on sixty, seventeen going on one hundred. Their eyes were like dull plugs of glass. Their gestures were slow and oddly disjointed. In fresh spray paint on the wall behind them was a black bat with fangs.

And what exactly do you propose we do, Captain?

He inched up the shotgun until the muzzle was resting on the door, then sighted down the barrel. If nothing else, he thought, I can get at least four of them—nail four of them to the pavement. Exhale, inhale, hold and squeeze...all in memory of Gabby Salinas.

But even as he felt his hand begin to tighten and the pressure on the trigger ease, he knew that he didn't have it in him, not anymore. In all, he must have spent ten or twenty minutes frozen around that shotgun, sweating like a pig while those Desmodos continued laughing in a crack-induced stupor. Then finally replacing the shotgun beneath the dashboard, he simply drove on.

Eventually responding to a radio call, he found himself talking to a Whittier Boulevard pharmacist, who claimed the Desmodos had threatened to murder his wife if he did not continue to pay his "protection tax." Then farther east along the avenues, he watched from a black-and-white while a team of paramedics zipped up the bodies of three more Desmodo victims, who had been literally gutted in a Burger King parking lot. He also spent a fair amount of time that evening drinking in a half-empty bar called the Smog Cutter. When he finally returned to his condominium on Third Street, it was just about midnight...or three o'clock in the morning at Stony Man Farm in Virginia.

IN ALL, FLORIO SPENT about four hours tracking down Carl Lyons. He began with a telephone call to a mutual friend in San Diego, who had also known Ironman in his days with the LAPD. Next, he called a woman with the Drug Enforcement Clearing House in Houston. Then finally, acting on a hunch, he placed another half a dozen calls to Washington, before he found someone who promised he'd get back to him.

But at some point just before dawn, in those five or ten minutes when even the worst neighborhoods of Los Angeles are silent, he picked up the ringing telephone to hear Ironman's deadpan greeting, "Hello, Hector. How the hell are you?"

For the most part Carl Lyons just listened, occasionally asking tactical questions. What was the Desmodos' estimated field strength? Although he didn't initially understand why Florio hadn't simply called in one of the federal assistance teams, he definitely seemed to understand the Dr. North syndrome.

"Look, I can't claim that you owe me," Florio said at last. "In fact, it's probably the other way around. But if my credit's still good with you, I'd like to take out another little loan . . . under the table."

"You've got to understand that I'm not working alone anymore," Lyons said. "I've got a couple of guys with me, and sometimes they can get pretty wild."

"Well, I don't have a problem with that."

"And your good Dr. North?"

"To hell with North. I've got people dying out here. Anyway, all I'm doing is asking an old friend to help with a little problem in the streets. I don't need any three-year psychiatric study to authorize that. All I need is an answer from you."

Although there were at least two or three second-ary questions concerning logistics, this time the an-swer was yes.

3

The three Desmodos eyed the van warily: a gray Ford, with blacked-out windows, a coiled antenna and electric side mirrors. It had been about six o'clock in the evening when the van appeared, gliding out of the back street and coming to rest beneath a pellet-riddled billboard. Now it was at least seven-thirty, and nothing had changed. No one had gotten out of the van. No one had entered. And except for those occasionally shifting side mirrors, there were no signs of life at all.

The three Desmodos—Julio, Dog and the Masterblaster—had been sitting on the steps of a gutted Taco Bell when the van first appeared, just sitting around drinking, smoking and watching the streets. Earlier that afternoon they had ripped off the local Pick 'n Save for about sixty-five bucks, but it had actually been a slow day, an easy day, a good day to just kick back with a couple of 'ludes and a wine cooler.

"Maybe we should go hit a Burger King?" Dog had said.

"Hey, I don't want no burger," Julio had replied.

"I ain't talking about eating, man," Dog had then said. "I'm talking about sticking a .38 in the window and getting some more cash...and maybe a little ass."

"Nah," the Masterblaster had said. "We're too busy looking good right here. Too busy just looking good."

Then the van had appeared.

Julio was the first to notice it, at first wondering what kind of radio the coiled antenna served and whether or not there was also a tape deck. Then after a while Dog and the Masterblaster also took an interest, but mainly because it just kept sitting there...no one getting out, no one getting in.

"Maybe we should check it out," Julio said.

"Yeah," Dog replied. "Let's check it out."

But that was at least thirty minutes ago, and the Masterblaster still hadn't made up his mind.

In all questions of planning and procedure, the Masterblaster always had the last word. He was by no means the toughest—Julio outdid him in that department. He wasn't even the fastest—speed was Dog's specialty. But whenever a tactical question arose, you could always count on the Masterblaster. It was as if he had some kind of sixth sense. He always knew, for example, which liquor stores routinely carried the most cash, and which proprietors routinely carried weapons. He was also pretty good at picking women, always knowing which ones went down easy and which ones were screamers. At the moment, however, he sensed something he hadn't sensed in a long time— trouble.

It was exactly eight o'clock when the Masterblaster finally decided to move. Apart from a few wandering drunks and a couple of exhausted hookers, the streets were mostly deserted. The surrounding windows were either entirely black or else dimly lit by televisions. They moved in slowly at first, the Masterblaster flanking the muscular Julio, while the wiry Dog brought up the rear. When they came within a dozen feet of the van, weapons were withdrawn: snub-nosed .38s and a six-inch switchblade. Julio also had a foot of lead pipe, just in case there were skulls to crack.

And as if in response to this show of arms, the electrically controlled side mirror slowly shifted to track them again.

Five or ten minutes passed, before the Masterblaster worked up the nerve to lead his team closer. Not that there was anything obviously wrong; he just couldn't seem to shake that sense of trouble... bad trouble coming down hard and fast. Then stepping in a little closer, he failed to glimpse the shadow of someone watching from behind the blackened windshield.

But if the Masterblaster was still slightly apprehensive at this point, Julio was definitely ready for action. It was one thing to occasionally show a little discretion, but who ever heard of shying away from a few frightened tourists in a Ford van? Besides, he had gradually been developing a truly awesome hatred for the thing; it was invading their territory. He had grown to hate the headlights, the fenders and the little side mirror.

But in the end it was the door that really pissed him off. Because when he stepped in with the length of lead pipe, it was the door, suddenly swinging out to smash his face, that dropped him like a rag.

CARL LYONS HAD NOT expected to drop the punk. At best he had hoped to just stun him. But having gained an unexpected edge, the Ironman wasn't about to lose it. He flung himself out of the door like a furious bear, using his momentum to land a skipping side thrust into the gut of the taller Desmodo. He followed with an elbow, which laid out number two.

There was still the third Desmodo, a lanky boy with the name *Masterblaster* tattooed on his neck. But by this time Ironman had been joined by two allies: a lean Hispanic named Rosario "Pol" Blancanales and a stocky warrior named Hermann "Gadgets" Schwarz. Thus when the lanky Desmodo leveled his revolver, he found himself literally double-teamed—first with a Gadgets Schwarz rising kick, then with a devastating Blancanales back knuckle. As he fell, clutching his groin and spitting blood, the first two Desmodos finally struggled to their feet again. But catching a glimpse of Ironman's eyes, they turned and ran.

"Maybe we should run them down," Blancanales said.

Carl Lyons nodded. "Yeah, maybe," he said, glancing at Schwarz.

Schwarz in turn looked back at Blancanales. "Yeah, I think one of us should definitely run them down."

It was exactly twenty-nine minutes after eight, approximately fifteen hours since Able Team had arrived in Los Angeles. A desert wind, locally known as the Santa Ana, carried smells of the barrio: grilled meat, red pepper, vegetable rot. The night sounds were typical—distant echoes of screaming tires, bad music and wailing sirens. Now and again there were also gunshots, mostly from small-caliber weapons.

"All right," Lyons finally said. "You two wind-bags secure the prisoner, I'll go chase the rabbits." And taking off his jacket to reveal a tight-fitting T-shirt over his muscular torso, he moved out along the empty stretch of pavement.

He started at a fairly easy pace, content merely to keep the two Desmodos in sight. Then at about seventy-five yards and closing, he broke into a sprint.

JULIO COULD HARDLY believe it. The crazy tourist was actually chasing them, actually trying to run them down on their own turf. It was so outrageous he almost wanted to laugh...but instead of laughing he just kept running.

"You still packing?" he asked Dog as they continued along the refuse-strewn street.

"Just a blade," Dog replied.

"Well, then, let's just turn and stick 'im."

"Yeah, let's just stick 'im."

But neither boy even broke his stride.

They passed shops and crumbling tenements. Curious faces peered out to watch. They passed a shabby playground, and a couple of kids even hooted. But after glancing back over their shoulders and catching another glimpse of that awesome tourist, they just kept running.

They turned down an alley littered with the usual broken glass and rotting vegetables. They paused in the doorway of a closed bakery, and pressed themselves against the blackened bricks.

"Okay, this is what we do, man," Julio whispered. "When he comes in here, I'll distract 'im so you stick your blade right in his ribs. You got that?"

Dog nodded, with a nervous glance to the mouth of the alley. "Sure, I got it."

"Then after you stick 'im, I'll finish 'im off with the pipe. You know what I mean? I'll smash his fucking face with this pipe."

But hearing the approaching footsteps turn into the alley, they suddenly broke and ran again.

THERE WAS ANOTHER long and empty street beyond the alley, a fairly desolate stretch of thrift shops where the Desmodos had recently left at least four residents bleeding on the pavement. It was also not far from the spot where Gabby Salinas had been blown to bits, and the girl had lost her hand. The inhabitants along this wasted street believed they had seen it all; they certainly never imagined they would live to see the day when one middle-aged gringo chased two Desmodos.

There were about a dozen local residents on hand to witness the event. Most, including Sanchez the tailor and Cohen the pawnbroker, watched from behind the drawn blinds of their shops. But Señora Romero, convinced that another miracle was unfolding, actually stepped out on the sidewalk to get a better look. In short order, she was joined by the Alvarado girls, a dentist named Travanti and six or seven women from the sweatshop...all of them actually cheering.

Go. Go. Go. Go. Gooooooooo!

It was a long time since Lyons had performed for a cheering crowd. And although he couldn't be certain exactly what they were saying, it sounded pretty good. In fact it sounded great.... Only problem was, he didn't know how much longer he could keep it up.

Technically, Lyons was a sprinter, a fast-break man. Give him a clean start and a hundred-yard track, no one could escape him. But by now he had been at it for at least half a mile, and the legs were beginning to feel it.

He slowed his pace a little, sucking in air, filling his lungs.

The Desmodos were still a good sixty yards ahead, with not the slightest indication of tiring. He lowered his head, and started pumping. Fifty yards. He leaped the curb and turned on the power as the Desmodos slowed to take a corner. Thirty yards. He passed another woman cheering from an open window. Ten yards . . . and still closing.

There were now about four dozen local residents watching from windows and doorways, while a slightly larger crowd had gathered on the corner. Among them were recent victims of the Desmodos: a sixty-two-year-old grocer named Alvarez, who had suffered a broken collarbone attempting to defend his daughter, and a nine-year-old boy named Carlos, who had broken his wrist while defending his sister. There was also a little girl named Juanita, who had suffered a broken heart when three or four Desmodos had killed her kitten for the fun of it.

They were all cheering Lyons as he sprinted through the playground gates, hard on the heels of Julio and Dog. They liked the way he was moving, arms and legs like pumping pistons, head down, fists clenched. And, of course, they also liked the way Dog and Julio looked, glancing back over their shoulders in unmistakable terror. But the best part was when the gringo finally caught the two punks and tossed them against the chain-link fence.

Lyons faced them from about seven feet. The big one to his left had a six-inch blade. The thin one raised the length of pipe. They were all panting hard, and the big one looked like he might be hurting from the elbow in the face.

But they were definitely ready to fight, that much was clear.

He moved in slowly, feinting with a hip in order to draw them closer. Although the first rule when facing an armed opponent with your hands is to control the weapon, Lyons initially struck with a low kick to the thin one's knee. He struck with the side of his shoe in what is called a knife-edge, and is more or less a whipping blow designed to stun and disable. Then using the momentum of the half turn, he spun into a circling rear kick that caught the tall one in the face.

Blood and mucus flowed from the tall one's nose, while the thin one crumpled to a knee in agony. There were more cheers from the ragtag spectators, and someone even tossed a red carnation over the fence. Lyons struck at the tall one again, this time with another rising kick to the groin. Then grabbing the hand that held the knife, he slammed another elbow into the boy's gut. He responded with an agonized sigh, and collapsed to the pavement. But when Lyons turned to face the thin one, the boy had already gone, scampering up the chain-link fence and then tearing across the trash-heaped lot.

Lyons watched him for five or ten seconds before deciding it was hopeless. Even if he had had the energy to run him down, he would never have been able to find him in that maze of tenements and alleys. Actually, he wanted one of them to get away…to go back and tell his little playmates that the fun and games were over.

Reaching into his back pocket, Lyons withdrew a pair of plastic handcuffs that had recently become popular with members of the LAPD antigang unit. Then slipping the cuffs on the tall boy and yanking him to his feet, he moved back out to the street. Although none of the local inhabitants actually worked up the courage to speak to him, it was pretty obvious from their eyes how they felt.

"WELL, IF YOU'RE THROUGH playing for the crowd," Blancanales said when Lyons returned to the van, "maybe we should run these punks in and grab a bite to eat."

Lyons glanced down at his prisoners, and grinned. "Yeah, well, I guess they've had enough for today."

The Desmodos had been cuffed against the side of the van. Although the tall one obviously had a broken nose, he still remained defiant.

"I wonder if their mothers know where they are," Schwarz said to Blancanales.

"Kind of hard to believe they ever had mothers," Blancanales replied. "More like they just crawled out from under a rock."

They were keeping an eye on the Desmodos from about a dozen feet away, while at least thirty of the local residents still watched from the corner. The street had grown oddly silent again, with only the wind whistling through littered alleys and the sound of television voices from behind tenement windows.

There was also the noise of the shortwave radio in the van, as Lyons called for backup and an ambulance.

"How old do you think they are?' Schwarz asked after a long silence.

Blancanales glanced at the tall one again, then shrugged. "I don't know. What difference does it make?"

Schwarz shook his head. "No reason. They just look pretty young to me, that's all."

"Yeah, well, I think you'll find that babies can also bite, know what I mean?"

"I want you to just forget everything you ever heard about the gangs," Lyons said as he returned to stand beside his two colleagues. "The Desmodos have nothing to do with gangs. They're an army, and the sooner you come to terms with that, the sooner this job will be over."

"I'm not killing kids, Carl," Schwarz replied. "I'm telling you that right now. I'm not killing kids."

"No one's going to ask you to kill a kid . . . unless, of course, he's trying to kill one of us. Because one way or another that's what it might come to. Now you want to get fancy and try to disarm them, that's your business. But I think you'd better keep one thing in mind. An Uzi on full auto doesn't care who pulls the trigger. Could be a ten-year-old boy. Could be a sixty-year-old man. The result is the same."

They could hear the approaching ambulance now, and the undulating whine of the black-and-whites. Although the first Desmodo had lapsed into unconsciousness, the second continued to gaze at Blancanales.

Finally, Blancanales decided to attempt a rudimentary interrogation, but the kid simply told him to screw off . . . screw off and die.

"It's like this," Lyons said softly into the boy's ear when he realized Pol wasn't getting anywhere. "Three, four minutes the paramedics arrive. Now, they can either take you on a stretcher, or they take you in a Ziploc bag. It's your choice."

The boy slowly turned his battered head, and regarded the Ironman coolly. "Eat shit," he sneered. "Eat shit, and die."

Ironman smiled, glanced back over his shoulder to the empty valley of tenements and then leveled his gaze at the boy again.

"Oh, I get it. You're the smart one. You figure you'd rather piss me off, than piss off Falco. Well, that's fine. Except I got news for you, friend. Compared to me, Mr. Falco is nothing. You understand? Nothing."

But this time the boy just looked at him, the glazed eyes devoid of any recognizable emotion.

"All right, have it your way," Lyons said, and casually withdrew his automatic. Then, ordering Blancanales into the van, he pressed the muzzle into the kid's kneecap. "Now this is going to hurt, but it's not going to kill you."

A full five seconds must have passed before Lyons finally slid the muzzle away and fired the weapon into the air. And although the boy might have been a little shaken, his gaze remained unchanged—cold, defiant and consumed with hatred.

"He tell you anything?" Blancanales asked a few minutes later as the paramedics carried the kid away.

"Yeah," Lyons replied. "He told me a lot."

LATER THAT EVENING while Able Team relaxed and watched clips from a Lakers' game in a rented room at the TraveLodge, it seemed that the entire east side was talking about them. For the most part the speculation centered on who they were, where they came from and what their ultimate mission was. There were those, such as Old Man Almeida, who claimed that the three strangers had probably just been passing through. And although they might have taught the Desmodos a nice little lesson, it would probably effect no lasting change. Then there were those, such as the Alvarado girls, who claimed that the strangers were probably some sort of special law enforcement team. And although they might not end the Desmodo menace, they were at least a start in the right direction. Then there was Señora Romero, who not only claimed that the three gringos were sent from God, but was so confident of their power that she actually went for a walk that evening...entirely alone, with only her rosary for protection.

4

"There are seventy thousand gang members in the greater Los Angeles area," Florio said. "Five hundred individual gangs. Some are worse than others, but all of them are bad."

It was half past ten in the evening. The LAPD briefing room was warm, an uncomfortable consequence of the Santa Ana winds and Proposition Thirteen, which had cut the city's funds and thus the air-conditioning budget. Schwarz and Blancanales sat slouched around the conference table. Lyons stood at the window. Florio faced them all from the opposite end of the room, sometimes pacing, sometimes just staring down at his hands.

"Up until a few years ago," Florio continued, "the south-central neighborhoods were pretty much dominated by two warring confederations: the Crips and the Bloods. On the east side you had the Cholos, the Cypress Park Boys and the El Chemos. But the problem was still an isolated one. You had your Saturday-night rumbles with your Saturday-night specials. You had a lot of dope, and a fair amount of theft. But that was about the extent of it. Today, the weapons of choice are AK-47s, Atchisson shotguns and full-auto

Uzis. We've also picked up heavier stuff, including claymores.''

"Meaning that these kids aren't fooling around anymore?" Lyons said. "That your point?"

Florio shrugged. "Well, let me put it like this. According to our people on the streets, some of those gangs are running six, seven million dollars a year in coke, and half that much again in China white. Now, once you start getting into those kinds of numbers, buying firepower is no longer much of a problem."

Florio moved from the conference table to a map of the city tacked to the fiberboard walls. He had also pinned up two computerized charts detailing the Central American drug routes into the Los Angeles basin.

"Now, as far as we can tell," he continued, "the local coke trade is controlled by fifteen or twenty high-rollers. These are the guys with the Mexican links, and these are the guys who distribute to the gangs. Beyond that there's recently been some evidence that a few of the brokers are even starting to form their own distribution syndicates, mainly through the contras and their Agency contacts. But I shouldn't have to tell you guys about all that."

Lyons responded with a thin smile, while picking at a Styrofoam coffee cup. "I never said I was an Agency fan, Hector."

Florio also smiled, a grim and slightly lopsided smile. "Hey, I don't trust the Russians, either. But at the same time I'm going to be real honest with you, Carl. We wouldn't have a cocaine problem in this nation if it wasn't for certain people in the CIA."

"And the Desmodos are part of that cocaine problem?" Schwarz put in. "Is that where all this is headed?"

Florio shook his head. "Not necessarily. I'm just saying that everything cuts two ways. Langley needed cash to keep the contras in business, so they turned to their opium old-boy network. Those guys passed the ball to the Central American growers, and the next thing you know every punk on the street is driving around in a BMW, cutting dope deals on his car phone and buying enough weapons to outfit a small army."

"But the Desmodos are cutting more than dope deals," Lyons said.

"Exactly," Florio answered, nodding. "They're cutting more than dope deals."

He passed to Blancanales a hand-drafted chart of the California gang links. "Now, first you've got to understand the mentality out there," he said. "Guy messes a Crip or a Blood, Crip or Blood is not necessarily going to waste *him*. They're going to waste his mother. No exaggeration. We had one case a couple of months ago where some dealer tried to cut in on the Bloodstones. The Bloodstones turned around and whacked his two sisters, his mother and his brother. So that's the first thing you've got to keep in mind. These people are animals. We're talking about a completely sociopathic society where the big ones eat the little ones, and then spit out the bones."

Next, he picked up a computer projection of national gang links and handed it to Schwarz.

"Second thing you've got to know," he began, "is that although a lot of the problems out there are the result of local frustrations, there's more and more evidence that some of the power has been imported. Now, I don't know from where, and I don't know how, but we're beginning to find that some of these gangs are essentially terrorist organizations.''

"Such as the Desmodos?'' Blancanales asked.

"Exactly,'' Florio replied. "Not that I've got any hard evidence, but just between you and me I think Gabby Salinas was pretty close to getting that evidence when they whacked him.''

"And the Desmodos came on the scene, when?'' Lyons asked.

"About eighteen months ago.''

"All of a sudden?''

"Sudden enough.''

"And with what sort of profile?''

Florio shrugged, with another lopsided grin. "I've seen some bad moves go down out there. I've seen kids with a quart of Liquid Plumber in their bellies, kids with the flesh totally cut away from their bones, kids that looked like nothing more than a hunk of raw meat. But the Desmodos are something else entirely—a totally synchronized killing machine.''

"Ever thought about just pulling their plug?'' Schwarz asked.

Florio shrugged. "Sure, we've thought about it . . . but first we've got to find the socket.''

A manila folder containing about seven typewritten pages was finally tossed to the table. Among these was a photograph, an oddly haunting distance shot of a shadowy figure emerging from a limousine.

"Falco,'' Florio said. "No first name as far as anyone knows, just Falco. Two, three years ago he was just another neighborhood dealer, running maybe seven kilos a month and grossing about sixty-five grand. Today we estimate that he nets about four times that amount with God knows how much volume.''

"And coke is still his mainstay?'' Blancanales questioned.

Florio shrugged again. "Maybe, maybe not.''

A second sheaf of papers was tossed to the table, this one containing three photographs of bullet-ridden bodies and what must once have been a woman's face.

"Like I said, it all started about eighteen months ago,'' Florio continued. "Kid walks into the station and starts babbling on about a new force in town. Says they call themselves the Desmodos, and they're literally out for blood. Well, we get reports like that every day, so I didn't take it too seriously. But then we started finding corpses. Two or three in a Tenth Street storm drain, two more in a Boyle Heights Dumpster, four in a Carpet City warehouse on Pico. Since then we've zipped up at least another thirty-five bags, and that's just on the east side.''

Schwarz slid one of the photographs into view, a wide-angle shot of four or five youths sprawled on the steps of a Burger King. Judging from their impact response and the holes in the adjacent wall, Schwarz knew that the load must have been substantial.

"Any idea what makes them tick?'' he asked.

Florio shook his head. "Are you kidding? We're talking about a generation raised on Methedrine and chain saw movies. I mean some of these punks are totally screwed up. They'll go out and whack some guy for the fun of it, then go home and watch it on the six o'clock news. And if they happen to switch the channel, they think it never happened.''

"And what about Falco?" Schwarz continued. "How's he get his kicks?"

"I'm not sure you even want to know about it."

Up until now, Ironman had remained silent and frozen at the window. Finally returning to the table, he began to study a photograph: a close-up of two thirteen-year-old girls who had apparently been raped by Desmodo warriors before they'd been thrown from the Pasadena overpass. Their hands were bound with electrical wire. Their underwear had been stuffed into their mouths. Some sort of steel rod seemed to have been inserted in their necks.

"Bottom line," he said. "What's Falco's profile?"

Once again Florio shook his head. "Bottom line? I think he's got a backer, a fully resourced, outside backer."

"And the motivation?"

"I'm not sure. Drugs? Influence? Maybe it's someone who just likes the power. But either way, Falco's connected. I'm almost sure of it."

"So then we're not just facing another bunch of gang bangers," Blancanales said. "That your point?"

"Yes." Florio nodded. "That's exactly my point."

"Well, what's to keep us from dealing with them on their level?"

As Florio started to answer, an obviously agitated patrolman appeared in the doorway to announce Dr. North's arrival.

"I hope I'm not intruding," North said as he stepped into the briefing room and slowly appraised Able Team. "I happened to be in the building, and I thought a few words were in order...particularly in light of that little incident in the barrio this evening."

Florio glanced at Ironman, then back at North.

"Incident in the barrio, Doctor?"

"Come on, Captain, let's not play games. I spoke with the boy that your officers assaulted. He told me about that little trick with the kneecap."

"I honestly don't know what you're talking about, Doctor."

"Well, I do," Lyons said.

Then for a while they just looked at each other: the studiously disheveled Dr. North in a herringbone jacket and a tattersall shirt; the menacing Carl Lyons in a black nylon windbreaker and cheap flannel slacks.

"As a matter of fact," Lyons added softly, "I know exactly what you're talking about."

North continued staring at the man for another three or four seconds. Then obviously sensing something genuinely disturbing, something he'd only seen maybe once or twice in his life and had never wanted to see again, he finally turned back to Florio.

"Of course I'm not an attorney," he said, "but I can think of at least four statutes that were violated, not to mention what that kind of behavior does to the larger community. Point of fact—if your officers continue to act like storm troopers, the community will continue to remain rebellious."

"With all due respect, Doctor," Lyons said, "it's not the community that seems to be the problem here. It's a cancer that calls itself the Desmodos. Now, I'm not a physician, but don't you think it's time we cut that cancer out?"

North, however, merely turned to Florio again. "There, Captain. That is exactly the kind of mentality I'm talking about. If you can't understand it, kill it. If you can't kill it, burn it. Do you have any idea what effect that can eventually create? It could take us fifteen years to reestablish dialogue with barrio leaders."

"That's assuming there are any barrio leaders left," Blancanales commented.

North returned the wiry man's glare for a moment, then shook his head.

"You know, it's really a simple question," he said. "It's my responsibility, both as a citizen and as a consultant to law enforcement, to ensure that this city's police force does nothing to further inflame the minority communities. Now, I have several means at my disposal to do this. I can lodge protests with the mayor. I can impede funding for any of your so-called special projects. And if need be, I can take my complaints all the way to Washington. It's really up to you, Captain, just how far I go. But I will tell you one thing. If you continue to utilize these...gentlemen from the dark side, then I will continue to stand in your way. Is that clear?"

After once more shying away from Ironman's gaze, North turned and moved to the door.

But before he left the room, Blancanales called out, "Doctor?"

"What is it?" North asked without looking back.

"I'd like to straighten you out on one point. We're not *from* the dark side. We *are* the dark side."

Dr. North slammed the door behind him as Lyons turned back to Florio. "I'm sorry about all that," he said. "I guess I should have kept my mouth shut."

Florio gave him a halfhearted smile. "It really doesn't make any difference at this point. The line was drawn a long time ago. What's the next step?'' he asked.

Lyons shrugged, massaging a slightly swollen knuckle he decided he must have bruised on a Desmodo jaw. "I suppose that depends on how fast you want us to move,'' he said.

"And if I were to say real fast?''

"Then I suggest we hit the streets again, and see if we can't find someone who's actually willing to talk about Falco.''

"I think you might find that's easier said than done.''

"Yeah, but if it was easy you wouldn't have called us out here in the first place, right?''

5

From the outside, the abandoned Red Car tunnel looked desolate and deserted. Drivers in cars heading in and out of central L.A. rarely paid it any attention. But there it stood, a silent, decaying monument of the long-defunct streetcar line. In a distant past, a more civilized past, it was possible to catch a Red Car at this point and ride in comfort clear to Venice Beach. The whole trip took about twenty minutes, and the fare was ten cents. But now the Red Cars were gone.

Inside the hollow grotto, the Desmodos had taken refuge. The ceilings were some thirty feet above the old wood and concrete floor, and the vaulted construction left the expanse of the main hall unobstructed by pillars. The warriors were not the only inhabitants of the hidden hall, not by far. Rats, up from the sewer, scurried back and forth in the dark corners. Now and then they served for target practice; the walls were spattered with the remains of several of the larger rodents. And there was human blood as well.

One whole wall was piled high with weapons: AK-47s, fully automatic Uzis, M-16s with flash suppressors, MAC-10s and Squad Rifles with infrared scopes.

There were also a fair number of heavy armaments, and a lot of pieces that had never been uncrated.

The Desmodos, at least seventy-five strong, stood or lounged in and around those massive columns, and everywhere hung the sweet and sour stench of dope. There were also several women, most of them very young, and most of them simply picked up off the street. Now and again one of them cried out, either in ecstasy or in pain, but generally they were too terrified to do or say much of anything.

On a crudely fashioned throne fifteen feet above the others, the Desmodo leader lounged on velveteen cushions. Beside him lay an exquisitely beautiful woman named Lara Cardinales. Several lines of Columbian coke had been drawn on a circular sheet of glass. For the most part Falco kept his eyes on the woman. Now and again he would trace a crimson fingernail across her naked shoulder or throat, while she remained unmoving. He also seemed to be fascinated with her half-exposed thigh and the silky sheen of her calves.

A noise near the entrance caught his attention, but his fingernail did not leave the woman's flesh until a guard began to shout. *"¡Mira! ¡Mira!"*

The response was instantaneous, with dozens of weapons cocking in unison. Then just as suddenly the weapons were laid aside as Julio staggered in from the sunlight. Although still shaken from his encounter with the gringo's fist, he was clearly not seriously injured. However, his breathing was a little ragged, he clutched his side and occasionally staggered as if in pain.

He made his way across the floor until he reached the foot of Falco's throne. Then more or less sagging to the floorboards, he dropped to his hands and knees. Falco stood up slowly, moved to the edge of the dais and peered down at his apparently beaten soldier. His eyes betrayed no emotion at all...not pity, not anger, nothing.

"Tell me what happened," he demanded in quiet tone.

The glare of quartz halogen lamps all but blinded the youth. He looked up at Falco. He had to squint until his eyes were almost shut. But he knew better than to raise his hand to try to shield out the light.

"Those bastards," he said, his voice breaking into a rough cough, "three of them...they got Dog and the Masterblaster, handed them over to the cops. I almost didn't make it out myself."

Falco extended two fingers to receive a cigarette. Then motioning for the woman to give him a light, he let his next question gush out with the smoke. "Who?"

"They're just some dudes. I never seen them before. But they were bad. They were real bad."

"But obviously not so bad that you couldn't elude them?"

"Yeah, well I...well, I got lucky, that's all. I saw my chance and took it. I mean, you know how it is. You see a chance and you got to take it."

"Exactly," Falco breathed. "You see a chance and you've got to take it."

"Besides, there was nothing I could do for Dog, man. I mean he was down for the count. And the Masterblaster, well, he was also in pretty bad shape.

Those dudes really thrash you, man. I mean those dudes were bad news.''

Exhaling again, Falco said slowly, "Yes, Julio, those dudes were obviously bad news."

"And that's the other reason I thought I should try to get out of there. You know, to tell you about them. You know, so we can do something about them. 'Cause I know you wouldn't want that kind of shit going down, right?''

"Yes, Julio. That is right."

"So I did a good thing, huh? I mean, getting away like I did. That was right, huh?''

"Of course, Julio, you did absolutely right. In fact, I think a little reward is in order."

Then, snapping his fingers, he extended his hand to receive a silver-backed mirror with two lines of cocaine.

"Here, Julio. From my private reserve."

The boy hesitated a moment before accepting the mirror, glancing over his shoulder into the mute stares of the others. Finally allowing himself a slight smile, he cautiously inhaled the first rail.

"Good, isn't it?" Falco whispered.

Julio nodded, shutting his eyes. "Yeah, it's real good."

"Then why don't you do the other line?"

"Yeah, why don't I do the line?" Julio laughed, and slowly inhaled the powder again.

Then for a moment Falco simply looked at him, lips slightly pursed in a frown, left hand tapping against his thigh. And although Julio might not have noticed that anything was wrong, the others had grown dead still.

"And now we must discuss one little problem," Falco finally said. "It's just a little something that bothers me, you understand."

"Sure." Julio grinned. "Whatever you want to know, I tell you."

"Then tell me this, Julio. Why didn't you stay and fight with your brothers?"

Julio shivered, and lowered his gaze. "It was like I said, they were bad dudes. They were real bad."

"Exactly my point, Julio. They were bad, because you let them be bad, because you didn't stand up to them, because you didn't stand up to fight for your brothers. Now, this is very serious. In fact this is one of the worst offenses of all—disloyalty."

Although Julio still did not fully understand, he remained grinning at the foot of Falco's throne. But the others knew. And no one even seemed to shudder as Falco swiftly picked up his modified Uzi and fired a 6- or 7-round burst into the boy's face.

At such close range, the hot metal slugs literally ripped the face apart. The body flopped backward, pumping blood from what was left of the head.

Falco laid down the gun, picked up the straw and did another line of coke. Then he leaned over and stroked Lara's thigh again. She hadn't moved during the whole episode. She knew better. Even as he began to trace the outline of her breast, she still remained entirely motionless.

"Tell me," he whispered, "do you think I made a statement?"

She responded with an involuntary sigh, then managed a slight nod.

"So do I," he said with a smile. "Most definitely a statement." Then rising from the cushions again to face his army in the torchlight, he casually pointed to Julio's body and ordered it to be removed.

TWO HOURS LATER, Falco sat with Lara Cardinales in a room high above most of the warehouse blocks and corrugated roofs of surrounding factories. The loft, despite arteries of rusting pipes along the ceiling, was a luxurious place. The walls had been fitted with red velvet panels, and the overall decor suggested an exotic European brothel. The furniture could not have been more lavish, with tooled heads of panthers cut into the backs of ebony chairs and deep-piled velour upholstery. Mirrors, strategically placed to double the size of the room, further contributed to the sense of dreamy opulence. There were also mirrors above the circular bed where Falco toyed with his woman.

Since receiving seven ounces of Iranian hashish, which he claimed had inspired him with Oriental visions, he had decided to dress Lara like a harem slave, replete with a gold chain around her left ankle and only a thin film of silk covering her hips. To complete the fantasy, he had also purchased a pair of silver manacles and a silk-wrapped whip, with which he now caressed her.

She mostly ignored his touches, fixing her gaze on the sputtering flame of a scented candle. Now and again, however, in order to humor him, she would shut her eyes and sigh. This went on for twenty or thirty minutes, until he finally sensed her distance. Then sliding the end of the whip beneath her chin, he slowly forced her to face him.

"What's the matter with you?" he asked. "You sad or something?"

She shook her head and tried to smile. "Nothing's the matter."

He studied her face for a moment, then gradually smiled. "Oh, I get it. You're pissed off because I whacked that guy, right?"

She bit her lip and lowered her gaze, but said nothing.

"Well, I wouldn't feel too bad for Julio, baby, he's not worth the grief. Besides, I got to teach these boys a lesson once in a while. Otherwise they ain't going to respect me. And you and I both know that there ain't nothing more important than respect, right? I said *right*?"

She nodded, briefly shutting her eyes again. "Yes."

"Yes, what?"

"Yes, my darling."

He grinned. "Yeah, that's good. That's real good. Now how about you and I maybe do a little more of that hash, and get crazy, huh? Do a little hash, do a little coke and get real crazy. What do you say?"

"Sure, my darling."

He snorted the coke first, then at least a quarter inch of the hashish. She, on the other hand, had learned long ago that it was always a good deal safer to fake it, to pretend to get high while actually remaining straight. Because when he said, "Let's get crazy, baby," he generally meant it. After ingesting the drugs on an evening earlier that week, he had gotten it into his head that the only way she could prove she loved him was by stepping out onto the window ledge and shouting it to the city. Quite apart from the humiliation, it was a good five-story drop to the pavement.

"Now that wasn't so scary, was it?" he'd said when she crawled back inside.

She had nodded with another forced smile. "No, my darling. It wasn't scary at all."

"That's 'cause I was with you. Even though I never moved from the bed, I was still with you."

He had tapped her breast with the tip of the whip. "In there, right there inside your heart. That's where I was...holding you, protecting you, keeping you safe and warm."

She lowered her gaze again, with yet another theatrical smile.

"I know you were there, my darling," she said softly. "I could feel you."

IT WAS NEARLY DAWN when Lara Cardinales was finally able to extricate herself from Falco's grasp. Slipping on her clothes, she noticed at least two bruises on her breast from where he had slapped her. Then silently treading past the mirror, she caught another glimpse of the lashes on her thighs. He briefly stirred when she drew back the bolt, but fortunately did not wake.

Once outside, she had to pause and take a deep breath. Although the day promised to be hot and smoggy, the morning air was still cool from the night winds. There were even cries of birds now and then, mostly pigeons that nestled beneath the crumbling roofs of factories or higher up beneath tenement eaves.

She moved slowly, casually, just in case Falco had posted a couple of guards in the street. As she approached the 450 SL he had given her the month before, she thought she caught a glimpse of at least one thin Desmodo watching from a darkened doorway. But as with everything else about the Desmodos, she couldn't be entirely sure. Then starting the engine and pulling out into the street, she was almost certain she caught a glimpse of Falco... watching from the window of his loft.

She drove swiftly with the windows down to blow away the scent of his body. She popped a couple of breath mints in her mouth to cut the taste of him. She even pressed a cassette of Mozart's sonatas into the tape deck and turned up the volume to drown out the memory of his voice.

Naturally there were moments, particularly after the bad nights, when she thought about leaving him—regardless of what he might do to her mother and sister. But then looking into his eyes, hearing his commanding whisper, she would realize that there was no leaving him... except possibly through death.

On this particular morning, however, she found herself filled with the sort of hope she hadn't experienced in months, hope that had been kindled by something that Julio had said—something about certain "real bad dudes," who definitely seemed to know what they were doing. Of course, she had no idea of how she might find them, or even what she would say if she did. But the thought that there was someone out there capable of sending Falco back to hell, did her a lot of good.

6

About twelve miles west of Falco's loft was a row of shops called the Little Pico Plaza. There was a Pick 'n Save, a Turbo Video, a Taco Palace and the Pleasure Dome massage parlor. Swedish Massage, read the warped plastic sign of the latter, and beneath that, in burned-out neon: Girls! Girls! Girls!

The fading green massage parlor's entrance was off one of Hollywood's grimmest alleys. The adjacent shops were filled with wigs and the faceless heads of mannequins. The surrounding walls were covered with fierce hieroglyphics. Two or three women listlessly watched from second-story windows. Children threw garbage.

It was half past four in the afternoon and the desert winds had finally died, leaving a typical yellow haze across the basin. Although Schwarz and Blancanales had been engaging in lively banter since scrambling into the van an hour ago, Ironman remained silent, taut, intense.

"Oh, I get it," Blancanales said, looking at the depressing scene outside the van windows, "this is where we find the real meaning of life."

Lyons told him to shut up, and wait in the van until needed.

"Does that go for me, too?" Gadgets asked.

"Yeah." And Lyons walked away from the van.

A long corridor led from the alley to the heart of the Pleasure Dome. The light from red bulbs was reflected through curtains of green and gold beads and a rank of mirrors fitted into the walls. Lyons entered the place with his best tourist grin and his hands jammed into his pockets. He hung back at the door briefly, then shuffled in.

He was greeted by a thin girl, lying on a fake satin couch. She wore cut-off jeans and a halter top. She puffed a red curl of hair from her mouth and slid into her easiest smile. "What can I do for you, honey?"

"Just looking for a good time." Lyons grinned. By now he was pretty certain that the mirrors were one-way, and the girl was high as a kite on smack.

"Well, you've definitely come to the right place," she said, twisting the tassled fringe of the couch. "Only problem is, nothing comes free. Now, our standard introductory treatment is fifty. But if you want the deluxe, it's going to set you back another twenty-five."

"You accept American Express?" Lyons asked.

"Sorry, honey. Just Visa and MasterCard."

There was more gold paint on a brass chandelier that had been fitted with tiny red bulbs, more warped mirrors farther along the corridor that led to the candlelit rooms.

"Now I've got a little confession to make," Lyons said as he moved closer to the girl. "The truth of the matter is, I was actually hoping to enjoy someone else's company tonight. Someone by the name of Dee Dee.'' Lyons had gotten her name from Captain Florio's files.

"She ain't available," the girl snapped.

"Not even for another fifty bucks?"

"No."

"How about a hundred?"

The girl stopped, turned and looked at him. "Look Mister, I know you've never been in here before, which means that if you want Dee Dee, you obviously got something else on your mind. And we don't do that sort of thing around here, so I suggest you just leave."

"And what if I don't want to leave?"

"Well, then maybe Solly here will make you."

Lyons heard the sound of tinkling glass and a deep voice shouting something unintelligible. He whirled as the curtain of glass beads exploded and a heavy man in black tights and a bright red undershirt appeared and planted himself on the purple shag.

"You got a problem, pal?"

"That depends."

"Upon what?"

"Upon whether or not you're going to let me talk with a girl named Dee Dee."

The man shrugged, glanced over his shoulder and began to tap his fist against his thigh. His arms were covered with tattoos. "Well, then," he drawled, "I guess you have a problem after all. Because we got a policy here, see? No special requests unless we know you. And we definitely don't know you."

"Well, what would it take for you to get to know me?"

The man smiled again and quickly glanced over his shoulder once more. "I'm not really sure...but maybe this would help." And he suddenly lunged forward with a slow but powerful roundhouse.

Lyons met him full on, with a whipping snap-kick to the groin. He followed through with a circling elbow that dropped the man to the floor.

"Stop it!" the girl screamed. "Stop it!"

But Lyons ignored her, pressing his heel into the man's throat. "Now, why don't we try it again, huh? Where's Dee Dee?"

The man coughed, spit out a mouthful of blood. "First door on the left."

"Thanks," Lyons said, and moved off down the corridor.

DEE DEE WAS a slender girl with dark eyes, Hispanic features and darker hair. Apart from black panties and a bra, she wore only a gold chain around her midriff. When Lyons entered, he had found her cowering against the far wall, clutching a short stiletto. Now, however, she sat on the edge of a gold-flecked stool, and the dagger lay out of reach on the floor.

"You a cop?"

Lyons shook his head.

"You look like a cop."

He met her gaze for a moment, then pulled a robe in a lurid shade of green from the doorknob and tossed it to her. "And you look like too nice a kid to be working in a dump like this."

She slid into the robe and tossed her hair from her eyes. But there was still no trace of anything in those eyes but hatred.

"Okay, what do you want?" she asked.

"I want to talk to you about your brother."

"I don't got a brother."

"Sure you do. Sixteen, five-nine, hair like yours. Goes by the name of Gato. Ring a bell?"

She shook her head, then gave him a hard sigh. "Okay. But his name isn't Gato. His name is Paulo."

She lit a cigarette, exhaling through her nostrils and gazing at a cheap print of the Acapulco coast. Strains of music from a radio came through the walls, a whiskey voice singing about cruel love.

"Paulo's a good boy," she said. "Let's get that straight right now. He's a good boy."

"So what's he doing running with the Desmodos?" Lyons asked.

She shook her head again. "Hey, man, you got no idea what it's like growing up in the barrio. You got no idea at all. So okay, Paulo joined the Desmodos, but that don't make him bad."

"Maybe not, but sooner or later it's definitely going to make him dead."

He moved to her side, and knelt to face her. Although she wouldn't meet his eyes, he knew she was listening hard. "I can help him, Dee Dee. I can help him get out of the Desmodos."

"Nobody can do that. Once you're a Desmodo, it's forever."

"No, it's not. But you've got to help me. You've got to give me something to work with."

She gave him a quick glance, then turned her gaze back to that dreamy print of a tropical shore. "What are you talking about?"

"I can put an end to the Desmodos and make sure that Paulo gets out alive, but you're going to have to tell me a few things."

"Like what?"

"Like where they hang out."

"Come on, man, get serious. How would I know something like that?"

"Doesn't Paulo ever see you? Doesn't he ever tell you things?"

She shrugged, took a long drag from her cigarette. "I don't know. Maybe. But never shit like that, man. Like nobody knows where they hang out."

"Okay then, but what *has* he told you?"

Another shrug, then another long drag of smoke. "I don't know. Just little things, just little things about . . . well, you know."

"What kind of little things?"

"Like some of the stuff that's about to go down. Like some of the things they got planned."

"And what sort of things have they got planned?"

She ran a hand across her mouth and glanced at the ceiling. "Look, man, if I tell you, you got to promise—"

"What kind of plans, Dee Dee?"

"He said they're about to move on Chinatown. Then after that, they're going to be moving on this big crack house. You know, taking over one of the black gangs' crack houses."

"Did he mention where these moves were going down?"

"Look, man, I got to have some assurances that—"

"Where, Dee Dee?"

"I think the crack house is in the ghetto on one of the avenues south of Hoover."

"And the Chinatown action?"

"I don't know. But listen, you got to understand the Desmodos got ears everywhere. I mean they got ears where you wouldn't believe. So if you start spreading this shit around..."

"Don't worry, I'll be cool."

He rose to his feet and moved to the door, very conscious of her watching him...hesitating...trying to decide.

Then finally as he laid his hand on the knob, she said, "Hey, mister. I'll tell you one more thing. Falco's got this thing with women—he likes to hurt them. Well, it goes both ways. I mean, he's got this one woman. Her name is Lara, and like he's crazy about her. I mean real crazy about her. Anyway, that's his one weak point. You want to screw him over, you find that woman named Lara Cardinales. 'Cause that's where he lives, man. Deep down, that's where he lives."

Lyons found the man he had clobbered, brooding in a chair in the outer office. On a little marble table beside the chair lay a short-barreled Colt automatic. One glimpse of Ironman's eyes, however, told him to keep his hands away from it.

Back in the van, Lyons found Schwarz and Blancanales brooding over cans of Diet Pepsi that they had picked up from the Pick 'n Save across the street. He shot them a look that told the two Able Team warriors to keep their cracks to a minimum.

"Enjoy the massage?" Blancanales asked.

"No," Lyons said, "But I liked the message."

They drove east from Hollywood, following a map Florio had sketched on the back of an envelope for the Heaven Dating Service. When they reached the avenues along Whittier Boulevard, they turned north into the brown hills, into what is sometimes called the Badlands and is often compared to the worst areas of Beirut or Mexico City.

"His name is Juan Ortez," Florio had said, "but everyone calls him Casper. Like the ghost, right? Casper the Ghost, because he's invisible."

Once into the hills, they followed the Coyote Pass, a road that winds between empty lots filled with tumbleweeds, junked refrigerators and rusting Chevys. Every square inch of brick and sandstone was covered with graffiti.

"Far as we know," Florio had continued, "he's the only person to have ever left the Desmodos alive. Now whether he's going to want to talk about it is another matter, but you probably don't have anything to lose... except your scalps."

From the Coyote Pass, they turned north again, following a badly paved road through wastes of cracked stucco and withered cactus gardens.

"This is the place," Lyons said as they approached a sagging shack at the end of a dirt road. "Pull over, Pol. This is it."

They waited for a while, waited and watched through the tinted glass. The shack was a pathetic looking structure, a one-room affair constructed from scrap timber and a rusting Pepsi Cola sign. Coils of barbed wire had been laid around the dirt yard. A mangy dog slept in the shadow of an outhouse.

"All right," Lyons said after another five minutes. "Let's go."

They stepped out of the van, and separated. Lyons took the center path. Gadgets and Blancanales circled around the rear. The dog stirred, but couldn't seem to muster the energy to bark. A cat slid in and out of the shadows by a sandstone wall. Then at last there were no sounds at all apart from chickens scratching in the weeds, and the cocking of a M-16.

"One more step," a voice from behind the door shouted, "and I'll blow your head off."

Lyons stopped, casually lowering his sunglasses for a better glimpse into the cracked window.

"Take it easy, Casper. I just want to talk."

The door slid back an inch or two, then slid back another couple of feet. But although the barrel of the M-16 was now visible, the figure behind it was still in the shadows.

"Who are you, man?"

"A friend of a friend," Lyons answered.

"I don't got no friends," Casper said.

"Sure you do."

A pause, then another step forward so that Lyons could now make out the boy's outline. He was a thin and wiry kid, about eighteen or nineteen. His hair was long and secured with a red bandanna. His jeans and T-shirt were ragged, and his feet were bare.

"What you want to talk about?" he finally asked.

Lyons shrugged. "This and that."

"Well, I got nothing to say about this and that. In fact, I got nothing to say about anything. So get the hell out of here. Get the hell out of here before I blow your head apart."

Lyons lowered his sunglasses again, and ran a hand across his chin.

"You're going to have to talk to someone sooner or later," Lyons said.

"Yeah, well it won't be to you, gringo. Now turn around and start walking, or I swear I'll blow you apart."

But by this time the barrel of the M-16 was well within Blancanales's reach, and shooting a hand out from around the corner, he grabbed hold of the rifle and pulled.

A shot cracked the hot silence, sending the chickens scattering for shelter. Casper tumbled to his knees, trying to wrest the rifle out of Blancanales's hands. But after two or three frantic tugs, Schwarz also joined the struggle, delivering a quick ridge-hand to Casper's ribs, then knocking the kid flat with a second strike to the back of the neck.

They dragged him inside the shack and laid him out on a filthy cot in the corner. It was a crude place, with straw mats on a dirt floor, a junked rocking chair and kerosene lamps. Except for a crucifix and a few pots and pans suspended from nails, the planked walls were bare. There was, however, at least a thousand dollars' worth of weapons in the corner, including another M-16 with a laser sight and flash suppressor.

"So tell me something," Lyons said, examining the M-16. "Who are you afraid of?"

Casper smiled, rising to an elbow and rubbing the back of his neck. "Hey, I'm a gun buff. I collect 'em."

Also among the array of weaponry were two fully automatic subcaliber Heckler & Koch MP-5s and an M-203 grenade launcher.

"You know, there are laws against possessing these kinds of weapons."

Casper shook his head, and smiled again. "So what are you going to do? Arrest me?"

"No," Lyons said. "I think we're just going to take you back down to the flatlands, and dump you on Falco's doorstep."

Casper slid off the cot, withdrew a bottle of tequila from a heap of dirty rags and took a long hard swallow.

"So that's what this is all about?"

"Yeah," Lyons said. "That's what this is all about."

Threading his way through piles of yellowed magazines, Lyons began to examine a stack of paperback books beside the kerosene lamp. In addition to a well-thumbed copy of *The Catcher in the Rye*, there were two Shakespeare anthologies and a dog-eared edition of *The Sun Also Rises*. Strange stuff for a kid from the Badlands.

"Way I heard it, you and Falco used to be pretty tight at one time," Lyons said. "In fact the way I heard it, you were a founding member of the Desmodos."

Casper looked at him, took another swig of tequila. "So?"

"So what happened?"

"What do you think happened? The guy's crazy, okay? The guy's completely out of his mind, completely paranoid. Like he even thought I was after his old lady."

"And were you?"

Casper grinned. ''Well, she's not bad, you know. I mean, she's pretty fine.''

''So you made a move on her and Falco came after you? That how it went down?''

Another grin, and another swig of tequila. ''Depends on who you're talking to.''

''Well, right now I'm talking to you.''

Casper laid the bottle aside and sank back to the filthy cot.

''Hey, you ever heard of Dr. Faust, man? Well, he was this German dude who lived a long time ago, right? He was kind of like this scientist or something, and he was doing okay but he was kind of frustrated, you know? He was kind of frustrated, 'cause he wanted to know all the secrets of the world, only he couldn't figure them out. So anyway, one day this devil comes to him and says that he'll give Faust all the secrets of the world if Faust just signs this little piece of paper saying it's okay for the devil to take his soul after he's dead. So Faust signs this piece of paper, and the next thing you know he's all messed up. I mean he goes really crazy, right? Well, that's the same thing that happened to Falco, man. He wanted to be the big man around town, but he couldn't get it together. But then one day this real smooth dude comes to him, and says, 'Hey, I can make you the king of the heap, but you got to sell me your soul.' So Falco, man, he just goes right ahead and does it. He just goes right ahead and sells the guy his soul. And before you know it, man, he's just completely out of his head. I mean, like he's really crazy.''

Among that stack of books was a little pamphlet called *The Pistol and Knife Fighting Guide*, and a thin black book called *How to Get Anything on Anybody*.

"So who's Falco's devil?" Lyons asked. "Who's the dude that bought his soul?"

Casper shook his head. "I don't know his name, man. But I know he's bad, real bad."

"Where did he come from?"

"Straight out of hell, man. That dude came straight out of hell."

"Falco ever give you any idea what the arrangement is?"

Casper shrugged. "He never said exactly, but it wasn't too hard to figure out. Like right after this dude shows up, suddenly Falco's got more shit than you can imagine. He's got Uzis. He's got M-16s. He's got AK-47s. He's even got those missiles."

"And in exchange?"

Another shrug and a slow smile. "Like I said, man, Falco sold his soul. Dude says 'Jump.' Falco says, 'How high?' Dude says, 'I want you to take your boys out and waste this creep.' Falco, he says, 'Hey, no problem. We'll go out and waste anyone you want.' I could give you all kinds of examples, but the fact is that dude has definitely cut himself a deal, you know? He has definitely cut himself some kind of weird, freaking deal."

"And is that why you left? Is that why you got out of there?"

"Hey, man, you got to understand that it was crazy. I mean it was really crazy. Falco, he'd whack some dude and then start talking about how he could feel that dude inside him. I mean like how he could really feel the dude inside him, moving inside his head, talking to him, feeding him this power. Weird, you know? Real weird.''

There were sounds of someone stirring outside, then what sounded like another cocking bolt. Blancanales moved to the window, but finally said it was just the dog.

''When was the last time you actually saw Falco?'' Lyons asked suddenly.

Casper shook his head. ''I don't know. Eight, nine months ago.''

''And you haven't tried to talk to him since?''

''What? You think I'm nuts? Falco, he'd eat me alive if he could.''

''Why?''

''Because I left him, man. I packed up my shit and I left. Which is something you definitely don't do when you're a Desmodo, especially when you're one of the field commanders. I mean like you can die or you can get your legs blown off, but no way can you leave. No way.''

''Okay, but what if you went back to him? What if you went back, and told him that you wanted in again? That you were sorry you messed up and you'd like a second chance?''

Casper smiled again, a slow smile while his eyes remained fixed on that bottle of tequila.

''Oh, I get it. You guys want me to be your snitch. You want me to bust him from the inside.'' Reaching for the bottle, he took another long swig. ''Well, you can forget that one, man. Like I may not dig my old buddy Falco too much, but I'm not nuts, either.''

''We might just be able to make it worth your while.''

"Yeah, well why don't you tell it to the funeral parlor, man. 'Cause those dudes are the only one's who'd win that game. Besides, I like hanging out here. I'm getting things done. I'm getting educated. Like I bet you never even heard of some of the guys I've been reading."

"You're probably right," Lyons said. "But then I don't have much time to read anything... except the obituaries."

The visit ended in the dirt yard among weeds and litter, where the dog still lay in the shadow of the outhouse, and the chickens still wandered through the brown grass. Casper had walked out with Lyons behind Schwarz and Blancanales, ostensibly to see them off, but probably to check the surrounding hills. Although he was no longer carrying his M-16, he had slipped a .38 Colt into the waistband of his jeans.

"How much longer do you think you can keep hiding from him?" Lyons asked.

Casper spit, squinting across the low hills to a couple of children moving along the crest of a ridge.

"Who said I'm hiding from him? I'm just on my... what do you call it? Sabbatical. Yeah, I'm just on sabbatical. Now, you dudes want to try and take out Falco, that's your business. But I'm doing just fine sitting on the sidelines."

"And what happens when he finally gets the urge to come looking for you?"

Casper patted the revolver. "Well, I ain't exactly unprepared, am I? Anyway, I kind of think Falco's got other things on his mind right now."

"What sort of things?"

"Like ruling the city, man. Like sitting up on that velvet throne of his ruling the whole damn city... which in case you haven't noticed, is no exaggeration. Sure, he has to listen to that devil dude, but just take a walk along the Strip, man. Just take a walk and talk to some of the people out there. Talk to anyone you see in the barrio, they'll tell you how it is. 'Cause Falco, he doesn't just live in that part of town, man. He owns it. You understand what I'm saying? He *owns* it."

IT WAS TEN O'CLOCK in the evening when Lyons and the others returned to their rooms at the TraveLodge. Among the briefing material that Lyons had picked up from Florio earlier that evening were more than twenty pages of horror stories relating to the Desmodos. There were reports that the gang had originally made their mark by slaughtering seven men and women in an east-side Burger King, simply lining the victims up against a wall and then spraying them with 9 mm slugs. There were further reports of internal gang atrocities, reports that Falco had literally disemboweled two of his own warriors for cowardice, while a third had been slowly crushed to death beneath the wheels of a black Mercedes. Finally there were two or three stories concerning the kind of things that Falco liked to do to women, reports of rape with electrical drills, mutilation with buzz saws and the forced consumption of lye.

In all, Lyons spent about two hours examining the material, two sickening hours. Then finally laying the pages aside, he grabbed a beer from the fridge and stepped out onto the balcony. It was a warm night, with humid winds from the southwest that faintly smelled of the sea. Although the view was restricted by the flanking towers of a savings and loan office, he could still sense what lay waiting for him out there... waiting among the gray ranks of tenements and rat-infested alleys.

"Nice place to visit," Blancanales said from the darkness of the doorway, "but I sure wouldn't want to live there."

Lyons nodded, took a sip of beer, but didn't bother turning around.

"I used to deal with gangs all the time when I was on the force," he said at last, "but believe me, it was never anything like this."

"Decline of western civilization." Blancanales smiled grimly. "We're like those Roman centurions trying to keep the barbarians from sacking the capital. We've got the weaponry and the tactics, but they've got the numbers and the raw savagery. The more we cut 'em down, the fiercer they get."

"Well, we sure as hell can't negotiate with them."

"Of course not. But by the same token, we can't beat 'em on their own ground, either."

"Maybe not," Lyons said, "but we can try."

7

Kuo Lin Fang sat on his stool behind the counter of his Golden Dragon Medicinal Herb Shop on Ord Street. As he had every day for the past thirty years, he tallied the day's receipts on his abacus. The clicking of the beads was the only sound in the room, which was cluttered with large and small bottles containing a wide array of herbs and preparations. Kuo's eyes had begun to fail, but his ears were sharp. They pricked up when he heard the door chime tinkling, indicating that someone was about to enter.

"Is that you, Cheng Lo?" asked the old man after a moment.

He grew tense when no answer greeted him. He squinted, but all he could see was a faint silhouette against the front window. Just the week before there'd been a robbery in a shop down the street. In the intervening days he'd heard each bitter detail at least five times, while playing mah-jongg with the shop's owner, his friend Xiang. He was just about to slide the money off the counter and into the drawer beneath it when the person spoke.

"You shouldn't leave the door unlocked after hours, Uncle. You know what's been going on around here."

"Cheng Lo," the old man said angrily, "you gave me a scare. Young men should be more respectful of their elders."

"You know that you have my utmost respect, Uncle. Besides, a little scare might do you good. Maybe you'll think better about leaving that door unlocked."

The old man resumed his reckoning. "Cheng Lo, you are a bright boy. You study kung fu, but you do not study the rites and customs. You do not pay respect. You must learn this."

Cheng Lo closed the door behind him. He twisted the lock. But it wouldn't hold secure.

"There, you see why this old man doesn't lock his door? The lock is broken!" Kuo burst into a dry laugh that ended in a short fit of coughing. "Beside...who would want to hurt us?"

Cheng Lo whipped his head around as the door burst open. It swung so far that it knocked over a small porcelain incense burner that stood behind it. Sand and ash spilled out on the marble floor. Smoldering joss sticks rolled under the counters. Cheng Lo stepped back instantly and without thinking took his fighting stance.

The two Desmodos who had come through the door hesitated, looked at the curious, Chinese boy and then glanced at each other.

"We don't want trouble," said Cheng Lo, drawing his right hand back in the hooked, eagle's beak position of kung fu.

"Shit," the first Desmodo said with a note of disgust.

The other pulled out a butterfly knife and whipped it into position. Then the first began to talk rapidly. "Look. We're not here to kill you, but we will. This is our territory now... Desmodo ground. We take care of our own. You cooperate, and everything will be just fine."

"We pay no protection," said Cheng Lo defiantly.

"He's mine," said the one with the knife.

The other nodded slightly and his partner lunged toward Cheng Lo. With one smooth circular reverse roundhouse kick, the Chinese boy knocked the knife loose. It clattered on the floor. The beaten Desmodo became enraged. He leaped forward, but as he did, Cheng Lo caught him squarely between the legs with a front snap-kick. The Desmodo's face froze. He slumped to his knees, knocking down a row of glass jars containing ginseng roots.

Now the first intruder withdrew a short-barreled Uzi from his jacket and brandished it in a wide arc. "Shit," he said as he pointed it at Cheng Lo. "Shit. Listen. You move... you die."

He approached his kneeling partner and grabbed him by the shoulder of his vest. He yanked him back to his feet, but the Desmodo could barely stand—the pain was too great.

"Kill the slope," he managed to say between clenched teeth.

Cheng Lo eyed them closely. He moved slowly, retaking his ready position, once again drawing his hooked hand up in front of him. Then, for a moment, nobody moved or spoke. And suddenly, the first Desmodo seemed to relax.

"Yeah," he said, more to himself than to his companion. "Yeah. Kill 'em..."

The first burst caught Cheng Lo across the chest. Two of the bullets ripped through his heart, and he was dead before he hit the floor. Kuo was jabbering in Cantonese when the second burst from the Uzi smashed into his forehead. The wall behind the counter was sprayed with blood and bits of his skull.

"Shit," the gunman repeated.

Then he grabbed his companion by the collar again and hoisted him to his feet. There was no crowd outside as they ran from the store and down Ord toward Broadway. The injured one hobbled with great difficulty and only slightly diminished pain. In less than two minutes, they had disappeared into the thick of the city.

FLORIO'S MEN WERE on the scene within the hour. They bagged the bodies, dug the slugs out of the wall, poked around the broken glass and porcelain. But they already knew all about it. It was a Desmodo job. As recognizable as an old family photo.

"So what happens now?" Florio asked when he was finished inspecting the scene.

Carl Lyons faced him from the corner of the bloodstained room. "Ever been to a Chinese funeral? Pretty elaborate affairs."

It was dusk, and the night was coming on quickly. The usual crowd had gathered along the crime scene tape. The restaurant signs were starting to light up.

"Maybe we'll get lucky," Florio said. "Find ourselves a witness."

"Don't count on it," Lyons replied. "These people are too scared."

"So then what? We go home, grab a beer, turn on the tube? Because I'm not turning my back on this, Carl, not anymore."

"I'm not suggesting that you do."

"Well then, what the hell are you trying to tell me?"

Lyons moved from the bloody wall to the bullet-shattered window and the long view of the alley twisting between lacquered columns and sloped roofs. "All I'm saying is that they're still out there. Maybe not all of them, but the ones that did this are still out there."

Florio also moved to the window, gazing out to those tortuous alleys below the blinking neon.

"It's been a long time since you walked these streets in a uniform, Carl."

"What's that got to do with anything?"

"I'm just saying that a lot has changed since you were a cop around these parts."

"Yeah, well some things never change. This little incident tonight was a test. The Desmodos are just flexing their muscles, trying to see how far they can go before we try to face them down. And that's exactly what I'm going to do...right here, right now. Face them down."

THERE WERE TWO LANES leading from the medicinal shop to the New Mandarin Plaza, two shadowy lanes between ranks of forgotten bakeries, a handicraft shop and a nightclub called the Dream of Heaven. There was also a brothel with a woman in clinging silk, leaning from a lacquered doorway. But either she hadn't seen anything, or else she was too scared to talk.

Lyons moved down this lane cautiously, flanked by Blancanales on his left, Schwarz a few paces behind on the right. In addition to their Sterling MK-7s, with NATO specification loads, Blancanales now carried an Atchisson full-auto assault shotgun with a fourteen-inch "urban barrel." At close range against Uzis, however, the Atchisson was probably only even money.

They must have walked about a hundred yards before they caught a glimpse of two, maybe three sallow figures amid the darkening shadows of the plaza. Then along the railing of a restaurant called the Blue Swan four, maybe five more figures crouched among the shadows of flapping banners and dangling lanterns.

"You better try and get some elevation," Lyons whispered to Blancanales. "We'll draw them out from here."

Blancanales flashed Ironman a quick grin. "Elevation, huh?" He immediately began scanning the horned roofs, the peaked towers and tangle of television cables. "Yeah, elevation."

Lyons and Schwarz waited exactly seven minutes before moving out again. At sixty yards, Schwarz tore a spare magazine from his field jacket and set his Atchisson to full auto. At forty yards, Lyons also switched to full auto. Then, taking a moment to consider the surroundings, the dozens of civilians undoubtedly crouching on the other side of those walls, he finally switched to a 3-round burst mode.

They heard what sounded like a gently shutting door, but was actually a cocking bolt. Then came a frantic whisper, and then the first six rounds slammed into the brickwork above their heads.

There were screams from a neighboring cocktail lounge, and the echo of closing shutters all around them. Lyons caught a glimpse of another flickering shadow along the balcony overhead; it slid back into an alcove as four or five more 9 mm slugs splintered the woodwork behind him.

"I think we got some live ones," he whispered to Schwarz, and withdrew two magazines from his webbing. Then, reaching behind him, picking up the top of a trash can and sailing it into the gloom, he watched as another dozen rounds flashed from the shadows.

"Looks like they still think this is their ground," Lyons said.

"Looks that way, doesn't it?" Schwarz replied.

"Probably about time we went to work then."

"Looks that way."

They sprinted into the shadow of a low wall as the shrieking whine of high-velocity slugs ripped the air above them. Silently they formed a plan of attack by means of glances, nods and hand signals. After the count of three, Lyons suddenly swung the barrel of his MK-7 over the wall, and let loose with a short burst as Gadgets sprinted for the cover of a Dumpster. Then they waited, each counting off three seconds, until finally Gadgets rose again and blasted into the elusive figures on the balcony above.

There was a muffled grunt, a choked scream, then what sounded like a watermelon slamming into the pavement.

"Bingo," Lyons whispered.

But his satisfaction was short-lived, as a dozen more rounds from at least three locations tore chunks out of the plaster around him.

Another brief exchange of glances, nods and hand signals. Then the Ironman fired to cover Schwarz as he darted forward into another blackened alcove adjacent to a restaurant called the Gold Duck. Although there might have been a dozen patrons and employees inside, the place had grown silent since the shooting stopped. There was an occasional whisper, an occasional cry. But finally all Gadgets heard were the sounds of those ominous footsteps along the alley.

He waited, watching the shifting shadows on the brickwork, listening as the footsteps drew closer. Then flipping the selector switch to a 3-round mode, he stepped out and fired.

Two Desmodos were crouched among the garbage cans, two wiry boys with a riot of tattoos along their arms and MAC-10s in their hands. Although Schwarz had fired blind, fired into shadows and toward the footsteps, he dropped the first one with three clean shots to the chest. The Desmodo shuddered as he fell, blood spattering up into the neon. But as Schwarz leveled his Sterling to take out the second, a sudden burst of return fire sent him back into the alcove.

Lyons appeared, approaching silently from the opposite end of the lane, pressing himself against the far wall of the alcove.

"We've got at least six upstairs," he whispered.

"Yeah, well let's worry about them later."

"What are you talking about?"

Suddenly there were screams from within the restaurant, and at least three more shots from the MAC-10.

"That's what I'm talking about," Schwarz said. "That scum has taken himself some hostages."

"All right, let me see if I can't find another way in while you keep him occupied and away from the door."

Then flipping from the 3-round mode to the single burst, Lyons slipped off along the alley.

THE DESMODO who had taken refuge inside the Golden Duck restaurant was known as Sleepy. He was a lean kid with sullen features, his left eye permanently drooping with scar tissue—hence the nickname. In addition to the MAC-10, he also now held a twelve-inch, razor-sharp carving knife. The blade was almost, but not quite, touching the throat of a fifteen-year-old girl named Kim Lao. The MAC-10 was aimed toward the nine remaining patrons and employees huddled on their knees between tables in the far corner of the restaurant.

There was a hand-painted mural on one wall, a delicate landscape with human figures outlined among willow stalks and a white crane perched on a temple roof. Although Sleepy kept his eye on his prisoners, now and again he couldn't help stealing a glance at the mural. He particularly liked the way the artist had painted the willows, bending in a breeze that he could almost feel against his neck. He also liked the crane, which seemed almost about to sail right off the canvas and into the night. But most of all he liked the power, the raw power pumping through his veins as the PCP continued to spread.

Although he had ingested the PCP more than an hour ago, he was only now really conscious of the rush...the clean, churning rush of invincibility. Tensing the hand that held the knife to Kim Lao's throat, for example, he couldn't help but feel that he actually controlled her life. One tiny flick of the wrist, and the blood would start to spurt all over the place. And, of course, the amount of effort required to waste one of the girl's parents or another patron was even less a factor. One minuscule twitch of the index finger, and goodbye Chinaman.

He shifted his gaze back to the mural, and that tenuously poised bird on the sloping roof. He let his chin rest on the girl's shoulder, and inhaled the scent of her sleek black hair. He pulled her a little closer to feel the perfect curve of her back and the swell of her breasts...an absolutely perfect moment.

"Hey, baby, you scared?" he whispered in her ear. "Huh? You all freaked out?"

He felt her shuddering, felt a cool tear splatter on his arm.

"Yeah, you're scared."

He shifted his gaze to her father, an old man with a weathered face. "What are you looking at, Pop?"

The old man seemed to shudder.

"What's wrong? You don't think I'm good enough for your little girl here? Huh? That it? You don't like no sleazy spick touching your precious baby?"

He let the hand that held the knife slide down from her throat until it pressed against her breast. "Well, let me tell you something, Pop. She digs it. She digs it real good.''

A new thought came into Sleepy's head. What if instead of blowing Pop away, he simply blew the old man's mind? That was the sort of thing Falco was always doing, getting real crazy and then just blowing people's minds. Like the time he torched the Virgin Mary right in front of all those nuns. Or the time he fed this little kid's dog about fifteen rounds of hot lead . . . just getting ripped, going crazy and blowing people's minds.

And he definitely knew how to blow the old man's mind.

He shifted the blade of that knife an inch, flicked his wrist and popped the first little button off Kim's blouse.

"Hey, Pop, guess what we're going to do?"

He popped another three buttons off her blouse, and slowly pulled the cloth aside to reveal her bra. "What do you think, Pop? Is your little baby looking good or what?"

He heard her whimper as he sliced the bra away, and caressed her nipple with his thumb. He saw the old man tremble with rage as the blade severed the clasp on her skirt.

"Know something, Pop? I think your little baby's all grown-up."

He slid his hand along her hip, and smiled as another tear splashed on his arm. He was also pretty pleased about the reactions of the others, about the way the waitress fixed her eyes on the linoleum and the chef kept eyeing the door.

"Now we're really getting somewhere," he whispered to the girl as he gradually lowered her skirt. "Now we're really getting somewhere."

Then finally forcing her to kneel while he grabbed a handful of her hair, he actually felt their minds starting to blow, actually felt the beautiful horror filling him with a power that nothing could match....

Except possibly the ugly-looking dude in the doorway.

GADGETS BRACED HIMSELF against the wall, and took aim with the Atchisson. Given the spread of the Atchisson's shot, he knew he couldn't waste the Desmodo without hitting the girl, but he still took careful aim...drawing the punk into the sights, and contemplating the pressure of the trigger.

"Let her go," Schwarz shouted. "Let her go and drop the gun."

Predictably, however, the boy only sneered, yanking the girl back up to her feet for cover.

"You want to watch, too, turkey? Huh?"

"Shoot him!" the girl's father yelled. "Shoot him!"

But the youth just gently pressed the blade of the knife into the girl's naked belly.

"He ain't going to shoot me, Pop. He ain't going to shoot me, 'cause he's too scared of hitting your little baby." Then softly whispering to the girl again, "Now we're having fun. Now we're having lots of fun."

There was the noise of shattering glass, and what sounded like a sliding latch. But although the Desmodo briefly turned his head, he quickly directed his attention back to the doorway.

"What happens when you're done with her?" Schwarz asked. "Huh? What happens when there's nothing left of her and I just sit back here and I blow your damn head off?"

"Ain't ever going to be done with her," Sleepy sneered. "Even when I cut her into little pieces, I ain't going to be done with her. Besides, you can't hurt me. I'm indestructible. I'm totally indestructible."

More faint sounds came from the kitchen, a squealing hinge and a footstep on damp tiles. But Gadgets just kept talking to the boy, locking his attention on a vision of the blasting Atchisson.

"You got any idea what this thing will do to you, punk? Huh? You got any idea at all? I'm talking about maybe a hole the size of a basketball. I'm talking about smearing you all over the walls. So you just think about it, punk. You just think about what this thing is going to do to you."

Again, however, the boy merely smiled . . . slid the blade of the knife to the base of Kim Lao's breast, and smiled.

"Hey, you want to watch me cut it off, man? You want to watch me cut one of them off? Well, then just keep talking, man. Just keep talking, and I'm going to cut off her tit."

"But don't worry, baby," he whispered to the girl. "I'll do it real fast, so it won't hurt at all."

There were two more sounds from the kitchen: a cocking bolt and the sliding of a screen.

The boy sneered again as the first thin line of blood sprang from Kim Lao's breast. "Now, tell me the truth?" he whispered to the girl. "Does that hurt? Well, does it?"

"Not at all," said Lyons softly. "Not at all."

He had entered with his Sterling held in combat readiness, his legs slightly parted, back straight. He aimed for the boy's left shoulder because it was the only really safe shot, considering the girl's position. Then as Sleepy whirled at the sound of his voice, he squeezed off the first shot.

The boy screamed, not in pain but in rage. He screamed, dropping the knife and spinning with his MAC-10. Lyons squeezed off two more rounds to the chest, but the boy didn't even seem to notice. He just kept coming, blood pumping from his shoulder and stomach, saliva spraying from his mouth as he screamed again, "I'm invincible, you asshole! Invincible!"

Lyons managed to get off two more rounds before the boy was on him; the Desmodo didn't even bother to fire his MAC-10, he just swung it like a bludgeon. Lyons met the charge with a powerful snap-kick, although it didn't slow the boy down.

But when Lyons rolled clear of the firing line, literally throwing himself into a corner, Gadgets let loose with his Atchisson.

He fired twice, first to the base of Sleepy's spine, then to the back of his head. The impact slammed the boy against the wall, sending blood and white tissue at least fifteen feet across the tiles. There were screams from the opposite corner, as Sleepy's jaw disintegrated and a solid arc of blood poured from his mouth. Then suddenly it became very quiet, except for the sounds of the softly sobbing girl and the soothing voice of her father.

Outside the restaurant, it was also very quiet…and very still, as if the entire neighborhood had withdrawn in order to allow the fight to continue. Above and to the left of where Lyons and Schwarz now watched from the street, Blancanales crouched among the rustling television antennae. Here and there more shadows shifted on the balconies, but still nothing definite.

"Maybe we scared them away," Gadgets said, gazing up to the dark red tiles, to a sagging staircase and then to a warped neon dragon. "Maybe they all got scared and went home to Mama."

"Don't count on it," Lyons said.

He glanced up to Blancanales, signaled with an upraised thumb, then started moving out. A few dusty blinds briefly parted to reveal frightened eyes, but not even the cops were actually out on the streets.

Again there were footsteps. Rubber soles moving through small puddles and across a stretch of broken glass. And then, the sound of a magazine snapping into place.

"How do you feel about drawing fire?" Lyons whispered.

Gadgets grinned. "Love it."

They moved to the mouth of the alley, and crouched behind another row of trash cans. From this vantage point, they could see six or seven suggestive shadows weaving and bobbing along a far balcony. Lyons carefully sifted through the trash until he found a Coke bottle. He grabbed the bottle by the neck, and heaved it against a far wall.

Two flashes of automatic fire exploded from the balcony, two quick bursts that powdered the brickwork and splintered more wood.

"Need I say more?" Lyons said, smiling.

From the mouth of the alley, they moved to the doorway of a laundry. As they pressed themselves against the bricks, Lyons noticed a dark shape heaped amid the trash. At first glance, he thought it was a dirty mound of discarded clothing that even the finest Chinese laundry hadn't been able to clean. But moving closer, he realized that what looked like the head of a mop beside the heap, was actually a young girl's hair. He was able to make out a thigh, and a gaping wound at the throat.

The girl could not have been more than twelve or thirteen, while the tatters of her dress suggested an even younger child. Apparently they had raped her first, muffling her cries with a filthy rag and securing her hands with electrical wire. Then they had cut her throat. He guessed she must have taken at least fifteen minutes to die . . . fifteen minutes of pure torture.

"What do you say we even the score?" Gadgets asked, also staring at the pitiful body.

"Exactly what I was thinking," Lyons replied.

They had advanced to the shadows of a dripping arch, where a strip of darkened pavement fell away to an arcade. Gadgets proceeded another twenty feet to the doorway of a jewelry store. Although the shadows had moved on the ledge above, nothing was obvious until Lyons sent another bottle crashing against the bricks.

Four more quick bursts flashed from the darkness. A dozen or more bullets sang off the tiles. Gadgets responded with what is sometimes called a "discreet burst," three or four rounds directly to the heart of the matter . . . in this case into the half-formed outline of a figure on the ledge.

A loud cry pierced the blackness. A quivering form emerged from a doorway, and stumbled to the edge of the drop. Then pumping out another round, a bloody shadow finally rolled into the neon, shivered for a moment and went still.

Silence.

"Ramon! Ramon!" a hushed voice called out.

Six more long bursts of withering fire from the balcony.

This time Lyons responded first, spraying half a magazine into the windows above the balcony, shattering at least four hundred dollars' worth of glass, but definitely missing the real mark.

"Go for it," he whispered to Gadgets. "Go for it!"

Gadgets shot a quick glance over his shoulder, nodded and then sprinted forward. At thirty feet, the pavement around him came alive with glancing slugs, but he just kept moving until he reached the darkest shadows beneath the balcony.

"Ramon?" another voice whispered.

"Hey, shut your face," someone in the darkness ordered.

Gadgets heard another cocking bolt, another magazine jamming into place as he pressed himself even deeper into the shadows.

"Hey, man, I think he's right below us. I think he's right below us, man," the voice from the darkness said.

But although the walls around were solid stone, the balcony was relatively thin, little more than a strip of wood planks. Thus when Gadgets finally stepped out and fired, spraying randomly into the plaster above, he was rewarded with at least two agonized screams and the sounds of bodies dropping onto the planks.

And then more silence.

Schwarz waited exactly four minutes before advancing from the alcove, along a corridor and up the staircase to the balcony. He moved on the balls of his feet, keeping his weight forward and his breathing modulated. Once, passing the doorway to a fortune-teller's, he definitely caught a glimpse of someone watching. But when he turned, ready to blast the face to nothing, he realized it was only a frightened child.

He found the first Desmodo on the second flight of stairs. The torso looked as if it had been bathed in blood, the eyes staring and empty, the right hand still clutching an Uzi. Apparently he'd been hit at least twice, first in the groin, then in the throat.

He found the second Desmodo at the top of the stairs, sprawled facedown amid a litter of spent shells and broken glass. Although at first Schwarz thought he saw a sign of life, it was only a trick of the light.

But the third one was still alive—huddled in a corner, clutching a sucking wound and gazing up at gently swaying lanterns suspended from the peaked roofs. As Gadgets drew closer, the gaze fell to meet him...the frightened and imploring gaze of a twelve-year-old boy.

"Oh, my God," Schwarz whispered. "He's just a kid!"

He sank to one knee, and gently lifted the boy's hand away in order to examine the wound. The boy responded with a shallow sigh, and a bubble of blood formed at his lips.

"Look, kid, you're going to be all right," Schwarz told him. "You just hang on." Then he screamed over his shoulder, "Ambulance! Somebody call an ambulance!"

But in response, he only heard footsteps and another cocking bolt.

Even as Schwarz reached for his weapon, he knew he was too late, that behind him stood a fourth Desmodo already squeezing a trigger. So this is it, he thought, this is how you buy it.... He wasted another split second because he still couldn't tear his eyes away from the dying boy's gaze.

But as he finally turned, hopelessly trying to dive for cover as that fourth Desmodo leveled his Uzi, four clean shots from Blancanales's Atchisson virtually blew the Desmodo's head away. Between glimpses of Politician and the staggering Desmodo, Schwarz actually saw bits of bone and brain flying into the night sky. Then just as suddenly it was silent again, and he sagged back into the mess of blood and plaster.

"You all right?" Blancanales asked as he slid out from between the eaves and onto the balcony.

"Yeah," Schwarz breathed. "I'm fine. But this one needs an ambulance bad."

Blancanales stopped to examine the boy beside Schwarz. "No, he doesn't. He's dead."

"WHAT HAPPENED out there?" Lyons asked.

Schwarz shrugged, staring out at the black-and-whites, the paramedic teams and the gently swaying lanterns above.

"What do you think happened?" he said. "I got some. I gave some. End of story."

"Is it?"

"What's that supposed to mean?"

"I think you know."

Lyons and Schwarz were slumped to the pavement, their backs against the side of the van. Blancanales dozed a few feet away, with another diet soda between his knees. Thirty or forty cops were either milling about in the plaza or patrolling the back lanes. But only the news teams seemed to know what they were doing, and they were just getting in the way.

"Look, I'm going to say this once and once only," Lyons said at last. "Man goes down, you call for help if it doesn't endanger your position. Otherwise you stay quiet. And either way you never, never stop thinking. I shouldn't have to tell you all this, not after all these years."

Schwarz slowly turned his head to the side and looked at Lyons. "Why don't you get off my back?" he said with a sigh.

"Hey, I'm not on your back. Some drugged-out punk with an Uzi was on your back. So let's stop playing games. You screwed up and you know it. If Pol hadn't been there to cover your ass, we'd be zipping you up in a bag right now."

As if to emphasize the point, two medics passed with yet another body from the alley. Schwarz watched them for a moment in silence, then finally whispered, "He was just a kid, Carl."

"So was that creep in the restaurant."

"That was different."

"Yeah? How do you know?" Lyons shook his head, ran a hand across his tired eyes. "Look, I'm not saying that this is the cleanest job we've ever done, but you saw what those punks are capable of doing. You saw what that creature was doing to that girl, right?"

"Yeah," Schwarz breathed. "I saw it."

"So what's the problem?"

"I also saw that kid on the balcony."

There was the unmistakable sound of another bagged body being tossed on the stretcher, then one of the paramedics saying, "Man, look at the size of that hole. Will you look at the size of that hole!" There were also sounds of weeping, coming from a group of women gathered at a restaurant entrance.

"Okay," Lyons finally said. "So you ended up tagging some little brat. So what are you going to do about it? You going to sit around all night and moan? You going to sit down and let the next one nail your ass? Or nail my ass? Or Pol's ass? Because that's what it's going to come down to. I don't care how old they are, sooner or later it's going to come down to us or them. So I'm asking you, Gadgets, what are you going to do?"

Schwarz took a deep breath, still staring out at those gently swaying lanterns and the lines of quivering neon.

"I think I'm going to be seeing his eyes for a while," he said. "That's what I'm going to do. I think I'm just going to keep looking at that kid's eyes for a while."

8

Falco stood at the darkening window, gazing down at the maze of factories and warehouse blocks. Although Lara could not see his features, she could sense the tension . . . the rage.

"Why don't you come to bed?" she asked.

He stretched an arm across the cold glass, and clenched a fist. "Who are they?" he whispered. Then again through clenched jaws, "Who the hell are they? Joey, Rico, Marko and Slash—all dead. And for what? Huh? Nothing. Nothing!"

Here and there across the loft lay further evidence of Falco's rage: a shattered mirror, a fractured panel, fragments of broken glass. Typically, he had also belted the boy who had first told him what had happened to his boys in Chinatown.

"Not that I ain't going to even the score. That's one thing you can count on, baby. 'Cause I'm definitely going to find the men who wasted my boys, and cut them into little pieces."

She reached across the bed, and picked up a bottle of whiskey from the nightstand. "Come on, my darling, have a drink and come to bed."

He turned from the window to face her, his lips twisted into a furious grimace. "You think I'm losing it, don't you?"

She shook her head. "Of course not."

"Yes, you do. I can see it in your eyes. You think these guys are too much for me. You think they're going to take me down." He stepped to the bed, grabbed a fistful of her hair and wrenched back her head. "Well, I got news for you. I eat guys like that for breakfast!"

He let go of her hair, picked up the whiskey and staggered back to the window. She was pretty certain that he was peaked on coke, that he'd had at least four or five clean hits of the stuff.

"Hey, I ever tell you about Colonel Atiff?" he asked suddenly. "My main man, Atiff. Very cool dude, you know? Very hip to what makes this place tick. Some assholes start giving me trouble, all I got to do is have a little word with Atiff. Because Atiff, he knows I got the right stuff. He knows I got the goods to make it happen. So all I got to do is call Atiff and he's going to kick butts. And you can believe in that, baby. You can really believe in it."

She rolled onto her side, pulling the sheet across her bare legs. She knew he was telling the truth. More than once she had seen a mysterious Arab, handing out advice, handing out money, handing out the weapons that Falco had used to build his little empire. Exactly what Atiff's motives were, she wasn't sure. But he was real. He was definitely real.

"And I'm going to tell you something else about Atiff," Falco continued. "That dude has connections. I want to know about those animals that whacked my boys, I just ask Atiff and bingo—I know all about them.''

He turned to face her again, with the whiskey bottle still dangling from his hand and traces of blood in his nostrils. Although he was still obviously consumed by rage, she sensed another chemical shift in his mood.

"But you know, baby, there's one kind of problem that Atiff can't help me with,'' he said. "One kind of problem I got to handle on my own. And you know what that problem is, baby? Huh? Do you?''

She shook her head, inwardly shuddering at the smoldering rage in his eyes.

"It's you, baby. The problem is you.''

He moved to the bed again, grabbing another fistful of her hair. "Now, I want you to do exactly what I say, baby. You understand? Exactly what I say.''

She nodded, but still couldn't face his gaze.

"I want you to go into the bathroom, and fill the tub with water. You make it nice and warm if you want, but I want it filled up good.''

He released her hair and she slid off the bed, moving in a trance down the mirrored corridor to the bathroom. She knelt on the tiles to turn on the taps, mechanically testing the temperature with her wrist just as her mother had taught her. Then not knowing what to do next, she sat down and waited.

He called out twice, asking if the tub was full, before finally appearing in the doorway. Then he told her to turn off the tap and slip out of her negligee. But when she started to step into the water, he suddenly grabbed her by the throat.

"No, not like that. Like this," and he forced her over the edge of the porcelain as if to wash her hair.

"Now we're going to play a little game," he whispered. "We're going to play a little game to teach you a lesson, to teach you never to doubt me again. You understand? Never again."

She remained absolutely motionless, as he slowly unbuckled his belt. She felt an idle hand caress her thigh, then a finger run along her spine. She caught a glimpse of his shirt falling to the floor, then the labored breath as he struggled with his jeans. Then at last, she felt the whole of him, collapsing on her.

But the worst of it was the water, her head and shoulders pressed underwater for at least sixty agonizing seconds. Then again, grabbing another fistful of hair, he forced her under again... until her eyes were wide with the horror of it, and her lungs felt as if they would explode.

She came up thrashing, sucking in air with painful gasps.

"What's the matter?" he whispered. "You don't like that? Huh? You don't like it?"

She shook her head, gasping for another breath. "Please."

"Please what, baby? Huh? what?"

"No more."

"Oh, you don't dig it, huh? Well, I got news for you, baby, you're not supposed to like it."

He pulled her from the tub and threw her to the tiles. She lay very still as he gently ran his hands along her thighs.

"See, it's like this, baby. You don't dig it, 'cause you think you're going to die, right? You think I'm going to keep you down there till your little lungs burst. But what you don't understand is that that's the whole point. 'Cause just when you think you're going to die, baby, just when you think your lungs are going to explode, that's when you're closest to me. That's when you can really start to feel me inside of you. And it's a beautiful thing, baby. It's a real beautiful thing.''

Even after he had left her alone, she still remained on the floor. For a while she heard him moving through the loft, drinking, pacing, cutting another line or two of coke. Then at last he was silent, and she heard nothing except the pigeons rustling in the eaves.

9

Just after dusk, the last of the cars carrying the shipment of cocaine had been unloaded and had driven away. The big yellow house at the corner of Gage and Budlong was quiet. The neighbors probably knew, at least suspected, that the local Crips used it as their crack house. But no one was about to do anything about it. The cops knew, or should have known. But it was a small and relatively quiet operation. At least it had been until now. Roughly five hundred pounds of the white powder, worth anywhere from five to eight million dollars on the street, had just been stockpiled in the lower rear bedroom. There were about twenty of the black gang members inside the house, all tense, all trying not to show it.

There'd been rumblings during the day. Someone had said something about the Desmodos during the unloading, but no one had wanted to hear it. The average age of those inside the house was eighteen. Moses was thirty-one, and the undisputed leader of the gang. Other younger lords had risen and fallen, but Moses remained, the stable pillar in a social structure that was otherwise pure chaos.

Now, even he was on edge. The darkness outside enveloped the house. Under normal circumstances there would have been music playing and at least three or four couples going at it in various corners of the house. Now it was all but silent. True, Ruben Santos had to show up. True, there were two million dollars in three suitcases on the dining room table. But there was something else present that had begun to capture the attention of everyone there. It was a pure and abstract terror. The only significance anyone associated with it was that single, uncomfortable name: Desmodos.

A car pulled up out front. Everyone stopped, riveted to the echo of two doors opening and closing. The guard at the front window turned around as soon as he recognized someone.

"It's Santos. He's here. He's got three guys with him. One's got an Uzi. Can't see the others."

Moses stood up slowly and slapped the table with the palms of his hands. "Sheeeeit. Look at us! Some faggot beaner comin' here and we're all actin' like old women. Sheeeeit. C'mon, brother, bring out those suitcases. Let's not keep this asshole waitin' around here any longer than necessary."

The guard opened the door. The first of Santos's men stepped across the threshold. He was more than six feet tall and had a bushy mustache that drooped down over the corners of his mouth like a perpetual frown. He hesitated, quickly surveyed the interior of the house, then turned to his master, nodded once and continued on into the living room.

Ruben Santos entered next. He was five-ten, slim and sported a white, woven flax hat from Trinidad. He looked as if he should be carrying a gold-tipped cane, but in its place he held some type of wand, just fourteen inches in length and crowned at one end by a transparent crystal about the size of a walnut. The crystal was held in place by a platinum eagle's talon. Above his right eye was a three-inch scar. It made Santos look like he was always winking or about to wink. He had a thin smile on his lips as he greeted Moses.

"Amigo...I understand that the merchandise has been well received. Have you had a chance to sample it? I'm sure you'll find it of the highest quality. You know, I was thinking on the way over here that you got a very good deal on this buy."

Moses stepped aside as the three valises were set on the table. "We got the shit. Here's your money. Pleasure doing business with you."

Ruben Santos frowned almost imperceptibly. He walked over to the table, held out his wand and with it opened each of the cases.

"Just like that..." Santos said when he had satisfied himself as to the contents of the suitcases.

"Just like that," Moses repeated.

"Well," Ruben Santos said, gesturing to two of his men to come and take the valises, "everything seems to be in order here. If you can move this much merchandise within a month, we can do business again—"

"Someone's outside," interrupted the Crips guard at the front door.

Instantly, everyone in the room was on their feet. A dozen automatic weapons were out, and almost in unison the sound of the slides was heard. Only Santos maintained any sort of calm. He nodded toward the cases on the table, indicating to his men that they were to take possession of the money regardless of this distraction.

"Who the hell is it?" Moses demanded.

"Can't tell . . . can't tell," the guard said nervously. "Could be the police. It's a goddamn white man."

"What is this shit?" Santos asked sternly.

"What are you askin' me for?" Moses retorted. "How the hell do I know he didn't come with you? What the hell are we gonna do now?"

Santos nodded to the tall man. He walked over to the window and looked out. "There's two or three of them. I just saw this one give some sort of signal. They're not cops...maybe DEA...I don't know. Juan, give me your Starlite scope..."

One of the others set down the valise of money he was holding and walked over to the window. He withdrew from his coat a MAC-10 automatic pistol mounted with a Starlite scope, and handed it over. The big man sighted through it. For a moment, everything inside the house was perfectly still.

"Shit," whispered Santos's guard. "I don't believe this. I know this asshole. He was with the DEA bastards who raided Contreras's airstrip in Ecuador two years ago. Shit. He's bad news. He's not human."

The atmosphere in the house thickened almost visibly.

"What the hell is going on?" Moses demanded.

"You don't seem to know," Ruben Santos said, "and we don't seem to know." Santos turned his attention to his big guard at the window. "Mijo, shoot the bastard."

"Hey, man, I don't wanna get him pissed off. I seen this guy take out a dozen of Contreras's men. Let's get the hell out of here."

"I can't believe you, Mijo. What do you suggest we do, just walk out here and say, excuse me, bad white man, while we take our money and drive outta here? Get your shit together, man."

There wasn't time for a response to Santos's question. The whole house was rocked by an explosion outside. Santos's car was a ball of flame.

"Shit!" the big man with the MAC-10 yelled.

A second later, two of the Crips backed into the living room from the kitchen, followed closely by Blancanales. Almost simultaneously, Lyons came down from the upstairs with another two.

"Everybody stay cool," Lyons said. "We're not cops. We don't want to bust your deal up. The Desmodos are coming, and we're going to wait for them."

"What the hell!" said Moses. "You guys gotta be kidding. What are you two crazy sons of bitches doin'?"

Ruben Santos stood staring at Lyons. He had to admit this crazy gringo had some sense of style. There he was, outnumbered by a factor of ten and confronted by enough firepower to literally chop him to bits, and he was coolly telling everyone to stay calm. And he meant it!

"Who the hell are you?" Santos asked, unable to control his curiosity.

"As far as you're concerned, I'm the Lone Ranger," Ironman said, taking another couple of steps into the room.

"And who's this?" Moses quipped, nodding toward Blancanales. "Tonto?"

"Tonto's still out front," Santos's big guard said. "And he's sitting on the grass with a goddamn machine gun pointed right at us."

"That's right," Lyons said. "So why don't you boys just keep me real happy, and that way nobody gets whacked." Suddenly he assumed a commanding tone of voice. "Okay, everybody around the kitchen table. Right now! Let's go, right now. Just make yourself nice and comfy for a little sit-down time."

Santos looked over at Moses, the novelty of the moment having quickly worn off. "Look, man, if this turns out to be some sort of stiff job..."

"Sheeeit," Moses said, throwing up his hands. "How many times do I got to tell you? I don't know who the hell these crazy assholes are!"

Then again above the squabbling voices, Ironman calmly said, "Okay now, everyone just take a seat around this table so we can tell Tonto out there to back his finger off the trigger. It's got enough bang to blow all that dope and all that money all the way to Beverly Hills...and they've already got enough dope and money down there."

"Not to mention blowin' your white assholes away with us," Moses pointed out as the rest of the Crips, and Santos and his men pressed in around the table.

"I suppose you've got a point there." Lyons smiled. "But on the other hand, that's the price of an insurance policy these days. Let's call it mutually assured destruction. Right? And let's remember that it's kept the world safe...so far."

"Sheeeit!" Moses said, "you talk some crazy shit . . . even for a white man. Now, just what the hell you be plannin' to do?"

Ruben Santos sat down and leaned back in his chair. The whole scene was so unbelievable to him that the potential danger seemed remote.

"Like I told you," Lyons said, taking a position near the front door. "We're just going to wait for the Desmodos to show up. Keep them from ripping off this little deal you've got going here. Now surely you, ah, gentlemen can't object to that, can you?"

"What you callin' a little deal?" Moses asked.

Santos remained silent.

"And what makes you think we couldn't handle those Daze . . . mongos . . . ourselves?"

Before Ironman could respond, the answer became clear. The shrill whine of a heat-seeking missile pierced the air.

"What the . . ." Moses yelled.

"Incoming!" Blancanales cried out.

The rocket exploded into the rear of the house. The whole back half was instantly destroyed, soaring up in flame and scorched wreckage as fragments of timber sailed at least sixty feet into the air. And in another second, what remained of the house was a searing inferno.

Then came the screams, some high and piercing, others hardly more than a whimper. A Crip, half-charred to the bone, staggered out of the billowing smoke, while another simply sat staring at his severed arms.

Blancanales remained very still beneath three dead Crips, their bodies absorbing a veritable wave of flame. He realized they were the only protection he had, and for a moment, he continued to lie there.

Lyons had been blown right through the front window by the initial impact. He landed on the front lawn and rolled to a stop at the sidewalk. Aside from a few cuts to his face, however, he hadn't been hurt. As he finally rose to his feet, gazing back at the raging inferno, two or three more people stumbled out, cloaked in flames and screaming.

Twenty feet away, lying against the wheels of a blistered Chevy, Gadgets sat shaking his head. The force of the explosion had blown him clear off the lawn, but he, too, was okay.

Then at last came Blancanales, emerging from the flames with a smoldering Crip still clinging to his back. After two or three seconds he shed the lifeless body and, dazed, he stumbled down from what was left of the porch. After another five or ten paces, he realized that his jacket was burning, and calmly tore it away. Then, finally starting across the lawn, he collapsed to his knees.

"Looks like somebody else had an invitation to this dance," Gadgets said to Lyons once they had regained their wind and once the shock had worn off.

"Looks that way," Ironman replied. Then glancing back to the flames, he asked, "Anybody still alive in there?"

The Politician smiled grimly. "You ever been the main course at a weenie roast?"

No sooner had Blancanales spoken than a natural gas line in the house exploded, sending a renewed wave of flame billowing into the air.

"Anybody see any Desmodos?" he asked.

"Well, that seems to be part of the problem, doesn't it?" Lyons replied. "I mean, if we could just—" He stopped as something else exploded in the house, sending up black smoke into the darkening sky.

Within five minutes two police choppers were circling overhead. Their searchlights crisscrossed, lighting up the flaming house as it began to burn itself out. Able Team just stood on the sidewalk and watched. There was nothing else to do. Neighbors gathered and formed their own perimeter several yards off. One huge, black woman was howling about the devil, genuflecting wildly as she ranted.

Another few minutes passed and police cars rolled up. Hector Florio stepped out of the second car to arrive and walked over to Lyons and his men.

"Don't you think you got a little carried away, Carl?" Hector asked.

"I kind of wish I had," Lyons answered.

"You mean—"

"Exactly... signed, sealed and delivered."

"Now the question is how? And the next is who? And the most important question is what do we do about it?"

Two or three paces away, Blancanales gently prodded Gadgets in the ribs. "You know something, pal? I kind of get the impression that Mr. Lyons here is pissed. I mean I think he's *real* pissed. What do you think?"

But what with the approaching fire trucks and the fascination of the flames, Schwarz didn't even bother answering.

"I didn't see him leave the party," said Blancanales.

The fire had almost burned itself out by the time the firemen got their hoses on it. As soon as the water was turned off, Lyons, Schwarz and Blancanales began poking around the soggy ashes. Bodies were burned, not just beyond recognition, but so that hardly anything was left. Some of the gun barrels had started to melt. The whole scene looked like a miniature Dresden. Under one of the bodies, Blancanales found Santos's peculiar wand, the crystal still in place. He bent and picked it up—it was still hot enough to scorch his fingers.

"Damn it," he yelled, letting the infernal thing drop on top of the charred body. He stuck his fingers in his mouth to cool them off.

"Must be Santos," Lyons said. He had come over to see what Blancanales was yelling about. "Late of the Cartagena network."

"Friend of yours?" Blancanales asked.

Lyons shrugged. "Not exactly."

"That's good. Because once they clean away all that ash, I don't think they'll even have enough left to bury."

10

Falco's footsteps echoed like tiny gunshots on the pavement. From a distance and in the shadows, he might have been a ghost, the sort of fanged and menacing ghost that inner-city residents thought they'd often glimpsed along these wretched back streets. His velveteen cloak, filling with the night breeze, almost looked like bat wings. The black fedora, worn low over the left eye, further suggested something unholy. Finally there were the boots, high-heeled and edged with razors.

When he lit a cigarette, his face briefly flared to life, then he tossed away the match and started moving again. He glanced back over his shoulder at the black Mercedes where Lara waited. At last he turned to face his two nervous warriors.

"So, Jojo, what do you got to tell me?"

Jojo was a slender boy, with pinched features and vaguely slanted eyes. Beside him stood a somewhat huskier youth, known as the Pope because his brother was a priest.

"Not too much." Jojo smiled. "I mean we did what you told us to do. I mean like we really blew the shit out of that place."

"Yeah," the Pope added. "Like we really blew that place to hell."

"But?" Falco's raised eyebrows actually lifted the fedora. *"But?"*

"But like they just walked out of there. You know? They just walked on out."

For a moment it seemed that Falco was on the verge of smashing his fist into Jojo's face. Then just as suddenly it passed, and his voice actually became quite calm.

"So you failed. Is that what you're trying to tell me? You were sent to rid me of this scum, and you failed?"

"Yeah," Jojo said softly. "We failed."

"But you got to understand how it was," the Pope added. "I mean like there was no way they could have gotten out of there alive. There was just no way. When that silky hit, the place just went up in smoke. So it was just like a fluke, man. You know what I mean. It was like just a fluke."

Falco turned, gazing back along the alley to the outline of Lara in the black Mercedes.

"Sure," he said softly, "just a fluke."

Although still obviously frightened, Jojo moved close enough to Falco to actually feel the man's breath, to actually inhale the stench of his cheap cologne.

"Look, I ain't trying to make excuses," Jojo said, "but I don't think we're dealing with ordinary guys here. You know what I mean? They have some kind of power."

Falco slowly moved his dark gaze until it fell on Jojo's eyes. "What are you talking about?"

"Well, I know this guy, see? His name is Valdez, and he used to be in the Special Forces in Nam, you know? Then after that he used to do some kind of special security work for these big companies in Arabia and places like that. Only then he met this girl named Ellie, and so he moved back into the neighborhood and took a job with—"

"Just get to the point," Falco said.

"Well, I was talking to him the other day, right? I was talking to him, and I kind of mentioned that there was these new guys in town who were kind of like cops, except a whole lot worse. So anyway, he said he knew all about these guys. In fact he'd even seen them work before in some place like Mexico or something. And he said that they're definitely not cops, man. Definitely not just ordinary cops."

Sensing a softening in Falco's mood, the Pope also approached now. "That's what I was trying to tell you," he said. "It's like these guys aren't just ordinary dudes, you know? It's like these guys are real bad."

"Who did Valdez say they worked for?" Falco asked.

Jojo shook his head. "Well, he didn't really know for sure, but he thinks it might be for the Feds. You know what I mean? Like these guys aren't local talent. They were specially imported."

Falco shifted his gaze back to the waiting Mercedes, and the flickering television glows behind the tenement windows.

"Did Valdez say that these guys have a name?" he asked. Then suddenly facing Jojo again, "Well, did he? Did he say that these guys have a name?"

Jojo shrugged, exchanged a quick glance with the Pope. "I think sometimes they're called Able Team. You know, 'cause they're able to get things done, see? 'Cause they're suppose to be able to take care of guys like us, see?"

"Yeah," Falco breathed. "I see."

After returning to Lara, Falco virtually said nothing. He slid into the Mercedes, turned the ignition and slowly drove out to the boulevards. Although it was well past nightfall, a number of local residents were on the streets. There were kids tossing pennies on the tenement stoops, vendors selling ice cream and pretzels. There were girls in plastic sandals and cheap dresses from the local discount store, boys in polyester disco shirts and blue jeans. There were old men, old women, babies and mothers...all of whom should have been too scared to leave their homes at night.

"Look at them," Falco sneered. "Three bozos come in town, and suddenly everyone's having a party."

Beside him, Lara remained silent and stiff. She had seen Falco in these moods before, and knew better than to speak unless spoken to.

They turned left on Ninth Street, moving into the heart of what was sometimes called Macondo. It was a four- or five-mile stretch where hundreds of frightened Central Americans had settled.

"So what's their story, huh?" Falco murmured. "They think suddenly I'm history? They think these three goons come into town, and suddenly Falco ain't going to bother them no more? Just look at them!"

They passed the little Alverado plaza where dozens of children had gathered around the mariachis. They passed a rank of open stalls, filling the air with odors of fried meat and red peppers. They passed a convenience store where even a woman in a wheelchair had the nerve to meet Falco's gaze.

"That does it," he whispered to himself. He swerved over to the curb, and withdrew his razor from beneath the dashboard.

"Where you going, my darling?" Lara asked, trying to sound casual, trying to sound as if she didn't know what he was about to do.

"Just wait here."

"But I don't know if we've got time to—"

"Just shut up and wait here."

He left the engine running, slid out to the sidewalk and moved rapidly into the convenience store. It was a small place, filled with all sorts of junk that only the poor would buy: cheap sunglasses, plastic handbags and digital wristwatches with Day-Glo faces. The proprietor was a thin man with white hair and a melodramatic mustache. Apparently the woman in the wheelchair was his daughter.

"Hey, let me see that," Falco said, pointing to a crucifix hanging on the wall behind the counter.

"I'm sorry, *señor*, but that's not for sale."

Falco smiled, shook his head. "I didn't ask if it was for sale, Pop. I said let me see it."

The old man hesitated, then finally lifted the crucifix from the wall, and handed it to Falco. It was an ornate piece, with the Lord's eyes in black pearl and the crown of thorns studded with diamond chips.

"Yeah, this is nice," Falco slurred. "This is real nice."

He picked at an eye with a fingernail, pulled at the tiny gold nail that held the palm in place.

"Yeah, Pop, you really got something nice here. I bet you feel real safe with this thing around."

"Please, *señor*, it is very old and very valuable. Please let me have it back."

"Hey, what do you think, Pop? You don't think I'm a religious guy, that it? You don't think I believe in God?" He brought the crucifix to his lips as if to kiss it. "It just so happens that I'm a very religious guy. In fact I'm so religious that I'm even going to pray for you."

The old man started trembling, his left hand opening and closing in a kind of spasm. "Please, *señor*, please."

But Falco merely grinned.

By now the old man had slipped into a kind of trance, first muttering to himself, then reaching out and grabbing Falco's wrist.

"Give it back to me!" he shouted. "Give it back!"

Falco smiled again, briefly glancing at the hand on the wrist, then suddenly he withdrew his razor and brought it down in a quick arc.

Blood spurted from a six-inch gash on the old man's cheek, then more blood from a two-inch gash across the bridge of the nose. The old man screamed, trying to twist away, but Falco held him firmly by the hair.

"What's wrong, Pop?" he whispered through clenched teeth. "Don't you believe in God no more? Don't you believe that God is going to save you?"

The old man struggled to turn his head until he could see the crucifix now lying in pieces on the counter.

"You will be punished for this," he whispered. "As God is my witness, you will be punished for this."

But again Falco merely grinned, and slowly dragged his razor across the old man's forehead, leaving another thin arc of blood.

"Yeah, I'm real scared, Pop. You got me real scared." Then gradually he let the razor slide down to the corner of the eye. "Now, how about we see what God has to say when I cut out one of these peepers. Huh? What do you think, Pop? You think God's going to get pissed off at me if I do a little carving in your eye?"

A fleck of blood appeared on the old man's eyelid, as Falco moved the razor still closer.

"So how about it, Pop? God going to punish me or not? Huh? Well, is he?"

"Yes," the woman in the wheelchair said. "He's going to punish you through my hands."

Falco released the old man, and slowly turned to face the woman behind him. Although she was half-hidden in the shadow of a doorway leading to the storage room, the shotgun across her lap could not have been more obvious.

"Now get out of here," the woman spit. "Get out of here before I send you back to hell myself."

Falco hesitated, with another thin smile. But finally sensing the woman's determination, noting that her finger had already begun to squeeze the trigger, he finally backed out the door.

FOR A LONG TIME after returning to the Mercedes and pulling back onto the boulevards, Falco remained locked in furious silence. Lara, sensing his rage, also remained quiet. Her eyes were fixed on passing faces, her hands pressed to the dashboard. Naturally she had noticed the traces of blood on his jacket and boots, but she kept her mouth shut.

It was half past ten in the evening when they finally returned to Falco's loft. Although the streets were still filled with people, the sounds were remote. Another insistent desert wind had risen, sounding like rushing water through the rainspouts.

"Fix me a drink," Falco ordered as he stepped out onto the balcony.

Lara complied immediately, pouring two fingers of whiskey into a glass, then half a can of cola.

"And draw me a line," he said, still not bothering to look at her.

She laid the drink on the table behind him, and tapped out a thin line of cocaine. Now and again strains of distant mariachis and echoes of laughter could still be heard from the streets below.

"I tell you what they call themselves?" Falco suddenly asked. "Huh? I tell you what those bozos call themselves?"

She stepped behind him, and pressed her head to his muscular back. Sometimes a degree of affection could calm him down.

"No, my darling, you didn't tell me."

"Able Team. You hip to that? Those three useless bozos are called Able Team."

He sucked up the cocaine, tossed back his head and grinned. "Able Team. Able Team."

He grabbed her wrist and forced her to face him at the railing. "What kind of name is that? Huh? What kind of bozo name is that? Able Team. Sounds like some kind of real macho fantasy.'' He finished his drink, and threw the glass over the railing.

"Sounds like some real redneck jive." He slammed his fist on the railing, shut his eyes, then slowly grinned again. "What do you think, baby? You think I should be scared? You think I should get the hell out of here before Able Team comes knocking on my door?"

She bent and pressed her lips against his knuckles, against the tiny tattoo of a bat on his wrist.

"I don't think they're anything," she whispered. "I don't think you even have to bother with them."

"Oh, but I want to bother with them. I want to bother them real bad."

He grabbed a handful of her hair, and lifted her head until she was only inches from his face and from those eyes that seemed as if they could suck her in.

"You know something," he whispered. "I can feel them. Right now. Right here. I can feel them...out there...waiting. And I like it. I like it, 'cause it's going to make it all that much sweeter when I cut them into little pieces."

IT WAS LATE when Falco finally fell asleep...three or four o'clock in the morning. Although the streets had finally grown silent, the winds had not died down. For a long time Lara lay by Falco's side, listening to the rattling papers, the singing wires and the occasional clatter of a trash can lid. Then finally whispering his name and receiving no response, she slipped out of bed and into the bathroom.

She examined her body in the mirror—the faint bruise on her left breast, the thin welts across her buttocks. She let her head fall to the glass, then caught another brief reflection of his sleeping form through the half-open door. Do it, she thought. Then again, watching him stir in the tangle of sheets, *Do it.*

She slipped on her jeans and an old sweatshirt, and groped in darkness until she found her shoes. He moaned when she lifted the car keys from the dresser, but did not wake. Then slowly lifting the latch on the door, she heard him moan again.

There were two Desmodos guarding the corridor below, two thin and wide-eyed junior members of Falco's elite team. They were both armed with MAC-10s that looked too big for their twelve-year-old hands. One of them was called Raoul, she remembered. The other one was called Little Frog, or something like that. As she moved down the stairs, she wondered if they had been listening at the door, listening to her cries and whimpers. Then she supposed that it didn't matter, that nothing really mattered anymore.

"Good night, *señorita*," Raoul said as she passed.

"Good night, Raoul."

"You want me to maybe walk you to your car?"

"No, I'm fine. Thank you."

"Are you sure? It's pretty wild out there."

She paused, glancing down the street. "But it's only the wind," she said, smiling, "and the wind can't hurt you, can it?"

In fact, the wind was comforting, almost reassuring—the palms thrashed like dancers and shredded newspapers skidded over the pavement like leaves. Maybe one day a real wind will come, she thought, and blow this city right off the map.

She drove slowly, keeping mainly to the darkened back streets. Ever since the appearance of the Desmodos, the walls along these streets had been covered with their graffiti: D for Desmodo, F for Falco, I for invincible. Here and there were bats with eight-inch fangs, dripping blood.

She passed a dozen pay phones before she worked up the courage to stop. Then it took her a long time to find a quarter. The wind had grown stronger, literally shaking the booth and hurling bits of palm fronds against the glass. Her hand, she realized, was shaking as she dialed the number.

Then, of course, she hardly knew what to say, and naturally she felt a little silly asking to speak to someone from Able Team.

11

The Desmodo faced Lyons from the deepest shadows of the factory. Rodents moved back and forth at a steady pace along a network of overhead pipes. But apart from the occasional squeal, there were no sounds except the Desmodo's footsteps.

The Ironman drew his .45, but kept it leveled at the concrete. Then after a couple more paces, he released the safety.

"You going to come out?" he shouted. "Or are you just going to stand there?"

It was late—three o'clock in the morning. Having received the invitation a few hours earlier, Lyons had spent the intervening time preparing—stationing his men on the roof of this crumbling factory, arming, watching, psyching himself up to meet a possible Desmodo defector.

"Look, you want to talk or not?" he shouted again.

"Yeah," came the muffled reply. "I wanna talk."

"Then get out here."

At which point a few more footsteps echoed before the Desmodo finally appeared—all four feet eight inches of him.

The boy, looking no more than eight years old, moved tentatively out of the shadows and across the empty room. The fact that he kept his hands plainly in sight was probably an indication that he had played these games before. He wore only jeans and a T-shirt to emphasize the fact that he couldn't possibly be carrying a weapon.

Nonetheless, Lyons kept his .45 at the ready. The barrel pointed at the concrete but the safety was off and the bullet chambered.

"So, kid," he said. "Let's hear you talk."

"It ain't about me," the boy said with only the faintest trace of fear. "I'm just the messenger. It's about someone else."

"Yeah? And who's that?"

"Just this person."

"What kind of person?"

"Someone who knows a lot about the Desmodos, someone who's willing to talk if you promise to play it straight."

"And where might this person be?"

"Around."

"Around where?"

"Just around."

Lyons took another step forward to study the boy's eyes. Although the invitation to this meeting had come in on a reliable line, Lyons couldn't get it out of his head that the Vietcong used to use kids like this one to set up GIs in Nam. Kid walks into a headquarters, says he's got information on Charlie, and nobody's the wiser till the claymores fire.

"All right," Lyons said at last, "what do I do to see this person?"

The boy shrugged, returning Lyons's gaze, studying the man as intently as he had been studied. "Maybe you already done it, okay? Maybe by just being here you can see this person, okay?"

Lyons took a step closer, moving into a thin shaft of light from the rafters above. "Where?"

The boy extended a stiff arm, pointing to an ominous alley beyond the factory gates. "All you got to do is keep on walking, just keep on walking till you can't walk no more. Then you'll see her."

"Her?" Lyons asked.

But all the boy said was "Just keep on walking."

THE ALLEY RAN for at least a mile, a long and narrow stretch of cracked pavement between loading docks and empty storage bins. There were no lights and no sounds, except for the occasional rat. As Lyons moved out, he caught a glimpse of Schwarz and Blancanales covering him from the corrugated rooftop. After a brief exchange of nods, he kept on walking.

For the first fifty or sixty yards, he mainly kept his eyes on those loading docks, figuring that the shadows beneath the planks could easily conceal a sniper. Then as the wall gave way to chain link, he began to scan the open ground, the weed-grown lots and train yards, a stretch of industrial swamp where bodies were always turning up among the trash heaps.

Twenty, thirty years ago, this stretch of Los Angeles wasteland had been a thriving industrial center, serving the entire basin. Then one by one the principal plants moved south, leaving mainly junk and ruins. For a while there had been talk of rebuilding here, blasting the place and starting all over. But like so much else in the city's east side, all that talk came to nothing, and these blackened lanes became the refuge for the rats and pigeon flocks that occasionally rattled Lyons now.

He caught a glimpse of something moving to his left, spun with his .45 extending from his stiff right arm, then shook his head as another rat slid into the sodden garbage heaps. Then he saw something to his left, repeated his spin, but again it was just a rat or else a gust of wind. Should have brought a Starlite scope, he told himself as he plunged into the deeper gloom between a rank of derelict tanks. Should have brought a howitzer, he thought as he entered the alley's depths, where even Schwarz and Blancanales could no longer track him.

It was very dark at the end, with a slow descent to some sort of ancient loading yard below a rusting footbridge. The pavement had given way to cobblestones, slick with oil and scum. The street lamps had burned out decades ago.

Lyons paused, trying to fix his eyes on a wavering figure in the distance. He took another slow step forward, keeping his center of gravity low and legs slightly bent in case he had to hit the deck. Then finally feeling his way to a nest of dripping pipes, he went for broke.

"Okay, I'm here."

Nothing except the breeze through a tangle of dangling electric cables.

Still nothing, except the rustle of frightened pigeons.

"Okay, I'll tell you what we'll do. I'll start counting to ten. If you want to talk, then just speak up. If not I'll be gone by the time I reach eleven. Fair enough? All right, here we go. One. Two. Three. Four. Five. Six. Seven. Eight. Nine. Te—''

"Yes," said Lara Cardinales. "I want to talk."

Lyons faced her from a dozen paces, across a tangle of moss-bound chicken wire and heaped rubbish. In a leather cloak and high-healed boots, she looked vaguely like a cavalier. And as the wind tossed her hair, spreading it across her shoulders, he also had to admit that she was really very beautiful.

But he still kept the .45 at the ready.

"So, you're Falco's woman," he said.

She bit her lower lip and nodded. "That's right. I'm Falco's woman."

"My condolences."

She shrugged. "I didn't ask you to come here for your sympathy."

"No? Then what do you want?"

She took another step forward so that he could finally see her eyes—gray-green and incredibly alive. "I want you to kill him for me."

He led her to the shelter of a low wall in order to eliminate at least one angle of fire. He glanced back over his shoulder to the rooftop above, wondering if Schwarz and Blancanales were still covering him. He glanced back to the opposite roof in case they weren't.

"What makes you think I'd kill him for you?" he asked.

"Because that's what you do."

"And what's your part in all this?"

"I'm going to help you…and maybe also I'm going to watch."

Although he hadn't touched her, he could sense her trembling, sense the fear behind her eyes.

"The first thing you've got to know is that they're all over the place," she said at last, "all over the city. Mainly they stay in the old Red Car tunnels beyond the tracks, but they're all over the place. The other thing you've got to know is that you can't go in the tunnel and get him, because he always has lots of guards and as soon as he heard the shooting he'd be gone. Also, if you try to get him in the tunnel lots of the little ones will die, the ones that aren't really that bad and can still be saved. Same thing if you try to get him in his loft. You try to get him in his loft, and he'll only slip away when the shooting starts, and then you'll just end up killing a lot of little kids for nothing."

"Where does he stay when he's not in the loft?" Lyons asked.

She shook her head, suddenly entranced by those softly rustling pigeons above. "I don't know. Maybe no one knows. He just sort of moves around. He gets drunk, gets stoned, then just sort of moves around."

"But if you need him, how do you find him? How would you contact him if there was trouble or something?"

She shook her head again, still watching the shadowy forms of pigeons above the loading docks. "I don't contact him. He contacts me. If he wants me, he gets me. That's all there is to it. He wants, he gets."

"But let's say you were with him one night. Let's say you were with him, and you were able to get to a phone or a—"

She cut him off with a hopeless sigh, and another shake of the head. "Look, you don't understand. You don't understand how it is with him. He doesn't make those kinds of mistakes. He doesn't turn his back on anyone, not even me. And besides, he's got eyes everywhere...everywhere. Even in a place like this. So if you want to take him, you've got to meet him head-on. You can't sneak up and shoot him behind his back. You've got to meet him face-to-face, and shoot him right there...right between the eyes."

She sank back to the wall, clutching her ribs as if chilled to the bone. A breeze, stinking of refuse and tar, had risen from the end of the alley, stirring leaves and bits of paper all around them.

"Tell me about his contacts," Lyons said. "Tell me about Falco's contacts," he repeated when she failed to respond.

At first she only shook her head, shivering with another gust of wind. Then she turned her head away and said, "I don't know too much about it all, but I know that there's this guy, this Arab guy."

"What's his name?"

"Falco calls him Atiff. Colonel Atiff."

"What's his role?"

"He just does things. Like if Falco needs something, Atiff takes care of it."

"You mean, he works for Falco?"

"No, he doesn't work for him. He just helps him. Like if Falco needs a certain gun or something, Atiff can always get it for him. And if Falco needs information, information about maybe some like you— same thing. Atiff gets it for him."

"You ever met him?"

"I've seen him a couple of times, but I've never really met him."

"What's he look like?"

"I don't know. He's kind of thin, thin and dark with a face like a hawk. And then he's also got these eyes, these eyes that are as cold as death."

"You have any idea where I might find this Atiff?"

She looked at him. "Yeah, sure. I've got his phone number right here."

"All right, what about Falco? How does he get in touch with Atiff?"

"I'm not sure exactly, but I know it's complicated. Like if Falco needs him or something, he's got to do things like make chalk marks on walls, stuff like that."

"And then what?"

"Then they meet, but never at the same place twice."

There were more sounds of pigeons overhead, then what sounded like two rats fighting over a shred of meat. The wind, too, had grown pretty insistent, and the woman couldn't seem to keep herself from shivering.

"I wasn't kidding when I said he's got people everywhere," she whispered. "Even in places like this, even right now he could have people watching, people who maybe followed you here, people who knew you were coming even before you knew it. Anything is possible."

He glanced up to the roof again and saw the vague forms of Schwarz and Blancanales crouching on the corrugated iron. "Those are my people up there," he said.

"No, not up there," she said. "Over there. In those shadows."

Lyons looked but saw nothing.

"Anyway, I've got to go. I've got to get out of here before they see me. Otherwise I'm dead. You know what I mean? If anyone sees me talking to you, I'm dead."

He grabbed hold of her arm, catching another glimpse of those exceptional eyes. "Listen to me, I can protect you. You help me nail Falco, and I can protect you."

She shrugged, glancing down toward those wavering shadows at the end of the alley. "Maybe you can. Maybe you can't. But first I think you should worry about just getting out of here alive."

Lyons waited about ten minutes until he was certain that she was gone, until he heard the Mercedes sliding out along the side streets. Then he waited a little longer, watching those shadows in the distance, trying to work out if it was really possible that the Desmodos had been tracking him from the start.

"So what's she like?" Blancanales asked after sliding down from the roof.

Lyons shook his head, gazing out three hundred yards to whoever or whatever might have been waiting. "Scared."

"Is she going to help?"

Another shake of his head. "I don't know."

Schwarz made sounds behind them, moving catlike with a Squad Automatic Rifle across his shoulders. When he finally approached all he said was, "You guys feel them, too, don't you?"

"Yeah," Lyons said, eyes still straining at the distant gloom. "We feel them."

12

A fog was now rising from the sewers and pouring out of the storm drains. Lyons, Schwarz and Blancanales watched from the shadows of the wall, then started moving forward again. Although Schwarz had withdrawn a roll of duct tape from his pack and secured a Mag-Lite to the barrel of his SAR, he didn't dare use it now.

It was the same walk that Lyons had made thirty minutes earlier, but in the reverse direction, a long and uncertain trek across a mile of littered pavement between loading docks and storage bins. This time, however, Ironman wasn't alone. He was with Able Team, but he also felt the presence of someone else out there.

It's quiet, too quiet, he thought. Even the rats and pigeons had grown dead still. Nothing was moving...except possibly the headlights of a car in the distance.

The car seemed to be approaching at a slow pace, fifteen, maybe twenty miles an hour. There were snatches of music and laughter, then nothing except the faintly knocking engine. At least two passengers were visible in black silhouette, one of them apparently hanging out the window.

"What do you make of it?" Lyons asked.

Blancanales unslung the Atchisson. "Two hundred yards and closing."

"All right, then, let's move," Lyons said. "Move!"

The Team scrambled to the edge of the loading docks, crouching behind a mess of trash and pools of foul water.

"This is nice," Blancanales whispered. "This is real nice."

By this time the approaching vehicle was less than eighty feet away. It was a black Chevy, with beaten fenders and tinted glass. A spidery form hung from the side window, apparently clinging to a roll bar. A second form, leaning out from the rear window appeared to be hunched behind a swiveling cannon.

Then as the engine suddenly roared and tongues of light flashed from the windows, at least a dozen heavy slugs slammed into the brickwork around Able Team.

"Shit," Schwarz shouted, "that's a fifty caliber!"

More slugs splintered the decks of the loading dock as the Chevy spun for a second pass. Fist-size chunks of brick exploded from the walls. A fragment of wood the size of a finger sliced Lyons's forehead. A screaming ricochet sailed off into the sky.

"We've got to get the hell out of here," Lyons shouted.

But the only place to go was beneath the loading docks. They found it cramped and foul, with rancid pools of water and a mess of rat litter.

"This is nice," Blancanales whispered again. "This is real nice."

But as the Chevy turned for another pass, he had already leveled the Atchisson. Although he couldn't aim for the windows, he finally had a clean shot at the tires.

He squeezed off four shells as the Chevy flew past. The left front tire exploded in a shower of sparks, as the wheel rim skidded on the asphalt. The Chevy swerved, rebounding off chain link and skidding into a heap of rotting crates.

Lyons fired next, spraying nine slugs between the fender and the grill. Two doors blew open, and two dark forms rolled off into the deeper darkness. But the driver, apparently struck in the chest, stumbled six or seven feet and then collapsed.

There was a momentary silence, with only the sound of escaping steam or else the escaping breath from the driver's sucking wound.

"What are you carrying?" Lyons asked.

Politician padded the pockets in his fatigues. "How about thirty rounds?"

"Gadgets?"

"I got enough."

"Then let's move out behind that SAR."

Schwarz withdrew the tripod, and set up beneath the lip of the dock. Then came the count…three, four, five. As Schwarz squeezed off the first dozen rounds, Blancanales and Ironman rolled out, sprinting for the cover of the trash heaps. Although at least twenty more rounds followed them into that mess, nothing came closer than a foot or two.

They waited, watching for flashes in the darkness. Then counting off another seven seconds, they started out again, moving low in the shadow of storage bins as a dozen more shots cracked out into the night.

"Looks like the first two may be behind those Dumpsters," Blancanales whispered.

"With what?" Lyons asked.

Another four or five shots cracked through the blackness, bullets zinging wildly off the pavement.

"AK-47s?"

"Then I'll take 'em out with this," he said, flipping the MK-7 selector switch to full automatic.

Blancanales squeezed off six more shots as Lyons sprinted forward into the shadows. The Dumpsters stood below another loading dock sixty feet up the alley. Steel shot pinged against steel as Blancanales squeezed another four rounds to cover Lyons's approach.

Again there was silence.

Lyons lay waiting in the shadows of another garbage heap. Once or twice he had heard the scrape of a boot heel on the asphalt, but hadn't quite been able to zero in on a location. Then catching a brief glimpse of a bobbing silhouette, he started crawling forward again.

At sixty feet another burst of automatic fire sprayed from behind the Dumpsters, split-second flashes of light from out of the utter blackness.

At thirty feet a frantic voice shouted something in Spanish, and more automatic fire flashed across the alley.

But by now Lyons was close enough to see feet beneath the slightly raised Dumpsters.

A breeze, smelling of cordite, had risen from the southeast. Fragments of another frightened exchange in Spanish echoed softly from behind the Dumpster. Finally inching forward another nine feet, Lyons was able to make out their shoes: one pair of suede boots, one pair of Reebok hightops.

He rolled a little closer to the lip of the dock. The stench of rotting vegetables and meat seemed to clot in his nostrils. He felt the putrid moisture seeping through his clothing, heard the terrified scampering of tiny paws.

Once, eight or ten years ago, he had seen a perpetrator taken out like this, a twenty-year-old robbery suspect cornered in a parking lot on Fifth Street and Grand. It had been a rainy Memorial Day weekend and, responding to a frantic dispatch, Lyons had found himself stalking the kid through darkened ranks of Toyotas and Fords until he had finally sighted two scuffed loafers beneath the tires of a Datsun. Although Lyons's first impulse had been to fire a warning shot, another young detective named Hatchenson had had other ideas. Extending a .38 revolver from beneath a neighboring Pontiac, the detective had virtually blown the kid's foot off.

But now Lyons was alone. There was no Detective Hatchenson. There was only that pair of suede boots and those hightop Reeboks.

Lyons slowly extended his Sterling, sighting down the tritium dots to the eighteen-inch space between the two pair of shoes. The breeze brought snatches of another whispered conversation.

"You see them?"

"No."

"There?"

"No."

Bits of paper rattled across the pavement between the shadows where Lyons lay and the Dumpsters. A bird, probably another pigeon, took advantage of the temporary lull to leave its hiding place and fly away to greater safety.

"You, out there," Lyons shouted. "You are in our line of sight. Throw down your weapons, and step out with your hands on your head."

Another whispered exchange, then the sharp crack of the AK-47s.

"I repeat, you are in our line of fire. Throw down your weapons and step out with your hands on your head."

"Eat me, shithead," came the reply as a second automatic burst flashed over the top of the Dumpsters.

"This is your last warning," Lyons shouted. "Step out now, or we will be forced to fire."

In response, two long bursts sent hot metal ripping into the lip of the loading dock, tearing off more chunks of timber only inches above Lyons's head.

He saw the muzzle of the second AK-47 slide out along the opposite end of the Dumpster, saw a dark face squinting along the barrel; the eyes stared into his own eyes. He shouted, "Don't do it, kid!" He waited another half a second, then couldn't wait any longer, and finally squeezed the trigger of his Sterling para-pistol.

Lyons actually saw the first pair of shoes explode; the Reeboks suddenly disintegrated into red pieces of canvas and flesh. He heard the howling wail of pain, and the clatter of the AK-47 as it slipped to the pavement.

The boots exploded a split second later, the gray suede ripping like the skin of soft fruit and pouring forth blood.

The screams mingled and became one. The dark forms writhed on the concrete, rolling out from behind the Dumpsters.

Lyons rose to his feet, glanced over his shoulder and saw Blancanales sprinting toward him. Then glancing back to the Dumpster, he saw that the kid wearing the Reeboks was still clutching an AK-47, while the guy with the boots had withdrawn a MAC-10.

"Don't do it!" Lyons yelled. But again he couldn't wait any longer than a quarter of a second. The first shot from the MAC-10 exploded in his ears, and he squeezed the trigger of his parapistol one more time.

The NATO specification rounds splattered into the contorted face, kicking up small fountains of blood.

"Noooo!" Lyons screamed as the other boy responded by bringing up his AK-47. This time Lyons didn't even hesitate an instant. He squeezed out four more slugs. The boy's chest erupted with dark stains from the chin to the belly, while the choked cry echoed all along the alley.

Then there was nothing else to do but watch, to simply stand there and watch them quiver in a silence that was broken only by the slap of Blancanales's approaching footsteps.

"I'VE HEARD about this kind of action before," Blancanales said. "Kid pumps himself full of PCP, and the only way to stop him is to pull his plug completely. You hit him in the leg or something, and he won't feel a thing."

"Oh, they felt it," Lyons said. "It just didn't seem to make any difference."

They were crouched by the Dumpsters, hidden in the shadows of corrugated roofing. The bodies of the two Desmodos had finally stopped quivering, the arms twisted at impossible angles, the faces still contorted with rage.

"So maybe we should wait it out," Blancanales said, "let 'em come back to earth a little."

But even as he spoke, there were signs of movement in the distance, hints of shadows flitting across the rooftops, the echo of another vehicle gliding to a stop behind the ranks of warehouses, the muffled thumps of slamming doors.

"You feel the same thing I'm feeling?" Lyons asked, scanning the sloping rooftops around them, the dark mounds of refuse, the long and narrow stretch of pavement ahead.

"The punks in the Chevy were just the advance guard. We haven't even begun to see the main force."

"What about Gadgets?"

"What about him?"

"Maybe I should scoot on back and have a word with him, maybe get him to set up in those Dumpsters."

Lyons took another glance to the rooftops above, to what might have been a figure crouched behind a junked-out industrial fan.

"I kind of think that Gadgets is just going to have to play it alone for a while," he said. "These guys are all around us. And I mean all around us."

"Well, what do you say we try and draw 'em out?"

"Be my guest."

Blancanales groped around in the filthy blackness until his fingers encountered a chunk of brick the size of a golf ball that had been blown off earlier by the AK-47s. He tested its weight in the palm of his hand, then tossed it over his head to the corrugated roof above. Immediately following the hollow clang of brick on metal, the air was alive with bursting autofire. At least twenty slugs blasted into the woodwork around them, while tracers crisscrossed above their heads.

"Bingo," Blancanales whispered as he and Lyons rolled beneath the lip of the loading dock.

Despite the slime and mess of rat pellets, they continued crawling until they reached the blackest end of the shelter. Then although it was momentarily silent again, the alley was suddenly alive with the flitting red lights of night scopes.

"Ever read about the Little Big Horn?" Blancanales whispered. "Or the charge of the Light Brigade? Cannons to the left of them, cannons to the right, volley and thunder, and so on."

"We'll just wait for 'em, that's all," Lyons whispered back. "We'll hold our water and wait."

"We're talking about at least fifteen more AK-47s," Blancanales replied. "That's what I count, anyway... at least fifteen."

"I know," Lyons said, "but we're still going to let them come to us."

Another seven minutes of silence passed, while the stinking moisture continued to seep through their clothing. Apart from the rustling of the pigeons, there were also the sounds of rats.

Then footsteps.

"First guest?" Blancanales whispered as the soft tread of rubber soles drew closer on the planks above.

A pause. A hushed call. "Hey, Choo-Choo."

Then another set of footsteps on the loading docks. "Shit, man, they got to be around here someplace."

You're right, Blancanales thought. We got to be around here someplace. And gently rolling on his back, he sighted the Atchisson between the planks.

The two Desmodos were standing almost directly over them, two more spidery silhouettes in jeans and leather vests. Their weapons were resting on their hips. Their gaze was fixed on the black slits between the wooden planks at their feet. Then as a trace of recognition appeared in their faces, as their eyes grew suddenly wide with horror and as they aimed their weapons, Blancanales squeezed the trigger.

He fired twice, blasting through the wooden planks and peppering their chests with steel shot. There were simultaneous grunts of pain and the thud of collapsing bodies. Then as the taller of the two pitched forward, Lyons found himself covered with a spray of blood.

"Let's move," he hissed. "Let's get the hell out of here."

They rolled from beneath the loading dock, then sprinted for the storage bins. Dozens of bullets descended on their shadows, slamming into the bins. But by now two forms were clearly visible on the sloping roof. Sinking to his knee, Blancanales slowly squeezed off three more shots.

Another agonized groan, then the sound of leather boots sliding across the corrugated roof, and the heavy thud of a body on the pavement.

"Can't keep this up all night," Blancanales whispered. And just as he slid back into the shadows, another racking spray of lead slammed into the pavement.

"Any idea where that's coming from?" Lyons asked.

Blancanales nodded to the rooftops behind them, then the two rooftops in front of them. "I think they call this a cross fire." He smiled.

There was a two- or three-minute pause, while four more beams from night scopes flitted across the pavement inches from where Lyons and Blancanales knelt.

Then suddenly, not eight feet away, a wavering shadow materialized into another silhouette. Slugs ripped into the steel next to Ironman's shoulder, and he fell into a long roll. Another spray from the AK-47 sent up flying sparks at Blancanales's feet. But as Lyons came out of his roll, he managed at least four shots into the form. The Desmodo stiffened, then wavered as if struck by a high-intensity wind before finally collapsing.

"Shit," Blancanales breathed. "These guys are *everywhere*."

They had rolled into the chipped doorway of another gutted warehouse. The breeze had grown stronger, bringing a new scent of charred rubber.

Lyons shook his head, huddling back against the wall with his MK-7 at his hip. "What were you saying about the Little Big Horn?" he whispered.

"Surrounded, outnumbered and definitely violating Indian land."

Here and there stray shots still sent up mists of powdered brick. Sinking to his knee, Blancanales fired back into the blackness of the narrow alley, although he really had no way of knowing where to aim.

"At this rate we're going to be at this all night," Blancanales complained.

"Or forever," Lyons replied.

"So what do you want to do about it?"

"We need an edge." He scanned the rooftops, then along the loading docks. But in the end all he said was, "Yeah, we have definitely got to get us an edge."

They withdrew into a warehouse that was illuminated by two thin streams of moonlight.

"Ever climb a greased rope?" Lyons asked, running his hand along a dangling cable suspended from the rafters below the skylight.

"Not since I was a kid," Blancanales said.

"Well, then, welcome back to childhood."

Lyons climbed first, hauling himself up hand over hand, with his legs coiled around the cable. At twenty feet, he glanced down to the blackness below, took a moment to marshal his strength, then started moving again. At twenty-five feet, he was able to see the glare of the moon through the dusty skylight. At thirty feet he could actually feel the breeze through broken panes of glass.

Blancanales followed when Ironman had hauled himself up on the rafters. Although smaller than Lyons, Pol pulled himself up with the agility of a monkey. Then also scrambling onto the rafters, he gently pushed through the panes of glass.

They moved through the skylight and onto the roof in stages, first Lyons, then Blancanales. The breeze had grown marginally stronger, and sporadic shots seemed miles away.

But the hulking form of a furious Desmodo stood virtually on top of them.

Lyons reacted first, scrambling to his haunches as the first 9 mm rounds punched through the corrugated roofing. Then, because he knew he hadn't time to level the MK-7 and fire, he shot out his legs for a scissors takedown that caught the Desmodo at the knee and sent him sprawling down the sloping roof. He seemed to hesitate before falling, frantically reaching for the storm drain before sailing out toward the concrete below.

There were more shots from the roof of the adjoining warehouse, apparently from a belt-fed AR-15. Although Blancanales answered back with his Atchisson, his primary concern was simply to get out of the way, to roll back to the far side of the sloped roof.

But Lyons had finally had enough.

He rose in a single, fluid motion, leveling the parapistol from the hip and spraying a full clip at the humped shadow on the adjoining roof.

There was a cry like a strangled cough, then a sudden glimpse of another staggering form sprawling off the end of the roof.

"Let's go," Lyons shouted. "Right now, let's go."

Blancanales sprang to his feet, leaping for the adjoining roof. Lyons followed an instant later, landing with a dull thud, before inserting another magazine. From this vantage point, some fifty feet above the narrow alley, three Desmodos were clearly visible on the loading dock below.

And another two were firing from a ventilation shaft that ran from the end of the roof.

Lyons returned the fire as he dived, knowing that it was an impossible shot. He almost did not believe his eyes when he saw the spray of blood in the moonlight. Then as the second Desmodo rose screaming from the blackened shaft, Blancanales literally blew off the head.

There was a moment's silence, except for that rising wind. Lyons and Blancanales crouched in the shadow of a rusting drainpipe that extended from the corrugated rooftop like some enormous smokestack. Beyond the pipes lay the blackened line of factories, then the equally black line of tenements. But what with the moon and a few stray lights from the overpass, three prone Desmodos below couldn't have been more obvious targets.

They lay on the loading dock, facing the opposite end of the alley, where Schwarz had remained with the SAR. Although they must have heard the shots above, they obviously didn't realize that their rear rank had collapsed and left them completely exposed.

Completely exposed.

Lyons withdrew his last magazine, and gently fed it into the MK-7. Blancanales performed the same task with another seven rounds of bird shot for his Atchisson. There were three or four more shots from below, and then it was very quiet.

"Now what?" Blancanales whispered, the shotgun just resting on his hip. "You want to paste another bunch of kiddies, or you just want to call it a night?"

Lyons flipped the selector switch from full automatic to a 3-round squeeze, but still kept the weapon down. Judging from the silhouettes, he guessed the boys below couldn't have been more than fifteen or sixteen.

Lots of the little ones will die, the ones that aren't really that bad and can still be saved.

"Keep me covered," Lyons finally said. "Just keep me covered." Then rising to his feet, he started forward.

He moved in a half squat, with the MK-7 in his right hand and his left hand extended for balance. As he neared the edge of the roof, he felt the roofing sag a little under his weight and heard the wind singing through the pipes behind him. Then as he moved another step or two, he could see them quite clearly.

They were lying very still, half-concealed beneath the lip of the dock. Two were armed with AK-47s, the third with another AR-15. Although he couldn't see their faces, he could nonetheless sense their fear—three thin boys lying in the darkness with weapons they had probably never fired before.

Then at last with a slight nod back to Blancanales, Ironman made his move.

"Freeze! You are within our line of fire! Lay down your weapons. Now!"

A second passed, a cold and tense second.

"Now!"

Another second.

"I said lay down your—"

"Okay, mister! Okay. We're laying down our weapons, see? Take it easy. We're laying them down."

There was a dull clatter as their rifles hit the concrete, then a few harsh whispers in Spanish.

"Now get on your knees," Lyons shouted, "and put your hands on your heads!"

Although two complied immediately, the third seemed to hesitate ... either reaching into the pocket of his jacket or else drawing something out of his trousers.

There was a hoarse shout, apparently from Schwarz, who had finally emerged from the shadows to press the attack. Next came a frightened scream, and Lyons thought he caught a glimpse of something in that third Desmodo's hand, something black and circular and roughly the size of a baseball. There was another hoarse shout and someone yelled out, "Grenade!"

Then at last, Schwarz fired.

He fired from the hip—one long and arcing burst that lifted the three boys into the air, left them suspended for an instant, then tossed them back down to a filthy concrete ramp. Blancanales whispered, "Shit," as the widening pools of blood began to spread from beneath the bodies and a hand continued to grasp at nothing. Then it was very quiet again.

"IT WASN'T LIKE YOU HAD a choice," Blancanales said.

"Sure," Schwarz breathed. "It wasn't like I had a choice."

"Well, ask Lyons. He'll tell you. You had no damn choice."

"Right. No choice."

They were resting thirty or forty feet from where those last three Desmodos lay. The grenade, a standard military fragmentation type with a three-second fuse, lay on the pavement between them—the pin almost, but not quite, pulled.

"I mean you've got to look at it this way," Blancanales said. "Egg like that goes off, Lyons is definitely Swiss cheese. Me, I'm lucky to spend the rest of my miserable life in a wheelchair. Know what I mean? That sheet metal would have offered no—I repeat *no*—protection. So why don't you just call it a wrap?"

But Schwarz just kept gazing out across the shadowy litter to where those bodies lay sprawled on the ramp. Now and again, he thought he saw them moving, miraculously coming to life. But it was probably just a contorting muscle or the rats, cautiously surveying the scene.

"You get a look at them?" he finally asked.

Blancanales shook his head. "Huh?"

"Those kids. You get a look at them?"

"Sure, I got a look at them. They were almost the last thing I ever saw."

"Well, how old do you think they were?"

"What difference does it make? Lyons tells them to drop weapons and kneel. They drop weapons and kneel, except for one and he pulls out that grenade. You come running up, see the whole thing about to go down, and cancel the guy's ticket right then and there. That's the way I'd write it up if somebody asked for a report, and that's the way it happened. So what's it matter how old they were?"

"It matters," Gadgets breathed. "It matters."

"Well, it doesn't matter to an AK-47, and it sure as hell doesn't matter to a grenade."

"WE'VE GOT SIX BODIES and still counting," Florio said. "I guess you guys are starting to get pretty serious about all this."

"Yeah," Lyons said. "I guess we're starting to get pretty serious."

It was nearly dawn, and the once deserted alley was now swarming with teams of paramedics and uniformed officers. A rank of headlights cut the gloom for at least two hundred feet. The crackle of radios had frightened all the pigeons away.

"Not that I'm necessarily complaining," Florio added after an awkward pause. "It's just that I'm not sure how to log this kind of action. I mean is this authorized counterforce? Defensive action? You tell me."

"It was a firefight, Hector. That's what it was."

A young patrolman had wandered behind the Dumpster and apparently encountered one of the bodies Lyons had virtually blown apart with the MK-7. There were sounds of scuffling footsteps, then "Oh, shit. Oh, my God," followed by retching noises.

"How do you suppose they pegged you?"

Lyons shrugged. "I'm not sure."

"The Cardinales girl?"

"I doubt it."

"Then who?"

Lyons turned, once more scanning the surrounding roofs that only a few hours ago had contained so much death. "Either they had us followed from the start, or else you've got a leak in the department, someone who knew we were going on a little excursion tonight."

Florio glanced past Lyons to a row of bodies laid out in the headlights and encased in plastic.

"A little excursion, Carl?"

"They must be like cats," Falco said as he paced back and forth.

The light from the halogen bulbs was harsh. He wore dark sunglasses. His eyes had become sensitive to the light. His movements had a sharp staccato rhythm, almost as if he were keeping time with some haunting melody. But there was no music. Several of the other gang members idled near the door, but everyone was silent. Atiff sat on a stool not far from Falco and didn't take his eyes off him.

"So now they only have seven more lives. What makes you so worried?"

"First they walk away from a silky. Then they walk out of that alley. And you ask me why I'm worried." He pressed a thumb and forefinger to the bridge of his nose. "You just don't have no idea what it means, do you? No idea at all."

Atiff seemed almost indifferent to Falco's anxiety. "It means they don't care about death. You cannot kill a man who doesn't care if he lives or dies. You can only wait. Wait until he makes a mistake."

Falco shook his head, and sank to what he called his throne. "You know, man, sometimes I think your Arab philosophy really does a number on my head."

"And your philosophy, my friend? What is your philosophy?"

"My philosophy is that I can kill anyone I want. Period."

"Then again I ask you, why worry?"

"Because I just don't like it, that's all. They know something is up. I can feel it."

"What do you mean they know something is up? You've killed almost a dozen cops since the first of the year. You think they didn't already know something is up?"

"They know we're planning something," Falco said, staring into Atiff's dark eyes.

"It doesn't matter," Atiff answered, ignoring Falco's glare. "Nobody can stop it now. Don't you understand that yet? No one can resist us. We are fighting a holy war, my friend."

"I didn't agree to fight your holy war, Atiff."

"It's too late for you to engage in such posturing. For as you say, they know something is up. In a day or two, they will trace down the rumors that you are being supplied by foreigners; and of course, they will find them to be accurate. And if they grasp the scope of our operations, they will order military forces in against us. And that might prove to be a significant setback in our operation. I'm afraid neither of us has any choice at the moment. We can only press ahead."

"Press ahead to what, man? Huh? To blowing up another ten million in crack. 'Cause I don't call that pressing ahead. I call that real stupid."

"If you live," Atiff said calmly, obviously tiring of this banter, "you will have ten times that much." He stood up, walked over to Falco and faced him from less than a foot away. "And if you fail and die, you won't care about it."

"Fine," Falco said with a bitter smile. "That's just fine."

Then, although he'd looked as if about to say something else, his attention was drawn to Lara. She entered the chamber from the rusting iron steps behind them, passing among the Desmodos without so much as a glance for any of them. The light from the quartz bulbs accentuated the angles of her face and torso. Falco could not behold her without experiencing certain involuntary responses of anatomy. And seeing her, he almost forgot his anger, his frustration and the colonel's incessant badgering.

She crossed the floor and stopped beside the two men. She looked back and forth from Atiff's cold countenance to Falco's hot, intense features.

Atiff tried, in an instant, to plumb the depths of her spirit, to look beyond her eyes. But if there was a deeper abyss of emotion than Atiff's own, frozen bottomless pit, it was Lara's soul. He found himself somehow suspended in her uneasy gaze, unable to fathom her, unable even to look for very long.

Lara quickly turned her gaze from Atiff's and smiled at Falco. For an instant, he felt comforted by her. But then the brief absence of his anxiety reminded him of its intensity. He reached out, grabbed her by both arms and pulled her forcefully to him. He pressed his mouth to hers and kissed her long and almost painfully. She finally had to gasp for air, but then she pressed their lips together again.

Falco looked over at Atiff, who feigned indifference.

"C'mon," Falco said, leading Lara quickly off toward the door. "We'll talk later."

Atiff did not respond. He only watched the couple as they exited the building. In their absence, everyone else inside relaxed. Several of the others began to chatter in Spanish and in English. Soon there was music playing while beer and handfuls of bagged crack were passed around. For the rest of the evening, the Desmodos forgot about their battles.

Atiff continued to watch them for a while. Then finally shaking his head in disgust, he slipped up the ancient staircase and into the street.

FALCO AND LARA SPED west on the Santa Monica Freeway. Three nights ago, while prowling through the Korean strip, a few of the Desmodos had wasted a student from the city college and ripped off a Honda Interceptor. As Falco drove the machine past the San Diego Freeway interchange, he was doing more than 135 miles per hour. It was a little past two in the morning. When they passed the Fourth Street exit, Falco ignored the highway patrol officer.

It was Lara who first heard the whine of the approaching siren. She turned back and brushed the hair from her eyes. A CHP cruiser was closing rapidly. She tapped Falco on the shoulder and yelled into his ear.

"Cop," she said, forcing her voice out through the onrushing wind.

Falco turned his head to see what she was talking about. The cruiser was nearly alongside of them now, and the officer was waving for them to pull over.

"Wanna have a little fun?" Falco asked as he slowed the bike and brought it to a stop along a desolate stretch of road. He put down the kickstand of the bike and got off.

"Watch," he whispered, kissing Lara on the cheek as he took a step toward the highway patrol car.

"Hold it right there," said the officer from behind his spotlight.

Falco winced and shielded his eyes.

"Put your hands on your head," the officer called out.

Falco squinted and complied with the order.

The patrolman stepped out from behind the door of his cruiser and took several steps toward his quarry. "I clocked you at 107," he said, "but I know you were doing a hell of a lot more than that back on the freeway. What's the big hurry, amigo?"

"It's a big bike," Falco said with a grin.

"Aren't you concerned about her safety?" the patrolman asked, nodding at Lara, who was now standing beside the bike.

"She can take care of herself," Falco returned coolly.

"Let me see some ID," the patrolman said.

"I got to take my hands down to show you my license," said Falco.

"Don't be a wiseass. Just take it out slowly and hand it over."

The officer was now close enough to Falco to see his face clearly. He immediately noticed his dilated pupils.

"Are you high?" the patrolman demanded.

"I'm high on life," Falco said, grinning broadly.

Falco was already reaching inside his jacket when the officer became concerned.

"Okay—hold it," said the patrolman, "face in the dirt! Now!"

They were the last words he spoke.

"Up yours, cop," Falco said as he whipped out the straight razor from inside his jacket and in one smooth movement cut a four-inch gash in the officer's throat.

The cop's hand had already clutched the butt of his service revolver. Automatically, his arm managed to withdraw the weapon from its holster, but that was all it could manage on its own. The .38 fell to the gravel. Blood from the officer's neck splattered over the revolver.

"Up yours," Falco repeated, as he turned to walk away.

Then gravity took over, and the patrolman's body crumpled like a rag doll. The knees gave way first. Then he fell facefirst onto the gravel. The last, confused sound the dying officer heard, aside from the rush of air escaping from his trachea, was the engine of the Interceptor starting up. The noise drowned out everything else, and as the bike pulled away, gravel and dust spewed over the now dead patrolman.

THE AIR WAS COOLER north of Malibu. The highway was virtually empty. Falco had slowed to a clean ninety miles per hour, while Lara remained clinging helplessly behind him. "Now, we go to your place," he had told her. "Now we go to your place and party, right?"

Lara's house lay on a bluff above the Pacific, eight miles north of Malibu. It might have not been the most exclusive lot, but Falco liked the seclusion. He also liked the long view of empty sand and limitless horizon behind. On this particular night, the sea lay still beneath a predawn fog. There was also a full moon, like a Chinese lantern suspended above the crescent shoreline.

In contrast to Falco's loft, Lara's house was virtually bare, the floors uncarpeted, the walls hung with only two or three abstract prints in muted pastels. The furniture was clean and uncluttered, made primarily of glass and tubular chrome. The bed, however, was pure Falco, with a lace canopy and silk sheets. And, of course, he had also insisted on mirrors along the bedroom walls and on the ceiling.

He told her to leave the lights off, and to fetch him a cold beer. Then he casually did a few rails of coke, and wandered through the living room out to the deck. There were times, usually toward dawn, when he would sit out on the deck for hours and simply stare at the incoming swells. Tonight, however, he was clearly much too agitated to leave her alone.

"So, baby, you having fun, or what?"

She nodded, but still couldn't face his eyes. "Sure, my darling. I'm having fun."

He smiled, and gently caressed the back of her neck. "How much fun?"

"Lots."

The caress grew more forceful, his fingers actually digging into her flesh. "You know, baby, I love it when you lie. Nothing finer than to hear you lie through those beautiful white teeth."

"I don't know what you're talking about."

"Take off your clothes."

"But, my darling, I was only—"

"Just take off your fucking clothes."

She complied meekly, keeping her gaze fixed on the redwood planks, but knowing that his excitement was rising at the vision of her body awash in the moonlight.

"Now, the rest," he said. "Everything."

She removed her bra, then the sheer panties. He reached out to touch a taut breast. Then, pinching the nipple between his fingers, he slowly drew her closer and down on her knees.

"You know what they do in Atiff's country to little girls who don't tell the truth?"

"Please, I don't want—"

"I'll tell you what they do. They hurt 'em. They hurt 'em real bad."

He drew up one of her tubular chrome chairs, and forced her to lie at his feet within casual reach of his right hand. Then running a finger along her leg, he began to whisper again.

"Sometimes if the girl is, you know, a real bitch, they tie her up to this big post in the marketplace and then they whip her with these big leather straps. Or sometimes maybe they brand her or even maybe cut off an ear or two."

He gently passed a hand over her left breast, then again over the small of her back.

"But, you know, I don't think that even something like that would do you too much good right now. I mean we done all kinds of bad things to you, and where did it get us? You're still telling me lies. You're still telling me how much fun you're having, and all the time you're lying. So what's the point of regular punishment for you? Huh? What's the point? That's why I been thinking that we need something special, something real special to teach you a lesson you'll never forget."

He reached into his jacket and slowly withdrew the straight razor he'd used to slit the CHP officer's throat. The edge was still coated with blood.

He wiped it carefully on the edge of the railing, then wiped it again on his trousers. Lara's eyes widened.

"So this is how it is, baby. You start telling little lies, and pretty soon you going to be telling big ones. And I can't let you get away with that, can I? So I got to teach you. I got to teach you right here and now."

She pressed her hands to the redwood planks, shutting her eyes and holding her breath.

"And besides, I know you like to bleed," he whispered. "All little bitches like to bleed."

He took the razor and carefully drew its edge along her naked abdomen, pressing only hard enough to leave a thin, red line. Here and there, a drop of blood pressed from between the edges of the tiny cut. A cool breeze arose, causing her flesh to stand stippled with goose bumps, while her muscles quivered with the colder touch of the razor's edge.

"Now, this ain't like my whip, baby. You start flinching and squirming under the blade, and you'll end up looking like hamburger. So you be still, and take it. You understand? You be real still.''

Then once again he drew the razor along the front of her body. But this time, he pressed more firmly, and a thin trickle of blood now accompanied it down toward her navel. But Falco didn't stop there. He kept going until the blade was hidden beneath the lacy curls of her pubic hair.

Lara clutched her face with her left hand and gasped a panicked breath. Falco, who was now kneeling before her, looked up and smiled. He let the razor drop to the deck and grabbed her by the buttocks. He pulled her body toward his face, and with the tip of his tongue he tasted the blood that trickled from the cut.

As usual, Falco's passion was quickly spent, and after a few minutes he was sleeping. Lara got up and slid back into her skirt. She left her blouse off so she could clean her wound and walked inside the house. She could hear the distant sirens.

What's the use, she thought as she went to the bathroom to wash out the cut. He's dead . . . we're all dead.

She finished washing and headed toward her bedroom. She lay in bed and watched the moon through the skylight. She knew in the morning she would wake, and he would be gone. And for several hours, sometimes days, she could live as if he didn't exist. But then, he would return; or worse, drawn to him like a moth to the flame, she would reenter his lordly and isolated world.

CARL LYONS AND HIS MEN arrived at the murder scene ten or fifteen minutes later than the rest of the police units that had been dispatched. Florio, who was always called whenever there was any hint of gang-related violence, was bent over the body, which was already cold.

"Desmodos?" Blancanales asked.

Hector Florio looked up into their faces.

"That's thirteen," he said as he stood up and brushed the gravel from his hands.

"Let's hope they're superstitious," Gadgets said.

"Doesn't matter," Florio answered, staring into the dark. "I am."

After an hour or more of close scrutiny of the scene, Florio directed that the slain officer's body be loaded onto a stretcher and taken away.

"At least I don't have to go and tell his wife," he said to Ironman as the two of them walked toward Florio's car.

Lyons, however, hadn't even heard his friend. All he said was, "It's too tight...too professional. There's just got to be another angle here."

"Regarding that so-called Arab link?"

"Maybe."

"So then what do you suggest?"

"I suggest we keep moving," Lyons said, "and fast."

"Look," said Florio, "we've been up since nearly dawn. I feel like I've been shot at and missed, shit at and hit. Let's get some sleep. We can get back at it in the morning."

"You don't really see it yet," Ironman said. "Or you see it but you just can't believe it. This ain't police work anymore, Hector. It's a goddamn war. You don't go to sleep in a war. You fight.''

''*You* fight, Carl. I'm going to sleep.''

Florio got in his car, started the engine and drove off. Then he stopped at the edge of the highway, put his head out the window and called, ''I'll be in my office by nine. I'll go back to war then.''

Ironman didn't respond. Gadgets and Blancanales were arguing over the type of motorcycle that had left the tire tracks near where the officer had fallen. Lyons called them over.

''We've got to get a line into these bastards,'' Ironman said. ''We've got to get some sort of perception on them.''

''What about the girl?'' Blancanales asked.

Lyons shook his head. ''Too unstable, at least for the moment.''

''Still, she came to us, didn't she?''

''All the more reason not to trust her.''

''Then what do you suggest?''

Again, however, Lyons just shook his head. ''I don't know. I just know there's something very strange about this whole thing.''

''Meaning you think she set us up?'' Gadgets asked.

''No...not intentionally at least. But I still don't want to depend on her, not now anyway.''

''So then what?'' Gadgets persisted.

Lyons clenched his jaw, gazing out to the flat, oily sea. ''Falco knows we're on to him, and he knows he can't shake us off. If he tries to hit us...fine; we can take him. But I don't think that's what he's going to do. There's something big, very big, in the works. I think they'll just speed up their timetable. So we've got to get some things done. Gadgets, I want you to check the records, look for anything that might tip us off as to what Falco's planning next. Pol, you check and make sure all our gear is ready. I've got a sneaking suspicion that we're going to be knee-deep in shit before too long. I want to make sure my boots don't leak.''

Schwarz and Blancanales each gave him a thumbs-up.

''Let's move. You two can go back to the hotel and get some sleep. And you can drop me at the station. I want to get a wire off to Stony Man Farm. They may have some intel on any Middle East infiltration of the gang communities. We're not just dealing with a bunch of hopped-up bad boys here. These guys are on a mission.''

LARA CARDINALES WOKE from a brief and restless sleep. It was 4:00 a.m. When she was a child, her mother had warned her about that hour, calling it *la hora d'el lobo*...the hour of the wolf. She'd never gotten out of bed at that time of the morning.

Now she knew what she had to do. She rose like a sleepwalker, and with each step felt she was dying a little more. By the time she reached the kitchen, her head was spinning. She had trouble keeping her balance. She made her way to the drawer where she kept the knives. Pulling on the handle, she opened the drawer. The glint of the steel blades caught her eye in the dim light. She reached in and took hold of a knife. She didn't care which. She tested the sharpness of the blade with her thumb. A tiny cut opened. It would do.

She made her way through the living room. The
sliding door to the deck was still open. Now each step
became heavier until walking was a monumental
chore. Finally, she reached the threshold. Her heart
was beating heavily in her throat and in her ears. She
raised the knife above her head and stepped onto the
deck.

Falco was gone. She let the knife fall. Its point stuck
in the soft redwood and it wobbled back and forth.
For a moment, she was relieved. Then her relief
changed to anger. She was shaking, dizzy. She walked
to the railing and leaned against it. Soon she was
breathing normally again. The little cut on her thumb
began to sting. She sucked on it and vowed it was the
last cut she would ever get. And then she just stood
and watched for an hour or more as the ocean swal-
lowed the moon.

14

"I've got somebody here I think you should talk to," Blancanales said into the phone.

A passing motorist leaned on his horn, swerving to avoid an old lady at a crosswalk. A couple of kids on skateboards careened through a motley crowd of commuters waiting for a bus. A bag lady stretched herself out on the sidewalk, oblivious to everything. It was ten o'clock in the morning, and already fiercely hot. Blancanales had to shout into the mouthpiece in order to make himself heard.

"What?" he continued. "Yeah. I was having a chili dog over at this place called Pinks. Sure. Great dogs. But there was this weird little character sitting in the back, and...well I think you should talk to him. I think I should bring him down, and let you talk to him. No, I'm not kidding. I think he can help. Look, you were the one who said we needed to get some sort of perception on the field. Well, all right, I think I've got a guy who might be able to give us that perception. Name? Well, he calls himself the Philosopher. That's right, the Philosopher. Well, it's not going to kill you to listen to him. Hey, Carl, am I ever wrong about this sort of thing? All right, so once I was wrong. But this time... Look, let me just bring him down to the station so you can talk to him. Fine. See you in fifteen.''

Blancanales hung up the phone and muttered to himself.

"Say what?" his new companion asked.

The Philosopher was a lanky black, with a veritable mushroom cloud of faintly blue hair. He wore loose-fitting turquoise trousers that fastened at the waist with a drawstring and a bright yellow silk shirt adorned with abstract renderings of pink and green birds. His eyes were deep and virtually radiant, with an oddly primitive wisdom. His skin was leathery, suggesting a lifetime spent in the sun. And although apparently frail, he seemed to possess an almost inhuman energy, which he attributed to a dietary supplement of almond paste, seaweed and something called a Green Turbo shake.

"So, mon. We go talk to your colleagues now?"

The Philosopher's accent was also fairly exotic, sometimes suggesting a Jamaican heritage, sometime simply L.A. jive.

"Yeah," Blancanales replied. "We go talk to my colleagues now."

"And they also professional killers?"

"What the hell makes you say a thing like that?"

The Philosopher smiled, slowly shifting his gaze to Blancanales's eyes. "Because I see into your soul."

By this time they had reached the Politician's rented car—a 1959 Chevrolet Impala convertible. Blancanales had seen the Dreamboats ad in the *L.A. Weekly* and he hadn't been able to turn down the opportunity to drive one of the beauties.

"Get in," Blancanales said.

"Different sort of cop car," the Philosopher responded.

"Just get the hell in."

The Philosopher slid onto the passenger seat and leaned back as Blancanales pulled away from the curb. When they reached the Rampart Street station some fifteen minutes later, the Philosopher merely smiled and whispered, "Exactly. Professional killers."

"JUST TELL THEM what you told me," Blancanales said.

Initially, however, the Philosopher merely grinned, gazing knowingly at Lyons and Schwarz, while contentedly nibbling on a doughnut. Then finally lowering his eyes to the doughnut as if to examine it on a molecular level, he murmured, "Glazed. Glazed with da cherry filling."

"Go on," Blancanales said. "Tell them about the Arab."

"Ah." The Philosopher smiled. "Dee Arab. Dee Arab of dee desert wastes, man of a thousand battles, eyes dat have seen too much and forgotten too little... Dee Arab."

"This is good, Pol," Lyons scoffed. "This guy is real good."

"Just wait a minute," Blancanales snapped. Then to the Philosopher, he said, "Look, remember when you told me how the Arab and the Desmodos—"

"Ah, yes. Dee Desmodos. Da very embooty-ment of evil. Da nightmare of all who dwell in the belly of dis jungle. The veritable—"

"Okay," Blancanales finally cut in. "Just get to the point."

The Philosopher shrugged, then at last without a trace of the previous accent, "The Desmodos are in league with this Arab, see? And the Arab is in league with some very big dudes."

"What sort of dudes?" Lyons asked.

"Libyans. The Arab is from Libya. You know, as in Khaddafi's Libya."

Lyons glanced at Blancanales. Blancanales glanced at Schwarz. The Philosopher returned his probing gaze to that half-eaten doughnut, and then smiled again.

"Now, naturally, you dudes got to understand that what I'm saying here is just the rap. Know what I mean? It's the rap you hear on the street. But I do happen to believe that those Desmodos definitely got a backer."

"And by backer you mean exactly what?" Lyons asked.

"I mean a *backer*. A big money, meaner-than-shit backer. A dude who gives them bread, keeps them fed and pissed off in the head. Now, 'course, this here is just the word on the streets, but them streets do talk. Understand what I'm saying? I mean like you walk down the streets, and you listen hard enough and you can here that ol' concrete whispering to you, singing you all kinds of little songs about what's been going down, and what's been going round, who's been getting screwed and who's been getting unglued."

"And what do those streets tell you about the leader of the Desmodos?" Lyons asked. "What do they tell you about a guy called Falco?"

The Philosopher took another bite of his doughnut, and shifted that dreamy gaze to the ceiling. "Falco," he said, smiling. Then again with a vaguely Jamaican accent, "Falcoo. What a mon. What a devil. What a bad dude. You know one time I see him. I really *see* him good, right down to da soul. He walk out of some fancy place on da Strip, and I happen to be walking too that night, just walking along and minding my own business. And what do I see? I see da Falcoo. I look up into his eyes and I see da Falcoo's soul. And it's black, mon. It's black like coal. Which, by da way, is why dee Arab come to Falco, mon. See dee Arab, he lookin' for a bad dude from da streets to make trouble for da people. See, dee Arab need to make a lot of trouble in the streets so dat America know not to mess with dee tribes. So dee Arab, he come to Falcoo and he say, 'Make me a war, mon. Make me a war that really scare shit out of America.' And Falcoo, he say, 'Okay, mon, I make you a real war.' Den dee Arab give Falcoo lots of guns and tings like dat so dee war can be a happenin' ting."

"Yeah," Lyons said. "I think we got it."

"But if you got dat, den you better get dis, too. Da streets, day don't just talk about Falcoo and dee Arab. I tink dey also talk about you. I tink dey talk about dees certain guys who tink dey can paste Misser Falcoo, but in fact dey probably going to get pasted demselves."

This time it was Schwarz who spoke, returning the philosopher's gaze full bore. "What are you talking about?"

"I talk about Misser Falcoo's ears. I talk about how dis Falcoo, he got ears everywhere. I talk about how he got ears wit all kine of bery important dudes who tell him all kine of bery important secrets. I talk about how you dudes got to be real careful or Falco goin' to nail your ass bad. Also I talk about how you dudes better start lookin' at dem high places, 'cause dat's where you goin' to get nailed. Now you understand what I'm talkin' about? Bery, bery high places.''

IT ENDED in the parking lot where Blancanales had escorted the Philosopher to a waiting black-and-white. The heat by now was relentless, although the Philosopher didn't seem to notice. His pockets were filled with at least three doughnuts he had picked up en route from the briefing room. He also seemed pretty happy about the prospect of riding in a black-and-white without handcuffs.

"What you think, mon? I tell 'em good, or what?''

Blancanales slipped on his aviator sunglasses, and gazed out to the shimmering pavement and limp palms. "Yeah, man, you told them good." Then slowly laying a hand on the Philosopher's shoulder, he said, "Assuming you were telling the truth."

"Hey, what you tink, mon? Course I tell da truth. Everything about dis Philosopher is true . . . except maybe da fact dat I don't always speak like dis. Know what I mean, Jack?''

"SO WHAT DO YOU THINK?'' Lyons asked.

Schwarz glanced at the empty chair now littered with doughnut crumbs, then back at Blancanales. "I think," Schwarz said, "that next time we shouldn't let the Politician here out on the streets by himself.''

Blancanales started to defend himself, but was silenced by one of Ironman's more menacing glares. "All right, so maybe we were just wasting time with that maniac. But there's one thing for sure. The Desmodos definitely have this city in their grip."

"Or at least somebody does," Blancanales put in. He moved to the chair where the Philosopher had been sitting. "Now, I'm not saying that he was the most reliable witness I've ever come up with. But on the other hand, I don't think we can totally discount everything he said. There's just too much parallel evidence. I mean what did the girl say? She said that Falco's being backed by some Arab. She also said that this Arab has a line into some pretty high places. Now you want to ignore all that? That's your choice. But I think we're definitely under somebody's microscope, and I don't like it. Anyway, it's not like this would be the first time that a foreign terrorist network enlists local help to wage its wars, a network with links to high places."

"And it wouldn't be the first time we're caught in the middle, either," said Schwarz. "But I'm sure as hell not going to take that idiot's word for it."

"But maybe I will," Lyons said. "Maybe I'll do just what he suggests, and take a look at dem bery, bery high places."

15

Dr. North often did his best thinking while strolling the campus grounds. He generally walked in the late afternoon, when the cooling breeze rose and the shadows began to stretch across the flagstones. He liked to take a southwest route, past the eucalyptus groves beyond the student union. Sometimes he even paused at the edge of the high lawns, because he still enjoyed watching the coeds. On this particular Tuesday afternoon, however, he kept mainly to the more secluded paths, to the paths that lay behind the parking complex where a man could be alone with his fears.

About ten years ago, North had made a fairly comprehensive study of fear. For the most part he had been concerned with the more common fears: fears of dark streets and urban prowlers, fears of skidding automobiles on rain-swept freeways, fears of malignant tumors, coronaries and dentists. But briefly, inspired by a short sabbatical in Bali, he had also examined primitive fear, gut-wrenching, white-knuckled primitive fear. Which, he supposed, was roughly the sort of fear he was experiencing now.

He paused where the path fell away to a particularly dark and tangled grotto of dwarf pines and white ivy, wincing with a quick vision of some swarthy killer waiting with a razor. He shook it off, continued on the flagstones, then nearly jumped out of his skin at the sound of a sparrow in the branches above. This has got to stop, he told himself. This has simply got to stop. But almost simultaneous with that thought, he heard footsteps on the path behind him.

He turned and took a few steps back, vaguely wondering what to do with his hands, desperately wishing he had remembered to pack the little Colt revolver he had purchased the year of all those robberies. He turned again, once more telling himself that his fears were silly, but at the same time scanning around him for some sort of weapon.

When at last he picked up a length of lead pipe that one of the groundsmen must have discarded after repairs on the sprinklers, there was a moment when he actually felt pretty formidable, pretty damn dangerous considering that he was basically just a flabby psychiatrist with occasional sinus problems.

Then he heard the voice from only inches behind him, a very soft but menacing voice literally whispering into his left ear.

"You know, Doctor, you're going to look pretty stupid with that pipe sticking out of your ass," Carl Lyons said.

Dr. North let the pipe slip from his hand and stepped back to face Lyons. Lyons responded with a thin smile, and casually jammed his hands into the pockets of blue jeans. There were distant sounds of giggling coeds and drums from the athletic field, but otherwise it was very quiet.

North assumed an indignant tone. "I demand to know why you were stalking me."

Lyons, on the other hand, could not have been more relaxed. "Is that what I was doing, Doc? Stalking you?"

"You know perfectly well what I'm talking about."

But Lyons only continued smiling. "All I know, Doctor, is that you are one nervous shrink. Now why don't you tell me what's bothering you? Who knows. Might even help."

They began to walk, following the flagstones to a flight of concrete steps above the medical quad. A couple of obviously tranquilized patients sat gazing at nothing along the low wall, but otherwise the grounds were empty.

"Why don't you just tell me why you're here?" North said.

Lyons shrugged. "I don't know. Call it a hunch."

"About what?"

"That maybe you know a little more about what's going on than you're letting on."

"Well, that's ridiculous," North said. "Utterly absurd." A third patient, a potentially pretty girl with tragically wasted eyes, mumbled some sort of greeting to North. The doctor, however, ignored her.

"You know, I never did much cotton to shrinks," Lyons said. "Not sure what it is. Just never did like them much."

"Perhaps it's because you fear they will find things out about you that you'd prefer to keep hidden," North replied.

Lyons seemed to think about it a moment, but then said only, "Nah. I think I just don't like 'em."

They had reached the edge of the treatment facility grounds, where an expansive view of the research facility dwarfed everything around it.

"I will tell you one thing, though," Lyons added. "You boys sure do know how to rake in the dough. I mean talk about a nice little setup. This place really takes the cake."

"This institute happens to be one of the foremost centers of its kind," North replied. "The work we do here is indispensable to the welfare of society."

"Oh, I don't doubt it for a moment, Doctor, not for a moment."

As they walked along one side of the hospital building, they passed another four or five clearly sedated patients, gazing blankly from behind a chain-link fence.

"Although I must admit that there is one thing I'm kind of curious about," Lyons said.

"And what's that?"

"Who the hell pays for all this?"

North assumed a slightly pompous pose. "The institute," he said, "is primarily funded through the public sector by means of various federal grants, chiefly from the National Institute of Mental Health. Does that answer your question, Mr. Lyons?"

"Yeah. That answers it . . . to a degree."

"And what is that supposed to mean?"

Lyons paused, gazing at the doorway of the high-security section. "Well, it's like this, Doctor. Now, I can fully understand how you might be able to snow the Feds into paying for some of the stuff that goes on around here. I mean you tell 'em you need a hundred thou to study some lunatic's brain. But what I don't understand is how you can convince them to pay for a six-million-dollar study of urban violence syndrome...particularly when everybody knows that your program is bullshit."

North colored slightly, but his voice remained calm. "The fact of the matter is this, Mr. Lyons. If I am successful in determining the cause of urban violence, people like yourself may no longer be necessary. And *that* would certainly be worth six million dollars to the American taxpayer."

"Couldn't agree more, Doctor. Couldn't agree more. Only thing is, me and my boys simply respond to the violence. We don't contribute to it."

North stopped abruptly, narrowing his eyes. "Are you accusing me of something, Mr. Lyons?"

"Maybe."

"Then I would appreciate it if you'd just come out and say it so I might file a proper complaint with your superiors."

"Well, that's just it, Doctor. I know you're doing something dirty, but I don't think I can prove it. Just the same, though, it's been nice talking with you."

"TELL ME, DOCTOR," Colonel Atiff said, "are you at all familiar with the tales of Hasan?"

It was nearly midnight, with another desert wind scattering refuse across the east-side boulevards. Although the crumbling parking structure where North had joined Atiff appeared to be empty, the wavering shadows and stirring bits of paper suggested dangerous movement.

"Well, there is one tale, I think, that is most appropriate," the Colonel continued. "It concerns a certain agent of the Hashashin, who had been employed to help rid the old master of a particularly troublesome caliph. As the day of doom approached, however, this agent began to demonstrate signs of cowardice. He began to complain that people were watching him, suspecting him, covertly accusing him of plotting the caliph's demise. So what was the master to do? Here he was about to triumph over his enemy, but yet the agent employed to bring about this triumph was proving to be bothersome. Very well, this is what he did. He arranged it so that the agent had no alternative but to murder the troublesome caliph. Then as a fitting reward, he arranged for the agent, also, to be killed...cut into little pieces, if I remember correctly, and these were then fed to the dogs. Now, Doctor, what seems to be troubling you?"

North moved to the edge of the railing and gazed down to the garbage-strewed streets and the narrow lanes between the blackened tenements. Although he had already popped two Valium tablets, he couldn't help feeling that the colonel's little speech warranted another.

"All right," he said, "so I'm worried. But that doesn't mean there's nothing to be worried about."

"Oh, I couldn't agree more, Doctor. Indeed, this little world of ours is fraught with dangers. But were it not, people like you and I would have no place in it. We would be purposeless, useless, adrift in a sea of boredom. Besides, I was under the impression that you *wanted* a degree of chaos, for how can you justify a six-million-dollar grant to study violence, if there is no violence. Hmm? Tell me that, Doctor.''

North turned from the railing. "Look, Colonel. I'm talking about a very specific problem here. I'm talking about the fact that I am now under suspicion, and I don't like it. I don't like it one bit.''

"No," Atiff said with a smile, "I don't suppose you do.''

"So how are you going to handle it?''

"Handle what, Doctor?''

"I told you. These people, this so-called Able Team.''

"Ah, yes. Able Team. Those persistent little dogs that continue to sniff at our heels.''

"My heels, Colonel. They happen to be sniffing at my heels. And if I'm not mistaken, it won't be long before they start biting.''

Again, however, the colonel merely smiled. "Well, in that case, Doctor, I suggest you get a tetanus vaccination in advance.''

North moved away from the railing, once more narrowing his eyes to ominous slits. "Look, Colonel. Let me make one thing very clear. You came to me, I didn't come to you. You originally hired me as a consultant, not a spy. Now that you've insisted I serve as a spy, I cannot be held accountable for the consequences.''

Atiff returned North's gaze, but this time without a smile. "Are you threatening me, Doctor?''

"Of course not. I was simply pointing out that if I fall, you will fall with me.''

Atiff smiled. "Yes, Doctor, I do believe you are threatening me.''

"Well, the fact is that if I am called to account for certain professional inconsistencies, you can hardly expect me to—"

"Die, Doctor. That is what I can expect you to do. I can expect you to die a most horrible death. Now, you want to talk to me about Able Team? Fine, I shall talk to you about Able Team. But if you ever threaten me again, I shall follow the policy of Hasan and cut you into tiny pieces. Do you understand? Very tiny pieces."

North returned to the railing, once more gazing down at the ruins of tenements. Atiff stood less than a foot away, his slender but muscular arms resting on the steel guard. Although the wind had subsided, the streets were still alive with shifting debris.

"I happen to have a theory about these men," Atiff said. "Now, of course, this theory has yet to be tested, but I feel confident that it will prove effective in the end."

He lit a cigarette, holding it like a peashooter, and apparently luxuriating in the first long draw of Turkish tobacco.

"When I was a child, living near Al Khums, I recall that one winter my village was plagued with a pack of wild dogs. Now, these were not ordinary dogs, but unusually bold and vicious animals. In fact, one evening they were even so bold as to enter the house of a farmer and steal a small baby from the cradle. And, of course, they made a meal of it. So, what was to be done? Well, the village elders thought long and hard on the matter. Should they try to shoot the dogs? Should they visit the herbalist and ask him to concoct a poison? What should be done?"

"Colonel, I hardly think that—"

"Don't interrupt me, Doctor, because I think you will find this story illuminating. Now, where was I? Ah, yes. The elders thought long and hard about how to rid their village of these marauding dogs. Then one evening the brother of the oldest and wisest man in the village appeared. He had heard of the problem, you see, and he had come to offer his many years of wisdom to help solve that problem. And this is what he advised. 'You must not concern yourself with destroying the entire pack,' he said. 'All you must do is capture one of the dogs, and kill it in a way that is so horrible and so frightening that the remainder of the pack will never again enter your village.' Very well, it was decided that one of the dogs was to be captured and brutally killed as a chilling example to the others. Now, unfortunately, I cannot recall exactly how the animal was killed. Perhaps they cut off his legs and stuffed them down his throat. Perhaps they boiled him alive in oil. Perhaps they cut off all his fur, and set him out for the ants to devour. Frankly I cannot remember. I do, however, remember this: never again did my little village have a problem with wild dogs."

The colonel tossed away his cigarette, and turned to face North. "So, Doctor. You are having trouble with a small pack of wild dogs sniffing at your feet? Very well, I shall turn one of them into an example so terrible that none of the others will dare sniff again. And poof! That will be the end of your problem. So go home now, and sleep well. But remember if you ever try to threaten me again, I will make you the example."

16

It was a night for suspicion, a windblown night of suspicion and distrust. Falco had determined that at least two of his warriors had been withholding crack profits from him, and thus he had been forced to order their execution. But even as he had stared at their bodies, stared into their lifeless eyes, he had known that it wasn't the end of the treachery...not by a long shot.

It was just after midnight when Falco returned to his loft. The windows had been left ajar, and the room seemed alive with billowing curtains. Lara dozed on the low divan. He roused her with a kiss, a surprisingly gentle kiss that merely brushed her lips. Then when she opened her eyes, he smiled and kissed her again.

"So," he whispered. "I find you sleeping like an angel, a beautiful angel from heaven."

She returned his smile, not really certain what had prompted this kindness, but not really caring, either.

"What time is it?" she asked.

He shook his head, brushing his lips against her lips again. "What does it matter? I'm rich, you're beautiful, so what does time matter?" Then slipping his hand into the pocket of his leather jacket, he produced a slender velvet box. "Here, I brought you something. A flawless little something for a flawless woman."

She took the box, opened it and withdrew a tiny gold heart suspended from a silver chain.

"Oh, my darling, it's beautiful. It's really beautiful."

He gave her another glancing kiss. "Also, I'll tell you something else about it. It's magic. It's got real magic in it."

She rose to an elbow, examining the pendant in the weak light of a Tiffany lamp. "What kind of magic?"

"Well, I'll show you. See how shiny it is? You can even see your face in it. Well, if you look at someone's reflection in this thing, you will always know if they're telling the truth. Let's say you're talking with someone, all you got to do is hold this thing up until you can see the reflection in their eyes and then you'll know if they're telling the truth."

She lifted the tiny heart to the light again, and turned it until she could see the reflection in his eyes.

"All right," she said softly. "Let me try it out. Now, tell me the truth. Do you love me or not? Hmm? Do you?"

He met her gaze in the tiny reflection, held it for an instant, then slowly nodded. "You know I love you, baby. You know sometimes maybe you make me sad, and sometimes I hurt you, but deep down where it counts I always love you."

She let her head fall onto his shoulder, shutting her eyes in a momentary trance of happiness.

But just as suddenly it was over, and his touch grew cold again, and his voice began cutting like a razor. "Now it's my turn," he said. "Now we are going to see if you're telling the truth."

He snatched the pendant from her hand, and dangled it in front of her face until it caught the reflection of her frightened eyes. "Okay now, baby, here's the question. You been faithful to me, or you been scheming behind my back? Huh? Which one is it, baby? Which one? You my faithful angel, or you a scheming little bitch?"

She slid off the bed and moved to the window, becoming framed against the blue panes of glass.

"Why do you do this to me?" she asked. "Why?"

He stepped up behind her, and slowly slid the strap of her gown away to reveal the smooth dark tones of her shoulder. "Just answer the question, baby. You been good, or you been bad? Which is it?"

"Falco, please."

"I want to hear it while you're looking at me. Have you been good, or have you been bad?"

She lifted her gaze to meet his eyes in the window's reflection, then saw those eyes again in that dangling pendant.

"I've been good, Falco."

He took a deep breath, holding her in his gaze for at least another fifteen seconds before finally whispering, "Yeah. Sure you have, baby. Sure you have."

She remained at the window, watching his reflection as he poured a glass of whiskey, did a rail or two of coke and finally withdrew a .25 Seecamp autopistol, with a stainless-steel finish and a seven-round capacity. He cocked it and laid it on the ebony nightstand.

"Now we're going to play a different game, baby. Now we're going to play a game we never played before."

Leaving the pistol on the nightstand, he returned to the window, and guided her back to the bed. The pistol lay in easy reach of her right hand.

"Now this is the way we play it," he said. "I'm going to stand at the wall, and I want you to think about all the bad things I've done to you. All the times I hurt you. All the times I made you feel like dirt. I want you to think about those things real good. I want you to picture them in your mind. Then I want you to remember how it felt, how it felt to be squirming under my whip or quivering under that blade. I want you to remember every little bit of it, and then I want you to pick up this .25 and do whatever you want to do."

She glanced at the pistol, then back at those vaguely hypnotic eyes, and shook her head. "Don't do this, Falco. Don't do this to me."

He stepped back to the wall, and slowly slid down to a squat. But the eyes never left her for a moment.

"Hey, you think I'm some kind of a monster, baby? Okay, well now I'll give you a chance to do something about it. Right now. Right here. You think about all the shit I did to you. You think about it real good. You let the emotions come right up to the surface, and then you pick up that pistol and just squeeze the trigger. Just squeeeeeeeze the trigger."

She glanced at the pistol again, trying to imagine the weight of it, the feel of the cool steel and the Lexan grip. But then she looked into Falco's eyes, eyes that had always left her helpless, numb, virtually nailed to the floorboards.

"Okay, I make it easy for you," he said. "I make it real easy. I'm going to remind you of all the things I did to you, okay? I'm going to remind you about that time I beat the living crap out of you in Vegas. You remember that time, baby? I beat the living crap out of you, 'cause you didn't want to make it with those hookers. You remember that now? Those hookers, they come over to our place one night, and I tell you to make it with them, while I watch. But you don't want to make it with them. So I tie you up to that big bed, and start whaling on you with that big cane I had. I start whaling on you real good, and all the while them hookers are just watching and laughing and feeling you up and everything. You remember that now? Okay, well, you pick up that pistol. Come on, I want you to do it. I *want* you to."

But even as her hand began to move, to slowly slide along her thigh toward the nightstand, she felt his eyes again, actually felt them draining her, leaving her listless and empty while her mind began whirling with images.

"Come on, baby," he cooed. "You hate me so bad? Well, here's your chance. Here's your chance to end it. All you got to do is just pick up that little .25 and put the bullet between my eyes. Come on, do it. Do it. *Do it!*"

Without warning, her hand shot out and swept the pistol to the floor. "Stop it!" she screamed. *"Stop it!"*

Then it was very quiet, with only the sound of the wind.

For a long time after he had fallen asleep, she remained by the window and watched. She watched the steady rise and fall of his chest as he breathed, the occasionally stirring hand. She watched the shadows shifting across his face, and the blinking glow of red neon on the opposite wall. Now and again she also let her gaze fall on the pistol—still lying on the rug, apparently cocked and ready to fire.

I'm invincible, he had once told her. I can't be killed, 'cause I'm already dead.

And as she glanced at that pistol again, she supposed that he had been telling her the truth after all. Totally invincible.

She turned back to the window, pressed her palms against the cool panes of glass and felt the tears roll down her cheeks. *And if he's dead, then I must be dead, too.*

She let her head fall to her shoulder, once more sensing the helplessness, the numb paralysis that entered her body whenever she stood in his presence.

But if I'm already dead, then what have I got to lose?

And very slowly, very cautiously, she slid away from the window and moved to where that pistol lay.

If I'm already dead, what the hell have I got to lose?

She picked it up, feeling the weight of it, the cold, hard mass of it in her hand. Because there were no sights on the Seecamp .25, she didn't exactly aim; she just pointed it at the base of his skull. Then taking a long and slow breath, she slowly squeezed the trigger.

Click, as the hammer fell on an empty chamber.

So that was his game. A clever little test for a helpless little girl.

Click, click, click.

17

Gadgets found sleep elusive. For more than an hour he had lain in bed staring at the sweep of headlights reflected off the motel room wall, listening to the night sounds of L.A.—all to no avail. Then he had turned on the television, and watched for a while some preacher in a sharkskin suit talking about the devil. "The devil is very powerful in this city," the preacher had screamed. "He's in your neighborhood. He's in your home. He's in your refrigerator."

Finally Gadgets moved to the open window and drew back the curtains. The air was thick and heavy. A marine layer, he thought. But it wasn't really a marine layer. It was a death layer, an invisible film that spread from every fatal act of violence, merged and then spread some more until you could actually feel it, smell it, taste it. Late-night and early-morning death along the coast, clearing by noon. He wondered how people could stand living in the same weather day after day, year after year...until some psychopath pumps a bullet in their head and they, too, became part of the death layer.

The devil is in your refrigerator.

The night seemed endless, a whirling void that left him dizzy, exhausted but still unable to sleep. He moved to the bathroom, poured himself a glass of foul-tasting water and drank it down with a grunt. He returned to the window, inhaling the equally foul air, then back to the bed, and lay very still until he heard the gentle tap-tap on the door.

Death? The refrigerator repairman?

"Gadgets, you in there?" Lyons asked.

Schwarz rolled off the bed, unlocked the door, but then turned back to the open window.

"I heard your TV," Lyons said, "so I figured you were awake."

"Yeah," Schwarz breathed. "I'm awake."

"You want to go get something to eat or something?"

Schwarz shook his head. "I'm not hungry."

"You want to just go get a beer?"

Again Schwarz just shook his head. "Actually, I was thinking maybe I'd take the van, go for a drive, see the sights."

Lyons moved to his old friend's side, briefly placed a hand on Gadgets's shoulder. "You all right, man?"

Schwarz took a long time to answer. "Sure, I'm all right," he finally murmured. "I think I just need to get out on my own for a while, maybe drive out to the coast or something."

"Okay," Lyons said, sighing. "Let me get you the keys."

NIGHT WINDS, stinking of exhaust and fried meat, kicked up loose papers all over the pavement, as Schwarz descended to the parking lot, and distant gunshots mingled with the echo of sirens. Across the street more than fifty wasted teenagers were waiting for the one o'clock showing of *A Nightmare on Elm Street*. As he shifted into drive and pulled out of the TraveLodge lot, he sensed that someone was watching from behind the windshield of a cut-down Chevy.

He drove slowly, just drifting with the flashing lights around him, from Santa Monica Boulevard up to Sunset, then back down to Fountain, where any number of hookers lingered in the shadows. According to local legend, the lifespan of an L.A. prostitute, from the time she turned her first trick, was less than seven years. Seven years before she succumbed either to AIDs or to one of the predatory johns who also prowled the shadows.

Then, like a ghost image in his rearview mirror, Schwarz caught another glimpse of the Chevy.

Relax, he told himself. You're jumping at shadows. Get out on the open road, and let the wind blow the cobwebs from your head.

He sped up at an intersection where two young teenagers called out from a doorway, "Hey, dude, you want to see what we got?" He slowed to avoid an obviously stoned boy who had wandered off the curb. He switched on the radio, turning the dial past a barrage of heavy metal, rap, jive and finally another frantic evangelist talking about the devil...this time the devil of the airwaves.

At the next intersection a second cut-down Chevy pulled in front of his van and stopped.

Six Desmodos converged on the van. Three carried sawed-off Remingtons, two carried AK-47s, one carried a .38 revolver. They came from both ends of the van, with a mixture of curses and orders. One of the Remingtons blasted the tires, while the butt of an AK-47 slammed into the windshield and at least five muzzles pressed against the glass.

Although Schwarz knew it was fruitless, knew it would probably just get him killed that much sooner, he couldn't help trying to take at least one down with him. He waited until the first Desmodo had approached the door, jamming a Remington against the glass and screaming, "Get out of the van, asshole!" Pulling down on the handle and throwing his shoulder to the door, Gadgets sailed out to meet the punk.

He struck for the kneecap first, because he wanted to inflict real damage. Then grabbing hold of the Remington's barrel, he hammered his fist into the punk's neck. He saw the boy's eyes widen with shock and pain, felt his expiring breath on his face, and heard the strained choke as he tried to inhale through a crushed windpipe.

A split second later, Schwarz heard his own breath expiring as the butt of another Remington crashed into his skull and sent him head over heels into the swirling lights of the city.

LIGHTS FLICKERED on the edge of Schwarz's vision. Faces peered from the edge of consciousness. Voices echoed in his ringing ears.

"Hey, I think you hit him too hard, man."

"What you talking about? He's alive, ain't he?"

"I don't know, man. He don't look too good."

"Sure, he looks good. He just got a little bump on the head, that's all."

"I don't know, man. I think you screwed him up. I think you screwed him up real bad."

Silence, except for music from a distant radio.

Schwarz clenched his right fist, then slowly tried to lift his arm. Hopeless.

He tensed his legs, and tried to rise. Completely hopeless.

He slowly lowered his gaze until he caught a glimpse of the ropes that fastened him to the massive oak chair.

He seemed to be in some sort of circular chamber, a damp and foul place far beneath the surface of the street. The walls of blackened brick, and the ceiling twenty feet above, might have been cut directly from the stone. In the distance, two diverging passages led into utter darkness, while a flight of concrete steps led to what looked like an iron door. Then by degrees, it all came back to him: the Desmodos, this city, his life, the pain.

"You know who I am?" Falco asked. "Huh? You know who I am?"

Gadgets gazed around him wearily. The cavern walls were lined with at least fifty silent Desmodos. The torchlight flickered on their sweating faces, accenting the cruel shadows of scars and tattoos. Falco slowly circled the stout oak chair, occasionally testing the nylon cord that bound Gadgets's arms and legs. In contrast to his jean-clad followers, he wore an exquisitely tailored velvet jacket, purple velvet slacks and high-heeled black boots. His hair was drawn back in a ponytail, and secured with a gold ring. The pinkie of his left hand had been painted bright red.

Then suddenly striking out with the toe of his boot, slamming it into Schwarz's shin, he said, "Hey, I asked you a question! You know who I am?"

Gadgets's chin dropped with the stabbing pain that seemed to shoot up from his shin to a secret and tender spot deep inside his brain. Finally regaining some semblance of control, he whispered Falco's name.

"That's right." Falco smiled. "That's who I am. Now, who are you? Huh? You Luke Skywalker? You James Bond? Who?"

Another glancing kick to the shin, then a cooling trickle of blood.

"Nobody," Schwarz whispered. "I'm nobody."

Falco smiled, thoughtfully smoothing a thumb and forefinger along his chin, gazing with that same faint smile at the impassive faces of his followers.

"Hey, you guys hear that? He says he's nobody." A third quick kick to the shin. "Well, ain't that the truth."

A girl approached, a stocky girl in jeans and a filthy tank top. She wore heavy construction boots, and her thick hair was cropped short like a boy's. Her arms bore evidence of heavy weight lifting, and her hands were deeply callused.

"This here is Bad Lucy," Falco said, smiling again. "Lucy, this here is Mr. Nobody. Say hello to him."

The girl placed her hands on her hips, and nodded. Although her features suggested that she was only fifteen or sixteen, her eyes suggested she'd seen a great deal of pain.

"Now, Lucy here has kind of a problem," Falco added. "I don't know what you call it. Maybe it's some kind of mental problem, you know? Anyway, she likes to hurt people. Like when she was a little girl, for instance, she used to get her kicks sticking needles under the fingernails of all the other kids in the neighborhood. So finally they sent her to one of those institutions, but that didn't help none. In fact, all she did there was figure out new ways to hurt people."

Falco snapped his fingers and another Desmodo, a slender boy with oddly innocent eyes, appeared with what looked like a flashlight, but was probably some sort of electronic stun gun. Falco took the gun, handed it to the girl and then turned back to Gadgets.

"How about we start with a little get-to-know-you talk, huh? Like, for instance, what the hell are you doing here, anyway?"

Schwarz shook his head, blinking into Falco's dark eyes. "I don't know," he said.

"You don't know? What kind of an answer is that? You don't know."

Gadgets braced himself for another jarring kick to the shins or a jolt from the stun gun, but it never came. All he felt were Bad Lucy's hands, gently toying with his hair, gently testing the muscles along his neck.

He had witnessed enough hard questioning to know that eventually he would have to tell them something, if only to buy a little time to even the score.

"Now let's try it again," Falco said. "I ask you what you're doing in this town, and then you give me an answer. Sound simple? You bet it is. So let's play, okay? What are you doing in this town?"

Gadgets shook his head again as if still only faintly conscious. "I'm just here," he said.

Falco bent closer, his lips only inches from Gadgets's face. "What's that you said? You're just here? Course you're just here. But now I want to know why. I want to know why you're here."

Then finally meeting Falco's black gaze, Schwarz said, "To kill you. I'm here to kill you."

Falco stepped back from the chair and lit a cigarette. He whispered something in the girl's ear, and Schwarz felt her hands again, softly testing his biceps.

"So," Falco said, smiling. "Now, we're getting some place. You came here to kill me, huh? You and your little buddies. You all jump in that fancy van, drive out here and plan to kill the urban monster. Well, that's cool. That's real cool. Only problem is, I'm already dead. So how you going to kill me if I'm already dead?"

Bad Lucy slid her hands along Gadgets's forearms, and gently pulled up the sleeves of his shirt. Her breath in his ear was hot and uneven. She smelled of a mixture of dope and cheap wine.

"Okay," Falco went on, "so you came here to kill me. Now, how about telling me who asked you to do this? Huh? Who asked you to come here and kill me?"

"No one," Gadgets said.

"No one? What kind of answers are you giving me? You're nobody, a nobody who was asked by no one to come here and shoot me. Well, that's not going to cut it, man. That's just not going to cut it."

Falco nodded to the girl, who still stood out of Schwarz's line of sight. There was a sound like a softly clicking switch, then an excited intake of breath. Finally as the girl's hand slid away and Falco casually took another drag on the cigarette, volts of electricity charged through Schwarz's neck.

He screamed, almost lifting the chair off the concrete as his body strained in agony against the bonds. Then just as suddenly it was over, and he slid into another swirl of torchlights and undulating voices.

"I think they call it the Immobilizer," Falco said. "You can get all sorts of different kinds, but Lucy says the Immobilizer is the best. Right, Luce?"

She responded with a dull nod, and in a vaguely mechanical voice, said, "Yeah. Immobilizer is the best."

"Tell him how it works. Tell him about the batteries."

Bad Lucy nodded again, this time with a warped smile. "It's got eight double As, and a membrane switch. You don't even have to touch the guy."

"But if you touch him it hurts even more, right?"

Falco moved back in front of the chair, casually flicking ash. The girl stepped behind the chair, once more smoothing her hands along Gadgets's shoulders.

"Okay, let's take it from the top." Falco smiled. "You're some kind of hotshot tough guy, right? You and your buddies are told to come out here and get rid of a certain freak named Falco. All right, so who's calling plays, huh? Who you guys working for?"

Silence. Another sharp intake of breath as the girl slid her hands away. Then nothing but white light and screaming pain as she jabbed the stun gun into Gadgets's ribs.

More silence as he felt his muscles quivering in spasms, and the vomit rising in his throat. At the same time, however, he was also suddenly aware that his struggles had begun to loosen the arms of the chair, to actually tear the joints apart.

"I hate this, man," Falco said softly. "I mean talk about a cliché. I ask who you're working for. You give me the macho treatment. Lucy here starts frying you. What a stupid boring cliché, you know? I mean this is like something out of a Rambo movie."

He lit another cigarette, while Lucy began to toy with Schwarz's sweat-drenched hair. "All right, I'll tell you what we're going to do. We're going to try it all over again, and see if you can't put a little originality into the script. You understand what I'm talking about here? This time I'm going to ask the questions, and you're going to say, 'Gee, Mr. Falco, I'll be happy to tell you the answer to that one.' Okay? So here we go again. Who are you working for?"

This time, however, Gadgets didn't even pretend. He simply shut his eyes, clenched his jaw and waited.

And as the searing pain tore through his body, he actually threw himself into it, straining with an incredible rage against the loosening ropes...until something snapped.

Falco was still kneeling on the concrete when the arms of the chair broke loose and Gadgets rose. He rose only to a half crouch, because his legs were still tied to the legs of the chair. But as a foot of jagged oak came off in his hand and he tumbled back into the girl, there was more than enough play in the ropes to allow him a jabbing blow.

Blood sprang from Lucy's left eye as Gadgets jammed the splinter of oak from the chair deep into her temple. She screamed, thrashing under him as Falco tried to pull her free. Then again, Gadgets felt the butt of a rifle crashing into his head, sending him back into the swirling lights.

COLD CONCRETE. The slightly warmer muzzle of a shotgun pressed against his throat. A stench of Bad Lucy's blood, mingling with his own. Agonizing pain along his spine as he stared out into the wavering torchlight.

"Bet you think I'm going to shoot you, huh?" Falco said.

He was standing above Schwarz, with the Remington extending from his hand. Some of the girl's blood had stained his jacket and white ruffled shirt, but he had not even noticed.

"Bet you think I'm going to just squeeze the trigger and blow you all over the tunnel."

Gadgets shifted his gaze to the right, and saw the dark form of Bad Lucy still slumped beside the remnants of the chair. The stun gun was still lying on the concrete.

"I mean, first you clobber one of my people so he'll probably never be able to talk again. Then you waste Bad Lucy. I mean, what do you expect a guy like me to do? Laugh it off? No, I can't laugh it off, no way. But by the same token, I ain't going to shoot you, either...least not yet. See, shooting's too easy, too quick. Bang, bang, and it's over. No, we need something with a little more flair, a little more imagination. Then maybe I shoot you, okay?"

Another Desmodo approached, a massive boy with a child's face and a thin scar along the hairline.

"This here is Chico," Falco said, smiling. "But don't let the name fool you. He may not be too bright, but he's strong as an ox. You try any macho shit with him, and he'll break your neck faster than you can say gringo."

Schwarz felt Chico's hands clench his wrists like a vise, and draw them up over his head. He winced as another stabbing pain shot up his spine to the center of his brain.

"Okay, now we're going to do something a little different," Falco said. "I mean you been such a tough guy, I think it's time to do a little tenderizing. You know what I'm talking about? Tenderizing, just like you do with a good steak."

Falco bent to whisper into Chico's ear. The muscular boy nodded, and Gadgets felt the pressure of the boy's weight settling on his shoulders and arms. Then in one fluid movement, Falco withdrew the razor from beneath his coat, and brought the blade across Gadgets's face in a downward arc.

Blood gushed from the three-inch slash. Gadgets clenched his teeth, but remained silent.

"Now, that wasn't too bad, was it?" Falco asked.

He swung the razor again, leaving another three-inch gash on the opposite cheek. The blood was now flowing down Gadgets's neck and across his chest. Although the pain was nothing compared to the electric jolts, it was enough to send him back to the edge of unconsciousness.

Falco lashed out twice more, this time to Gadgets's forearm, where the razor left a line of blood from the wrist to the elbow. In response, Gadgets gritted his teeth and twisted under Chico's hold until he had sufficient leverage to strike out with his knee.

Chico grunted, then spit out a mouthful of blood, but his hold didn't break.

"I told you he was a strong bastard." Falco laughed. "I told you." And he brought the razor down on Schwarz's other arm.

"Now we're getting some place. Now we're really getting down to basics." Falco slashed out twice more to leave long bloody lines across Schwarz's chest.

The phrase *cut to ribbons* passed through Gadgets's mind, and he felt himself sinking again into those swirling lights. But as Falco stepped back in with the glinting razor, whispering something unintelligible, Gadgets twisted his leg free and sent his heel driving into Falco's stomach. It was a weak blow and badly timed, but Falco still obviously felt it, reeling back and sinking to the concrete.

Twenty or thirty seconds passed before he rose to his feet again—twenty or thirty taut seconds. Then as he finally got up and glanced over his shoulder to the ranks of Desmodos, his lips formed into another thin smile.

"You know, I got to admit it, man, you're definitely one mean prick. Definitely one mean son of a bitch."

Falco jerked his head to the right, and Chico suddenly released Gadgets's shoulders. Falco jerked his head to the left, and four more Desmodos stepped forward. He picked up the razor, and slipped it back into his jacket.

"Now, I got some important meetings tonight, but maybe a little later we can play again. What do you say, tough guy? You rest up, and we play again?"

Schwarz wasn't certain what happened next... whether he walked under his own power or they had to drag him, whether he passed out along the passage or later in the cold cell. Once he thought he heard a woman screaming, although it might have been a radio. At another point the half-witted Chico kicked him three or four times, maybe breaking a bone or two, maybe just breaking more blood vessels. Then for a long time Schwarz floated in and out of consciousness, while the lights continued to swirl around him.

18

It was not quite dawn. The air-conditioning at the station was still not in operation, and the briefing room was filled with the stench of sweat and cigarette smoke.

"Look, there's still a chance he's alive," Florio said. "I mean we didn't find any blood in the street and we didn't find any blood in the van, so there's still a good possibility that he's alive."

"Yeah, but for how long?" Lyons said. "That's the question." To illustrate his mood, he nearly put his fist through the fiberboard wall.

"I think the captain's right," Blancanales finally said into the stony silence that followed Lyons's outburst. "We go busting into that Red Car tunnel, and they'll be waiting for us in full force. Then we not only stand a damn good chance of losing Gadgets, we also stand a damn good chance of getting popped ourselves."

"Listen to him, Carl," Florio added. "He's dead right. Falco is just waiting for you to go busting into that tunnel. He's just waiting for it. And the moment you make that move, he'll blow your man away. Besides, we don't even know for sure that they took him to the tunnel. I mean there's all kinds of Desmodo houses in this city, all kinds of places.''

Lyons stepped away from the window. Although he appeared calm, his right hand was still clenched in a fist. "Okay," he finally breathed. "How do you think we should play it?"

Blancanales also took a deep breath. "I think we should have a little talk with that Cardinales woman. Maybe she knows something, maybe she doesn't. But either way I think we should have a talk with her."

Lyons turned to Florio. "Do we know where she is?"

Florio nodded. "Assuming she's not with Falco tonight, you'll probably find her at her Malibu home. I'll take you there myself."

Lyons shook his head. "Not this time, old buddy. This time Pol and I have got to do it alone."

"Carl, if you're worried about—"

"Trust me on this, Hector. That girl starts giving us any shit, and I just don't think you're going to want to be there, not as long as you're carrying a badge. Know what I mean?"

Ten minutes later, Lyons and Blancanales were tearing down the Santa Monica Freeway en route to the coast. The sun had still not risen, and the road was virtually empty. In order to cut the chilling silence, Blancanales had switched on the radio. But the only thing he could tune in were a couple of raving evangelists and a requiem for the dead.

IT WAS ABOUT FOUR O'CLOCK in the morning when Lara heard the footsteps in the corridor—four o'clock, the hour of the wolf again. Her first thought

was that it was Falco, Falco stalking down the hallway either drunk or stoned or both. But even when
completely sober, Falco never had such a calculated
step. Yes, he moved with a kind of grace, but nothing
like the cat steps sounding on the floorboards now.

She slipped out of bed, went to the door and slowly
peered down the shadowy hall. Something might have
moved, she thought, but then again maybe not. From
the dresser she withdrew a little Smith & Wesson .38
revolver—another gift from Falco. She pulled back the
hammer, stepped to the door and peered down the
darkened hall.

Possibly.

She continued out the door, staying close to the wall
until she reached the staircase and a long view of wavering shadows in the foyer.

Probably.

She slowly raised the revolver until it was level with
what seemed the outline of someone crouching in the
doorway.

Definitely.

Gripping her right wrist with her left hand, she took
a deep breath and said, "All right, don't move!"

"Okay, honey," Lyons whispered as he grabbed the
barrel of her revolver. "We promise not to move."

They hauled her into the bedroom, and tossed her
to the floor. Blancanales then moved to the window,
while Lyons faced her from the doorway. Since the
firefight in the alley, Blancanales had traded in his
Atchisson for an over-under conversion, consisting of
an AR-15 above a Remington 870 pump. Lyons,
however, still carried the Sterling MK-7.

"So," Lyons said, "is this where Falco does it to you?"

She turned her face to the wall and shut her eyes, as if waiting for a bullet in the head.

"Well, is it?"

Apart from black panties, she wore only a thin negligee that barely covered her thighs. But she didn't dare reach for the robe on the chair; she didn't dare move a muscle.

"This is the way we're going to play it," Lyons told her. "I'm going to ask you some questions. You're going to give me some answers. Now, isn't that simple?"

"Look, I don't know where Falco is," she said. "I haven't seen him all night."

Lyons got down on one knee, and gently placed the muzzle of his weapon against her ear. "That doesn't happen to be one of my questions, honey. Now, let's try it again."

He ran a hand across his mouth, but otherwise nothing had changed. The muzzle of the MK-7 was still pressed to her ear. Her head was still turned to the wall, and her eyes remained shut.

"The problem's something like this," he said. "Your boyfriend grabbed one of my buddies tonight, and you're going to tell me everything you know about it. You understand? You're going to cut the crap, cut the little cat-and-mouse game, and you're going to tell me everything you know."

She trembled slightly, but otherwise remained absolutely motionless as she said, "Look, I have no idea what you're talking about. Falco hurts all kinds of people that he never tells me about. That's just the way he is."

Lyons increased the pressure of the steel against her ear. "Is that so? Well, let me ask you this. If he was to take a hostage, where would he keep him?"

"I don't know. Different places."

"The tunnel?"

"Maybe."

"Where else?"

"I don't know. He's got lots of secret places that I don't know about."

Then from the window, Blancanales said, "Come on, man, let me talk to her."

Lyons withdrew the pistol, rose to his feet and began to examine the contents of her dresser drawers: silk underwear, gold jewelry, bottles of perfume. "Falco buy you all this shit?" he asked.

She let her head rest against the wall, and shut her eyes again.

"Hey, I asked you a question. Did Falco buy you all this shit?"

"Yeah. He bought it for me."

"So how come you wanted me to kill him? Huh? If he's always buying you all this stuff, then how come you asked me to kill him?"

She opened her eyes, and slowly turned her head to look at him. "Because he's scum . . . just like you."

He moved back to where she was kneeling, and for a moment she thought he was going to slap her. But he finally just tossed her the robe, and sat down on the bed. "All right, let's start over again," he said. "Falco's got one of my people. Now, I want you to tell me how I can get him back."

She slipped the robe on her shoulders, continued to look at him for a moment, then simply shook her head. "Look, I'm sorry, okay? I'm really sorry."

"What's that supposed to mean?"

"It means that there's nothing you can do for your friend. It means that if Falco has him, he's as good as dead."

"How can you be so sure about that?"

"Because I know him, okay? I know how he thinks. He probably took your friend to teach you guys a lesson. To teach you guys to stay away. Because that's one of the things he does. He takes people and cuts them as an example for others."

"And what if we were to grab one of *his* people? In fact, what if we were to grab you, and threaten to cut you up into little pieces? Now you tell me, honey, you think Falco would listen to something like that? You think he'd listen if he were to get one of your pretty ears in the mail? Huh? What do you think? Maybe a couple of your little fingers? You think something like that would make him sit up and listen?"

But again she shook her head, while her eyes revealed absolutely nothing. "You can do to me whatever you like, but it won't make any difference. Your friend is already as good as dead, and that's just the way it is."

Lyons stood up, set the safety on his Sterling and moved to the door. "Yeah, well I got news for you, honey. My friend doesn't die too easily."

"MAYBE WE SHOULD HAVE TAKEN her with us anyway," Blancanales said when he and Lyons had gone back out to the van. ''Maybe we should have taken her as a bargaining chip, or just for the hell of it.''

Lyons shook his head. ''It wouldn't have done any good. Falco doesn't really give a shit about her. He doesn't give a shit about anybody, except himself. Besides, we're past the bargaining point now. We're at the point where we either take him out once and for all, or we go down trying.''

''So what's our next step?''

''Like I said, we either take him out once and for all or we go down trying.''

19

For a long time Schwarz lay very still trying to take stock of himself. Probable concussion. Definite lacerations. Half a dozen bruises. Then at last he opened his eyes, and a piercing white light of pain burst in his brain.

He took a deep breath and slowly tensed his right leg. Not broken. He took another long breath, tensing his left leg and both arms. Not broken. He clenched both fists so that veins stood out like highways along his arms.

Could be better, he told himself, but could be a lot worse, too.

There were the sounds of dripping water, and what he thought might be the wind through a ventilation shaft. There were also distant voices, like whispers from another bad dream. Someone was talking about a girl named Rosie. Someone else was talking about a girl named Lindy. Then he heard hysterical laughter. For a long time, his eyes focused on a gently undulating curtain of black silk. Then by degrees, he realized the curtain was simply blackened stone. There was a door that looked as if it was made of iron, and a nest of rusting pipes above.

He rose to an elbow, slowly scanning the surrounding gloom. Eight paces to the far wall, six to the near wall. A thin crack of light beneath the door, another faint glow from the ventilation shaft. Pure blackness from the drain below.

He collapsed back to the concrete floor, resting his lacerated arms on his chest. Must be some kind of boiler room, he told himself. But the stench of death suggested it was used for other things as well.

He waited five or ten minutes before finally rising to his knees. Five or ten minutes lying on damp concrete, staring at the ventilation shaft. Now and again he heard the rustling of rats, some obviously no more than three feet away. Again he heard voices. Someone talking about the effects of a 9 mm slug in the chest, then another burst of hysterical laughter.

When Schwarz finally rose to his feet, fighting waves of nausea and agonizing pain, he realized that he'd never be able to fight his way out, not in a hundred years. Then reaching up to the pipes above, he slowly started climbing to the light.

THE FOUR DESMODOS RESTED in the gloom: Paco, Ricky, Tooth and Sal. The radio had died about an hour ago. Fragments of crack lay scattered on the table, along with a clean gram of hashish. A half-conscious girl lay curled on a makeshift bed of newspapers. Her hands were bound with leather thongs. Her thighs were mottled with welts. Apart from the echo of the dripping pipes, it was very quiet.

Then they heard it—a long and howling moan, like something from the bowels of hell.

"What the hell was that?" Paco asked.

Ricky roused himself from the depths of a drugged sleep, and glanced at the captive girl.

The moan was repeated, like some furious ghoul calling from deep within the stone.

"Hey, man, we better check it out," Paco said.

But the others just looked at him as yet another haunting groan echoed from the walls.

"Okay, fuck you guys. I'll check it out myself."

Although barely eighteen, Paco was a bulky boy with well-defined arms and a barrel chest. He was also pretty proud of his hands, which had turned into virtual clubs after years of work on the heavy bag. But following another shuddering groan, he slid a Colt Python into the waistband of his jeans.

A long, dank corridor lay between the Desmodo's chamber and the darkened boiler room, at least sixty feet of weeping brick and stone. It was cold, with foul drafts from the tunnel's mouth and the network of ventilation shafts.

Initially Paco moved at a determined pace, comforted by the feel of the Python against his ribs. The howl was repeated, and he withdrew the Python from his waistband and began to move a little slower.

He paused at the boiler room door, pressing his ear against the damp steel. Yet apart from that syncopated drip, he heard nothing.

Then it started again...a low whispered moan, gradually building to an awesome howl.

Paco cocked the Python, and slid back the bolt of the door. Then flexing his legs, he put his shoulder to the steel, and slowly began to push. An inch, a blackened inch of empty brick and concrete. He pushed again, this time revealing a good five feet of the room. But nothing else...

Except for the echoing howl.

There was a moment just before entering when Paco was genuinely frightened. Although not superstitious, he couldn't help recalling stories he had heard as a kid, stories of prowling demons and angry ghosts, animated skeletons and grim reapers. He also couldn't help recalling the stories of werewolves and slavering hounds from hell.

But when he finally leaped into the boiler room, the Python extended from his stiffened arm, he knew that there were no monsters, that everything had a perfectly reasonable explanation. Fixing his eyes on a rusting grate, for example, he realized that the howling was coming from the ventilation shaft, which accounted for the haunting echo. Then noting a trace of blood on the pipes, he further reasoned that the prisoner hadn't really vanished into the walls, but had merely climbed into the crawl space. And as he finally noted a flickering shadow, it also passed through his mind that the prisoner was still very close, probably just crouched on a ledge.

But in the end, Paco had to admit that there were in fact monsters... living, breathing bloodthirsty creatures with nothing but death in their eyes. Because when Schwarz dropped from above, swinging down from the overhead pipes, it was as terrible as anything Paco could have imagined.

Gadgets struck with his heels first, a truly crushing blow to Paco's spine. Then the Able Team warrior dropped his weight on the rib cage. There was an audible crack of splintering bone, and an awful sigh of escaping breath. Kicking the Python away, Gadgets moved in with a furious ridge hand to the windpipe. He struck twice more as the boy collapsed, first smashing the face to the concrete, then dropping a knee to snap the neck.

ALTHOUGH MORE THAN twenty minutes had passed and Paco had still not returned, the others had lapsed into a stoned repose. Ricky had more or less collapsed at the table. Sal had sunk to a couch, and after watching the flickering candlelight play on the captive girl's thighs, Tooth had finally crawled to her side to leisurely toy with her.

"Hey, what are you crying for?" Tooth whispered as he slid a finger up to her cheeks and drew a lazy circle in her tears. "We ain't going to hurt you no more. Are we, Sal?"

Sal grunted a reply.

"In fact," Tooth whispered, "we're going to be real nice to you now. We're going to show you all kinds of neat things."

The girl responded with a frightened whimper, and tried to turn her head away. But out of the corner of her eye, she caught a glimpse of a man who was pointing an enormous revolver directly at Tooth's head.

The first to fall was actually Sal—when he caught a glimpse of the shadow beside him, he jumped up from the couch directly into Schwarz's line of fire. Gadgets fired twice, first with a gut shot that left Sal on his knees, then again to the head, shattering Sal's skull like a melon. His third and fourth shots caught the dozing Ricky, at the table, spun the boy around and left him coughing out a fountain of blood.

It was only then that Gadgets leveled the revolver at Tooth.

Schwarz hesitated before firing, hesitated while he realized what had been going on here, what that little mutant had been doing to the girl, what she must have been thinking and feeling.

Then slowly sinking his weight on his heels, arching his back and extending the Python, Gadgets finally squeezed the trigger.

Tooth screamed even before the bullet impacted. He screamed, knowing full well where Gadgets had aimed the bullet. Then still screaming, he crumpled to his knees as a river of blood began pumping from his groin.

Schwarz waited another ten or fifteen seconds before he shot Tooth again, this time point-blank to the forehead. Then he bent down, untied the girl and looked around for something with a little more kick. In the end, he settled on an Uzi. It was by no means his weapon of choice, but at least there was plenty of ammo.

"Do you speak English?" he asked softly, turning to the girl now huddled in the corner.

She nodded, but still said nothing. Although she was no longer crying, she couldn't seem to keep from trembling. Gadgets gave her his own bloody shirt to wear.

"All right, I want you to listen to me very carefully," he said. "You stay close to me, but you stay behind me. Understand?"

She nodded again, rose from her crouch and clutched his shirt to her breasts.

"Okay, then, let's go."

They started out slowly, keeping to the shadows and following the curve of the tunnel walls. Once or twice he heard her gasp as a rat scurried under her feet, but for the most part she kept her mouth shut.

They had gone about a hundred yards before Schwarz spotted the next three Desmodos. They were lounging on a brick ledge, passing what must have been a quarter gram of hash. Two were dark and wiry boys in denims and red bandannas. The third was pale and skeletal, with an obviously dead left eye.

Gadgets motioned the girl to wait in the shadows, then he continued stalking forward. At thirty feet, he could hear them. At twenty feet, he could smell them.

He caught the first boy reaching for a cigarette, caught him with a short burst to the ribs. The impact lifted the kid into the air, and sent a spray of blood spinning downward. Schwarz caught the second one attempting to slide off the ledge, caught him square in the back with a 3-round burst that left the boy facedown in the scum. By that time, however, the third Desmodo had managed to withdraw a revolver.

Schwarz skidded to his knees, tearing the skin as the slug slammed into the bricks behind. Then he went into a roll as another three rounds turned the bricks to powder. But as he came up to his knees again, wincing with pain, he also sprayed at least six rounds into his opponent.

He didn't waste a second to survey the carnage. He dragged the girl into the darkened alcove and reloaded. It was quiet again, with only the sound of the

dripping pipes and the wind through the maze of ventilation shafts. Then after jamming another magazine
into the Uzi, he realized that the girl was crying
again...huddled by the mossy wall, she cried softly
into her tiny hands.

He moved to her side, but didn't touch her. "Come
on now. That's not going to do us any good, is it?"

She shrugged, then shook her head.

"Besides, you keep it up and we might just end up
drowning."

She gave him the shadow of a smile, and let her chin
fall to her knees.

"That's better," Schwarz whispered. "That's much
better. Now, how about you doing something else for
me? How about you telling me your name?"

Then although her eyes remained fixed on nothing,
her hair a dark shadow across her impassive face, her
lips finally moved, silently forming two syllables—lee-
sa.

"Lisa? That your name, honey? Lisa?"

She nodded.

"Well, that's a real pretty name. Lisa. In fact that's
one of the prettiest names in the whole world."

Then although she still hadn't really spoken, he felt
the pressure of her fingers on his hand.

It was very dark beyond the alcove. Here and there
faint snatches of conversations echoed through the
ventilation shafts, but on the whole it was also very
quiet.

There were moments now when Gadgets couldn't
keep himself from thinking about Nam, about moving through Cong tunnels with a Remington 870 and
a Velcro-mounted Mag-Lite. But this had nothing to

do with Vietnam. This was a far more ancient kind of war. It was the kind of war that dying civilizations have always fought when the rot within society begins to feed on the surrounding tissue. It was the kind of war that Roman mercs had waged on the barbarians, British mercs had waged against the Mau Mau. It was the kind of war that had no heroes that anyone would ever remember.

Schwarz figured they had walked three hundred yards before he began to notice the change. Three hundred yards of inky blackness and the stench of forty stagnant years, then suddenly...a breath of fresh air.

He reached for Lisa and drew her to his side. He released the safety, and pulled out a spare magazine from his hip pocket. Then he simply waited, listening, breathing in the air from above.

"Now there's a chance we might just be able to walk out of here," he told her. "But if not, I want you to stay close and keep your head down. You understand?"

He started to move out, then realized she was still gripping his hand, still staring at him. "What's wrong?"

She hesitated, then leaning very close to his ear she said, "You never..."

"I never what? Come on, honey. I never what?"

"You never told me your name."

He nodded, then gently brushed a finger across her cheek. "You can just call me Gadgets."

They tramped another hundred yards before he saw the light—the light of dawn filtering down from the mouth of the tunnel. The breeze, too, was unmistakable now, with glorious scents of diesel fumes, burned rubber and smog. After another forty or fifty yards, however, he also heard voices.

And finally he even saw them.

There were about a dozen of them, apparently guarding the mouth of the tunnel. Four or five were seated on junk furniture that had been randomly arranged on the damp concrete. Another six or seven lounged against a far wall. Here and there the glowing tips of cigarettes cut tiny tracks through the gloom, while flickering sparks from a fire in a trash can circled up like insects to the vaulted ceiling.

Schwarz paused again in the shadow of stacked packing crates, which were apparently filled with AK-47s. There were also at least four cases of M-16s, and an assortment of assault pistols. But what he wanted now, what he would have given a year of his life for now, was a M-26 fragmentation grenade with a three- to five-second delay.

He felt Lisa's eyes on him, reached out for her hand and gave her a smile. He felt that cooling breeze on his face, and faintly smiled again. Then finally leading the girl out of the shadows, he started moving ahead.

A number of possible plans went through his mind as he walked forward. He thought about picking off the Desmodos one by one from the shadows. He thought about rigging some sort of explosive device, and setting off a box of ammo. He thought about climbing into a ventilation shaft, and coming down on top of them.

Then he caught a glimpse of Lisa's welted thighs, and remembered her sobbing on that heap of newspapers. He clenched his left fist until the pain shot up from his forearm and merged with the pain behind his eyes. Then he flipped off the safety on his Uzi, and kept walking.

The first Desmodo to mark Schwarz's approach was a bulky nineteen-year-old named Roto. Earlier that evening he had dropped a couple of caps of something called Ecstasy, which had sent him into hyperspace. Then after grabbing some old woman's purse, he had scored another gram of hash and really moved into the outer limits. So when he saw Gadgets, hulking out of the gray gloom with the slender girl behind him, he thought they were simply another hallucination.

"Far out," he whispered to himself. Then, noting the angry slashes across Gadgets's face and the holy terror in his eyes, he repeated his observation.

The second Desmodo to catch Schwarz's approach was a vicious sixteen-year-old who called himself Lupo. Although he was also wasted on hash, his primary high for the night had been a spike of China white and a thirteen-year-old girl he had grabbed out of a convenience store. The girl was now dead from the forced consumption of Liquid Plumber, but the China white was still going strong. So upon first noting Gadgets gliding forward out of the shadows, Lupo, too, wasn't quite sure what to make of it all.

Finally, the Able Team commando's approach was spotted by a rail-thin fourteen-year-old known as Snake. Although by no means sober after at least a dozen beers, Snake was still able to differentiate between reality and fantasy. When Gadgets's approach caught Snake's attention, the boy immediately reached for a converted subcaliber Heckler & Koch....

That's when Gadgets fired.

He fired from the hip, squeezing out a 3-round burst that ripped through Snake's throat like a buzz saw. But even as Snake started to fall, Lupo and Roto still weren't sure what was happening.

But when Gadgets fired again, catching Lupo in the belly and Roto across the chest, everything was suddenly very clear.

Roto screamed as he fell, sinking to the concrete in a wash of blood. Then Lupo was also screaming as he sagged to his knees with his hands across his stomach. Immediately, four more Desmodos reached for their weapons, an assortment of MAC-10s and Kalashnikovs, while a fifth boy, called Rocky, slid behind a Soviet-manufactured 12.7 mm heavy machine gun.

Schwarz squeezed off another load, spraying at least a dozen rounds into the scrambling shadows. Among those who had gone for their weapons was a boy known as the Seco. Particularly renowned for his skill with a knife, he instinctively reached for his eight-inch Lock and Load stiletto. But even before he could release the blade, three bullets all but severed his wrist. For a moment, he looked at it in bewilderment . . . the pumping blood, the dangling hand, the knife slipping through his fingers. Then he took another bullet in the throat and collapsed to the concrete with the others.

Gadgets threw Lisa facedown on the concrete when the Desmodos started returning his fire. Then crouching near her and feeding in a fresh magazine, he unleashed another spray of lead. At first he kept the spray low to nail the gunner behind the 12.7 mm. Then bringing the Uzi up again, he pasted two more Desmodos along the far wall, caught them clean across their chests and dropped them like wet rags.

He grabbed Lisa by the wrist, hoisted her to her feet and started moving forward again. Three slugs from a Kalashnikov whined above his head. He answered back with a 3-round burst from the Uzi, and watched as a squat boy shivered to his haunches in a profusion of blood from his scattered skull. He winced as another three rounds from a Kalashnikov shot past his ear, then he dropped to a crouch and blew the shadow away.

Schwarz heard a sound to his left, a cocking bolt and a 9 mm round feeding into a chamber. He whirled to meet the eyes of a boy who must have slipped past him, a thin boy who couldn't have been more than twelve.

A second passed, an oddly fractured second in which Schwarz just kept staring into those youthful eyes. Then another pointless second, while the boy slowly lifted a Browning P-35 Hi-Power. Even when Lisa began screaming, Schwarz still couldn't seem to unlock himself from those eyes, still couldn't seem to bring the Uzi into play, not against a child.

Then just as suddenly it was over.

The boy had lifted the Browning, leveled it at Gadgets's heart and started to squeeze the trigger. Gadgets had pushed Lisa aside, while dropping to a combat crouch. Still staring into those haunting eyes, he had finally squeezed off four more rounds. Then grabbing the girl by the wrist and pulling her back to her feet, he started forward again, tramping toward the light at the end of the tunnel.

It was now quiet in the tunnel, with only the distant roar of trucks interrupting the silence. Lisa was also very quiet, no longer even crying. Then as they at last emerged from the mouth of the tunnel and into the postdawn mist, there were also the sounds of birds... circling gulls driven in from the sea, restless pigeons on surrounding roofs.

"How you doing?" Schwarz asked Lisa.

She let her head drop against his shoulder and nodded. "Okay."

"You want to sit a minute?"

She nodded again, and he led her into the shadows between two rusting Dumpsters. From there they had a fairly unobstructed view across eighty yards of rubble to the tunnel. But apart from the circling birds, there was still no movement at all.

"By the way, you did real good in there," he said.

She gave him another slight smile, laid her head on his shoulder again, then asked why they called him Gadgets.

He took a deep breath, then shut his eyes and smiled. "It's kind of a long story."

"Will you tell it to me someday?"

"Sure. Someday."

After a couple of minutes, he hauled her back to her feet and they started moving out again.

He walked at a slow pace, with the Uzi dangling from his left hand, the girl still clinging to his right. The breeze felt cool and soothing on his wounds, and he couldn't have cared less about the derelicts searching for bottles among the surrounding trash heaps. He also didn't care about the pair of punks prowling the railroad tracks, nor even about the cops in the black-and-white that eventually brought him back to the real world.

20

"So what do we do now?" Blancanales asked. "Go for broke?"

Lyons glanced in the rearview mirror, then back to the nearly empty road ahead. "You got any better ideas?"

"Not really."

A thin mist had risen along with the dawn. The incoming draft stank of tar and rotting seaweed. Although Lyons had started out at a comfortable seventy miles per hour, he was now pushing the van for all it was worth. They sped past a motorist in a beat-up Toyota, who promptly hit his horn and gave them the finger.

"How long?" Blancanales shouted over the roar of the engine.

"What?"

"How long till we get to the tunnel?"

Lyons briefly glanced over to his friend. "What makes you think we're heading for the Desmodos' tunnel?"

Blancanales returned the glance with a grim smile. "Just a guess."

Another irate motorist mouthed an obscenity at them through his windshield. As they swerved past two sleepy women in a Yugo, Blancanales caught another screamed insult. "So what do we do when we get there?" he asked.

Lyons shook his head. "I'm not sure. But it's better than doing nothing. Besides, I thought you liked crawling around in rat-infested tunnels."

"Sure." Blancanales grinned. "Love it."

At the Harbor Freeway interchange, a Highway Patrol cruiser briefly gave pursuit. Then obviously having called the dispatcher to check the license number, the cop in the cruiser broke off the chase.

Lyons exited the freeway at Third Street, and they found themselves in an irritating gridlock. Backtracking to Beaudry Street and finally to Second, they reached the stretch of empty lots adjacent to the tunnel's mouth.

It was quiet, with only the sounds of the van's ticking radiator and car horns in the distance. Blancanales had already stuffed his pockets with spare clips for the Remington. Lyons withdrew the M-16.

"Okay, here's how we play it," Lyons said as he inserted a magazine and switched to full auto. "If he's in there, we get him out. If he's not in there, we find someone who knows where he is, and work on the punk until he talks. Anyone else who stands in the way gets wasted."

Blancanales shook his head with a lopsided smile. "And that's it? That's your plan?"

"Yeah. That's my plan."

"What happens if the whole team is in there? What happens if we're facing the whole damn nest?"

Lyons shrugged. "Like I said, anyone who stands in the way gets wasted."

They paused just outside the van, scanning the surrounding fields, the crumbling warehouse blocks and shattered factory fronts, then exchanging glances. Lyons said that they might as well just nut up and do it.

But just before he closed the door to the van, they heard the high-pitched ring of the cellular phone.

There was another exchange of glances, and Blancanales shook his head again. "Florio?"

Lyons nodded. "Probably."

"Calling to tell us to keep our cool?"

"Probably."

"You going to answer it?"

"No, you answer it."

Blancanales picked up the phone on the fourth ring. For the most part he just listened, then swore under his breath. Lyons couldn't be certain what was happening. But when Blancanales finally put down the phone and stepped back out of the van, he was definitely smiling.

"How about we call the whole thing off and just head back to the station?"

Lyons looked at him. "What are you talking about?"

"Oh, I just thought we could use a little breakfast, maybe a dip in the pool. Besides, I'm really not too interested in seeing a bunch of corpses this early in the morning."

"Pol, what the hell are you talking about?"

"That was Florio. Gadgets walked into the station about twenty minutes ago...alive and more or less well."

"SHIT," BLANCANALES SAID, smiling. "Look what the goddamn cat dragged in."

Schwarz lay half-reclining on a low couch in what the cops sometimes called the Rec Room. Florio was speaking softly on the telephone in the corner, apparently inquiring about a doctor. A pretty clerk in blue was arranging coffee and a platter of doughnuts. Quiet sobs came from an adjoining room where someone was attending to the girl Schwarz had rescued.

"You ever heard of the *Desmodus rufus*?" Gadgets asked. After receiving blank stares, he repeated, *"Desmodus rufus?"*

"Some sort of fungus?" Blancanales asked.

"It's a bat," Gadgets said. "A vampire bat."

Silence filled the room.

"The Desmodos are named after this Central American vampire bat, because they like to bleed people," Gadgets continued. Then he extended his arms. "They like to bleed people."

There was nothing the others could say. Schwarz's face was marked by two long diagonal cuts, one on each cheek, going to the corners of his mouth. The cuts were identical pink grooves that looked as if they had been etched into the flesh with an awl. His forearms were similarly marked from the wrists to the elbow. The bleeding, however, had stopped.

"How'd you get out?" Lyons asked.

It seemed to take a second or two for the question to register. "It's a long story," Gadgets finally said.

"He brought a girl with him," Florio said softly from the corner. "She's been through the wringer, but she's basically all right."

"Yeah," Gadgets said after another uncomfortably long silence. "She's basically all right."

Styrofoam cups of coffee were passed out, although Schwarz said he only wanted water. Then the clerk left the room, and the door was locked.

"Maybe you should just take it from the top," Lyons said.

Schwarz nodded, but it seemed to be a long time before he actually spoke. "Like I said, there's really not that much to tell. They picked me up, did their little number, and then I started getting mad. All in all, I'd say there are about thirty or forty of them down there."

"What about their equipment?" Blancanales asked.

"Place is an armory. You name it, they've got it. A lot of Eastern bloc stuff. A lot of Chinese stuff. I didn't see anything real heavy, but I'm pretty sure it's there."

"What about Falco?" Florio asked.

"What about him?"

"Well, did you see him?"

Schwarz let his head fall back, and shut his eyes with a strange smile. "Yeah. I saw him."

"And?" Blancanales put in.

"And nothing," Schwarz said softly.

Then, following another awkward silence, Lyons whispered to Blancanales that they should probably just let Gadgets rest.

Schwarz, however, said that he didn't want to rest, not now, not yet.

IT WAS HALF PAST NOON when Schwarz returned to the TraveLodge.

Once inside his room, he turned on the television, pulled out a medical kit, recleaned and dressed his wounds. Then he drew the blinds and stretched out on the bed. After fifteen or twenty minutes, he realized that he should have turned off the air conditioner, for he was almost numb with the cold. But he just didn't have the strength to move.

For a long time Schwarz lay still, wondering if the dripping of water he heard was simply his imagination and if the occasional rustle of papers on the table was actually the sound of rats. He thought about the girl, Lisa, and about his first kill in the boiler room. He thought about the kid on the balcony in Chinatown. He thought about the Politician, emerging from the burning crack house, about Falco, sneering from the shadows. Then he finally fell into a restless sleep.

While he slept, he dreamed—dreams of dark faces looming in darker doorways, dreams of grinning children with rats' snouts and whiskers. Later, hours later, he would also recall dreaming about a girl, who seemed to be dying very slowly in the blackness.

21

"Did I happen to mention what Hasan, son of Sabah, used to tell his assassins before they went out to kill?" Atiff asked.

Falco ignored him and continued to gaze at the carnage in the tunnel.

"Well, I shall tell you. He used to say, 'Go, my children, and slay my enemies. And when you return, I myself shall welcome you back into paradise where you shall have anything you desire. And even if you should die, I shall be here to welcome you back into paradise.' Now, of course, this all took place in a purer age, and Hasan's paradise was merely an illusion, but I think the sentiment is still appropriate, don't you?"

Falco rose from where he'd been examining three or four bodies slumped by the mouth of the tunnel. "I'll tell you what I think, Colonel. I think you'd better just shut your mouth. You hear what I'm saying? Just shut your mouth."

"Naturally, I understand your sorrow," Atiff said. "Indeed, I think it is only appropriate that a commander shed a tear or two for his fallen warriors. But you must not let your emotion come between us, because we still have much to accomplish together."

They began to walk, following the trail of bodies deeper into the tunnel. Although a number of black-and-whites had been prowling the upper wastes near the tunnel, the actual scene of Schwarz's fury had not been disturbed. Tooth and Sal, for example, still lay where he had left them. Paco still lay sprawled in the boiler room. There was a different feel to the tunnel now, a vaguely disconcerting sense of disaster.

"Now, of course, should you desire, I will be happy to arrange proper burials," Atiff said. "After all, they died for the cause."

Falco looked at him. "They died," he said, "because we underestimated the enemy. And because we were stupid."

Atiff bent to examine Paco's body, idly calculating the degree of physical strength Schwarz must have employed in order to crush the ribs and snap the neck. He was also intrigued by the apparent method of attack, the sudden fall like a shadow of death from that ventilation shaft above.

"It is possible," he said, "that you are right, that we may have slightly underestimated the men of Able Team. But I assure you that in the greater scheme of things, it really makes no difference at all."

Falco kicked the lifeless body. "Yeah, well maybe you should tell that to Paco or to Sal. Maybe you should tell that to some of the other stinking corpses around this place. Because they'd probably be real happy to hear all about your greater scheme. Like they'd probably really appreciate it if you told them some of your Arab stories right about now. I mean like they'd probably really get a buzz if you told them all about how that Hasan guy used to take care of his people, and what a great honor it is to die for the downtrodden people. So why don't you just go talk to them about all that shit and leave me alone.''

The colonel moved to Falco's side, and calmly withdrew a cigarette. ''You know something, my little brother? Were I not a patient man, I think I might be forced to teach you a lesson you would never forget.''

Falco slowly turned to face the man. ''You threatening me, man? Huh? You threatening me?''

Atiff took a slow drag on his cigarette, then let the smoke filter through his teeth. ''Let me see,'' he said with a smile, ''am I threatening you? No, I don't think so. I think I am merely trying to impress upon you a vital fact. I think I am merely saying that were I not a patient man, I should probably feel the need to punish you for insolence.''

Falco returned the glare. ''Yeah, well I'd like to see you try it, man. I'd like to see you try it.''

Then, although Falco seemed merely to turn away, the motion became a circling lunge as his straight razor appeared out of nowhere, flashing by the colonel's left ear. The colonel, however, sensed it coming, and deftly stepping to the right, he drove his boot into Falco's groin.

Falco crumpled first to his knees with an agonized moan, then face down on the concrete.

''Now listen to me,'' the colonel hissed as he kicked away the razor and planted his boot on Falco's neck. ''Listen to me very carefully. I have given you weapons to destroy your enemies. I have given you money to pay your whores. I have given you a cause with which to motivate warriors. In addition to all that I am now giving you a second chance. But if you ever attempt to defy me again, if you ever so much as contemplate defying me, I shall grind you into dust and scatter you over this trash heap that you call your kingdom.''

He removed his foot from Falco's neck, and watched as the leader of the Desmodos slowly rose to his hands and knees.

''Now, in a very short time we shall be making the consummate statement against the decay within this city. We shall be etching our place in history with the blood of our enemies. And when that time comes, I shall require every ounce of your loyalty. Do you understand, little brother?''

Falco coughed, then retched. ''Yeah, I understand.''

''Good.'' Atiff smiled. ''Very good.'' Then, grabbing hold of Falco's hair and wrenching back his head, he continued, ''Now there is only one other small word of wisdom that I wish to impart before leaving you. I want you to remember your place in all this. I want you to remember that although you may think you are the king of this little world, in fact you are merely my servant. Do you understand? You are nothing but my servant. And just as I created you, I can also destroy you.''

FOR A LONG TIME after Atiff had gone, Falco remained seated in the boiler room. He sat with his back to the far wall, and his knees drawn up to his chin. He sat with his eyes fixed on Paco's lifeless eyes, and his attention fixed on the dripping pipes. Now and again he heard the footsteps of his warriors passing through the corridor, but mostly there was only the drip of water on the concrete.

And just as I created you, I can also destroy you.

He pulled out a pack of cigarettes, lit one and took a long draw. He picked up his razor from the floor, and gently tested the blade with his thumb. He pressed the tiny cut to his lips, and tasted the blood. He let his head loll to his shoulder, and shut his eyes.

And just as I created you, I can also destroy you.

He sat for nearly an hour before he finally heard the door ease back, and the tentative step of a kid named Raphael. Opening his eyes, he looked at the boy and smiled. "What is it, Little Brother?"

Although only twelve years old, Raphael had been with the Desmodos from the beginning, primarily serving as a watcher. Recently, he had been watching even more closely, but now he didn't know how to report what he had seen.

"Well, you got something to tell me or what?" Falco persisted.

The boy nodded, but his gaze kept moving between the razor in Falco's hand and Paco's dead eyes.

"It's about your old lady, man," he finally said.

"Yeah? What about her?"

"It's about something she's been doing."

"Yeah? What's she been doing?"

"Well, just something I thought you should know about, okay? I mean, like I just thought you'd want to know about it."

Falco slipped the razor back into his jacket, then placed another cigarette between his lips.

"Hey, Raphael," he said. "You got something to tell me, man? You just tell me. I don't care what it is. Just tell me."

The boy nodded again, but this time fixed his eyes on his feet. "Well, a couple of the little guys say they saw her talking with these dudes, man. You know, they saw her talking with these certain dudes."

"What dudes?"

"We didn't get no name, man, but one of them was carrying a conversion. You know, a conversion? Like with a Remington pump on the bottom, and one of those automatics on top. So anyway, we just thought you'd want to know about it, okay? We just thought you'd want to know."

Falco withdrew his cigarette, and began to inspect the glowing tip. "What did these dudes look like?" he asked.

"Well, it was kind of dark, you know. But I hear that one of them was real white, you know? Like a real white guy. And the other one was kind of like us. But for sure they were both cops or something."

"And when was this?"

"Late last night."

"Where?"

"You know, Malibu. Like up in Malibu."

Falco took another long drag from the cigarette, then tossed it against the wall in a tiny shower of sparks. Otherwise, however, he remained unmoving, apparently unconcerned. "Hey, Raphael. You ever seen a shooting star?"

The boy glanced up briefly from the concrete. "Huh?"

"Shooting star, man. You ever seen a shooting star?"

The boy shrugged, then shook his head. "I don't know. I don't think so."

"Well, it's like this rock up in space. And like it just shoots across the sky burning like a torch until it burns itself out. And just before it burns itself out, it gets real bright. Like maybe the brightest thing in the sky."

He lit another cigarette, took a long drag and tossed it to the wall again in another shower of sparks. "It's like that, man. It's like this glowing thing in the black sky, and just before it burns itself out, it gets almost as bright as the sun."

He let his head loll back to the wall, then shut his eyes. "And that's how it's going to be with us," he whispered. "We're going to be like a shooting star. We're going to be the brightest thing in the whole night sky, just before we burn ourselves out."

He opened his eyes, with a lopsided grin. "You don't know what I'm talking about, do you?"

Raphael shrugged, nervously twisting fingers.

"You think maybe I'm all screwed up, don't you? You come in here and tell me that my old lady is maybe gone dirty, and I just sit here talking to you about shooting stars. So naturally you think maybe this time old Falco has really flipped his lid. But I got news for you, kid. I got big news for you. When the time comes and we start lighting up the whole damn sky, then you'll know exactly what I'm talking about. You'll see us burning up this whole city, and then you'll know. You'll really know."

22

At approximately the same time that Falco was contemplating Lara Cardinales's treachery, Florio and Lyons were discussing Dr. North. It was warm again, with smog-choked winds from the east. Lyons was exhausted, reclining in a chair opposite Florio's desk. An empty coffee cup dangled from his fingers.

"I'm only telling you all this because I think you need to know it," Florio said. "I don't necessarily want you to go out and bust the man's face."

Lyons shifted his head an inch or two until his gaze fell on the mess of papers scattered on Florio's desk. Although North's name had been deleted from the actual reports, the implications were clear.

"Why don't you just give it to me from the top?" Lyons suggested.

Florio took a deep breath, casually slid another sheet of paper into view. "Let's call it a possibility at this point," he said. "Let's say that Colonel Atiff seems to have connections with something called the Center for Middle East Studies. Let's also say that this particular foundation is nothing more than a laundry for all sorts of terrorist activities."

"And North's name popped up on the payroll, that your point?"

Florio nodded. "Roughly."

"So who knows about this?"

"Nobody. I got it from a friend in the Bureau, but he's not obliged to file a report for five working days."

"Which means what? We've got five days to play by our own rules?"

Florio pushed the papers aside, rose from his desk and moved to the window. "I can't let you tear him apart, Carl. I just can't let you do that."

"Hey, you saw what they did to Gadgets."

"I also saw what they did to Gabby Salinas, but I still can't let you take him apart."

Lyons smiled, staring at a water stain on the ceiling, a stain he'd been gazing at for some time now, trying to decide if it looked like a rat or a vampire bat.

"I've got no intention of tearing the good doctor apart," he finally said. "I just want to take a little piece. I just want to cut off a little piece to show him what it means to mess around with terrorists."

DR. NORTH LIVED on a leaf-strewn street about four blocks east of the Westwood Center. The house was a long, low Colonial-style affair, with white painted shutters and a wrought-iron gate to block a visitor's approach. Although there were only occasional burglaries in the area, the doctor had installed bars on the windows and an elaborate alarm system. For a few months, North had also kept a guard dog, a monstrous beast he had called Id. But after noting that the animal lacked the true killer spirit, he had finally got rid of it.

It was about eight o'clock in the evening when North arrived home. He had had a bad meal with colleagues in the cafeteria, and was also suffering from a minor headache. He didn't like the fact that his maid had left the windows ajar, letting in dozens of tiny moths.

North always enjoyed coming home to his house. He liked the emptiness and the stillness. He liked to wander through the half-lit rooms, gazing at his collection of artifacts gathered from a lifetime of travel. On this particular evening, he poured himself a drink and sank into a chair opposite his African mask display. He never tired of examining the masks, never tired of staring into the eyes and trying to fathom their primitive secrets. He had it on good authority that his collection was worth at least sixteen thousand dollars. And considering that he had picked up most of them for next to nothing from ignorant savages, he couldn't help but smile a little whenever he looked at them.

It was at least twenty minutes before he realized that one of the masks was missing, that someone had actually removed his Nigerian shaman's mask from its hook on the far wall. All sorts of alarming thoughts quickly passed through his mind. It was possible that the thief had known what he was doing, because that particular mask was easily worth three thousand dollars. North also recognized that the thief might not have stolen the mask for profit, but have simply taken it to mess with its owner's head. . . .

The thief achieved this last objective when he stepped out of the hallway with the mask over his face and a .45 dangling from his hand.

"Nice place you've got here," Lyons said, speaking before North had time to react to his presence.

North looked at him, then took another sip of his gin and tonic. "I suppose you realize that your presence in my house constitutes a felony," North said. "And frankly I've a good mind to call the police."

Lyons shrugged, took off the mask and tossed it away. He wasn't worried about the doctor's threat, for he had taken the liberty of yanking out the telephone cords.

"If I were in your position, Doctor, I wouldn't take the chance of threatening me with anything. I might get pissed off. Know what I mean?"

North finished his drink, then ran his hand across his mouth. "All right, what do you want?"

Lyons shrugged again. "Let's call it professional counseling, Doc. Let's say I've got a kind of emotional problem, and you're the only one who can help."

"Look, if you've come here to—"

"Now this particular problem I've got involves this certain guy, see? This certain guy who's been causing a lot of trouble for me and my friends. Now, normally I might just let it slide, but for some reason I can't seem to get it out of my head. I mean I'm starting to get real crazy on the subject...and when I go crazy on a subject, next thing you know somebody's not feeling so good. So anyway, I thought maybe you could help me out, maybe shed a little *perspective* on the area."

He slipped into a chair opposite the doctor, with a facetious grin.

"So what do you say, Doc? You think you can help me or not?"

North gave him a disgusted look. "What the hell do you want?"

Lyons let the grin sag. "Tell me about the Center for Middle East Studies?"

"I don't know what you're referring to."

"Really? Well, that's kind of odd, especially since you're on the payroll. Now, of course, one has to kind of read between the lines to see it all, but this so-called Center for Middle East Studies has definitely been paying you something. Say, two or three grand a month?"

North picked up his glass, realized it was empty, then jammed his hands between his knees. "Look, it so happens that I serve as a consultant to a number of study groups. There's no crime in that."

"Maybe not...unless, of course, one of those study groups turns out to be a front for a foreign terrorist network."

Lyons rose from the chair, moved to the far wall and began idly examining another item from the doctor's collection—the face of a hideous African demon fashioned from a human skull.

"Way I figure it," Lyons said, "the story goes something like this. Terrorists slip into the country, and set up a supposedly respectable academic group in order to launder money. You, as a supposedly respectable psychiatrist and educator, hook up with this group as a consultant. You get your money, they get your services and no one's the wiser...until people start dying."

North leaned forward, clenching his fists. "That's absolutely preposterous."

"Is it? I think I've hit the nail on the head."

"Besides, if the Center is involved in dubious acts, you can't possibly assume that I have anything to do with them. Groups of this kind are continually soliciting my services in order to gain credibility."

"Yeah, well, that's kind of the problem, Doc. See, the credibility isn't what worries me. It's the intelligence."

"I have no idea what you're talking about."

Lyons laid the skull on the shelf, and turned to face North again. "I'm talking about the fact that in addition to whatever else you've been doing for this so-called Center for Middle East Studies, I think you've also been supplying them with information, tactical information from the LAPD. Now, I'm willing to give you the benefit of the doubt. I'm willing to accept that maybe you didn't start out on the wrong foot, that maybe you just kind of fell into it. But the long and short of it is that it all comes out the same in the end— you're nothing but a cheap spy."

Then, although North's face suffered a number of odd contortions, his voice was very calm. "This is absurd," he said. "This is absolutely absurd."

"Yeah? Well, why don't you tell me about a greasy little Libyan named Colonel Atiff? Huh? Why don't we talk about Atiff?"

North rose from the couch, stepped to his desk and poured himself another drink. Although still apparently calm, his hands were trembling and his face was studded with beads of perspiration. "I think you had better leave now, Mr. Lyons. I think you had better leave before I lose my temper."

Lyons merely smiled and picked up another odd artifact from a shelf, a carving of some Indian deity with black pearl eyes and ivory teeth.

"You want to know what really bothers me about all this, Doc? I can't figure out why you did it. I mean you've got a pretty good thing going here, right? You've got your nice big office. You've got this nice big house. You're probably pulling down at least a hundred thou a year, not to mention all the dinner parties with VIPs. So why risk throwing it away for a measly two or three grand a month? I mean it just doesn't figure, you know. It just doesn't make sense."

"Look, I'm telling you for the last time. Get out of my house."

"Anyway, that was the problem," Lyons continued. "I just couldn't figure out why you were doing it. Then I remembered something you said the other day on campus, something about how you get all that grant money."

"I'm warning you, Mr. Lyons. If you don't get out of my house this instant, I will be forced to press charges."

"But then I started thinking, see? What if, in order to get those big grants, you had to demonstrate that there was a real need for your work? I mean let's say you're asking the Feds for two or three million in order to study urban violence, right? You're never going to get that kind of money unless it's real clear to everyone that there's one hell of a problem out there. Sure, there's always a fair amount of gang banging in the streets, but unless things really get outrageous you're not going to get the big bucks, right? I mean things would have to get pretty bad before you could go to the Feds and tell them, 'Hey, you guys better fork over some bread so I can figure out how to save your asses from the gangs.' And by that point Washington is so freaked out they just start cutting checks. Yeah, I've got to hand it to you, Doc. You really know how to operate."

"Mr. Lyons, I am going to give you one last warning, and then I am going to—"

"What, Doctor? What are you going to do? Because the way I see it, you're not in a position to do much of anything right now. After all, you just got caught with your pants down. You just got caught plotting with a foreign intelligence organization to create a climate of terror in an American city. And why? So you could justify a million-dollar grant in order to study that climate of terror. Now, that's what I call neat, Doc. That's what I call real neat."

Although Lyons acknowledged it was maybe not quite as neat as the .38 revolver that North had just pulled out of the drawer.

Lyons turned slowly, still toying with the gruesome little figurine he had picked up from the shelf. Although probably not comfortable with the handgun, the doctor obviously knew how to use it. And at seven feet, he could hardly miss.

"I imagine the police report would read something like this," North said. "Deluded into believing that I am somehow responsible for all this city's misfortunes, you broke into my home with the intent of doing me bodily harm. It was dark, you came at me suddenly, and in the end I had no alternative but to defend myself. I will naturally show a great deal of regret, but will explain that you were obviously suffering from paranoid delusions, possibly stemming from an earlier trauma. Now how does that sound, Mr. Lyons?''

Lyons shrugged with an easy smile. "Oh, it sounds pretty good . . . except that I'm not the one suffering from an earlier trauma. That man standing behind you, he's the guy that's really messed up."

As North spun around to face the leering Blancanales, and the double barrels of his over-under conversion, Lyons casually closed the distance. He went for the Smith & Wesson first, wrenching it easily out of North's hand. Then just as casually, he struck the doctor twice—first with a snapping elbow to the jaw, then with a back knuckle to the face.

The doctor collapsed like a slowly deflating bag, then sat staring at the blood dripping from his nose. His glasses had been shattered and his left eye was already starting to swell.

"All right, Doc," Lyons said. "The kissing's over."

North just continued to stare at the blood on his fingertips. Then finally dragging himself up to sit in the chair, he shook his head.

"There is not one shred of proof for any of your allegations," he said. "Not one single shred of proof."

Lyons stepped away as if momentarily beaten by logic. Then suddenly whirling and grabbing North by his lapels, he hauled the doctor out of the chair. "I want you to listen real carefully, Doc. Pol and I don't need proof. We're maniacs, okay? We just get these ideas in our head, and then start breaking necks. So forget about the proof, because this isn't a court of law. This is just you, me and Pol. And *anything* can happen."

North wiped another mess of blood from his nose, and sagged back into the chair. "Look, I don't know anything about it," he finally said with a sigh. "I only..."

"Only what, Doctor?" Then hauling him up by the lapels he repeated, "Only what?"

"I only know that they're planning something, something big."

"When?"

"I don't know. Soon."

"Where?"

"I don't know."

"Are the Desmodos involved?"

"Look, how can I possibly—"

"Answer me! Are the Desmodos involved?"

"Yes."

Lyons shoved North back to the chair, and turned to Blancanales. "What do you think, Pol? Should we blow him away or what?"

Blancanales hefted the conversion and dropped the safety on the AR-15. "I don't see why not."

"Look, I've told you everything I know," North whined. "They've got some sort of a strike planned, something that's going to take place in the next day or two. But I swear to God that's all I know."

"God, Doctor?" Lyons smirked. "I thought your kind didn't believe in God. I thought all you believed in were little chemical reactions in the brain."

"Why are you doing this to me?"

At which point Blancanales pulled the trigger, spraying the shelves with about eighty cents' worth of lead and shattering at least ten thousand dollars' worth of the doctor's collection of artifacts.

"It's called terrorism," Lyons said into the ringing silence that followed. "It's called mindless terrorism, and you might want to think about it before you play any more games with guys like Colonel Atiff."

IT WAS ABOUT TEN O'CLOCK in the evening when Lyons and Blancanales returned to the TraveLodge. Schwarz was propped on the bed amid sandwich wrappers and crushed soft drink cans. The television was tuned to KCOP's *Dance Fever*, but the sound was off. Although his wounds were still coated with salve, he had ripped off the bandages.

"You look like you're ready for the barbecue," Blancanales said upon entering the room.

Gadgets didn't even smile. "They just take me raw," he said. Then turning to Lyons, he added, "So how was your little meeting with the doctor?"

Lyons popped open a can of orange soda, took a swig and tossed it in the trash. "Stimulating," he said. "Real stimulating."

"Yeah," said Blancanales, "we're a whole lot more in touch with our feelings now that we've seen the good doctor."

23

It was a typical June morning in Los Angeles. Newscasters would repeat the same National Weather Bureau forecast that they announced on half the days of every year: late-night and early-morning low-lying clouds along the coast, clearing by noon. The light in the city was gray. The air in the basin was stagnant and virtually unfit to breathe.

Atiff found Falco standing on the balcony of Lara Cardinales's bedroom in her Malibu house, staring blankly out across the face of the water.

"A good day to die," he said in greeting.

"Yeah." Falco sighed.

He had been standing there for at least three hours since dawn. Now and again his thoughts had been disturbed by Lara's soft cries from the bedroom, but for the most part there was only the sound of the sea and the gulls.

"Do you see that bird?" he asked.

Atiff scanned the line of waves until his eyes fixed on a pelican gliding seaward.

"Watch how he fishes," Falco said.

Atiff watched as the big bird circled, suspended for a moment ten to twelve feet in the air. Then, pressing its bulky wings tight against its body, it speared through the crest of a breaking wave and vanished into the blue-green water. When the bird finally emerged again, a small fish flopped in its pendulous pouch.

"I used to be able to fly like that," Falco said. "I used to be able to fly and fish exactly like that bird. Then one day I woke up and forgot it all. I just forgot."

"We have a mayor to kill today," Atiff said softly.

"Why? So you can get your little friends out of jail? What did the scum ever do for you anyway?"

Atiff watched as the bird vanished into another wave, then rose again with a struggling fish in its beak. He took a long breath and turned back to Falco.

"Have you ever heard of the Mossad? No, I don't imagine that you have. Well, they happen to be highly professional killers. And we are playing a deadly game of chess with them. They make their moves. We make our moves. They murder a bishop, we capture a knight, and on and on it goes. At the moment, however, they happen to be holding three of our most valuable pieces. It's therefore time for our side to move, to press the attack on their queen. And to do this, we must have all our pieces on the board. Now do you understand?"

"I play craps, man. I don't play chess. But I get the point."

"Several months ago the Mossad murdered Abu Jinhad in Tunisia. Since then, we have been in chaos, unable to mount a meaningful attack. Jinhad was the heart of certain key operations. It's as if the heart of our struggle ceased to beat with his death. Now we must shock it back to life. Yesterday the first of these shocks began in Paris. And today, my friend, you and your vampires will complete the treatment in Los Angeles.''

Falco did not respond. His eyes were fixed on yet another pelican crashing through a breaking wave. Then finally withdrawing his little automatic again, he said, "Okay, Colonel, I'll fight your war... just as soon as I finish a little battle of my own."

LARA LAY ABSOLUTELY STILL. She had long since given up attempting to free herself from the nylon cords that secured her wrists and ankles to the bedposts. She had also given up trying to blot out the memory of the things Falco had done to her. But despite that, she found herself slightly embarrassed when Falco and the colonel entered the bedroom, and consumed her naked body with their eyes.

"Beautiful, isn't she?" Falco said. "Even after all the shit... still beautiful as all hell."

"We haven't a great deal of time, my friend," Atiff whispered.

Falco moved to the edge of the bed, and lazily ran a finger along the inside of her thigh. He smiled when she shivered at his touch, but otherwise his face remained impassive.

"You know, I think there was a time when I would have died for her," he continued. Then, running a finger across her belly to the left nipple, he said, "Yes, there was definitely a time when I would have died for her."

He turned his gaze to Atiff, who still hadn't moved from the doorway. "What about you, Colonel? You ever had a woman you would have died for? You would have killed for?''

The colonel pressed a thumb and forefinger to the bridge of his nose, clearly agitated now. "It is time we go, my friend. It is getting very late.''

"Even now that she's betrayed me, I still can't keep myself from worshiping her.'' He bent and kissed her forehead.

"Look,'' Atiff said. "If you want to take her, then take her. If you want to shoot her, then shoot her. But I must insist that we leave right now.''

"Yes, I thought about shooting her.'' Falco smiled. "You know, maybe sticking a .45 between those beautiful lips of hers and pulling the trigger. But then I thought, shooting is so obvious, so predictable. I mean, like I dedicate my whole life to her and she stabs me in the back, and all I can do is shoot her?'' He bent to fondle the right breast, while leaving a chain of kisses along her throat. "No, you don't shoot a woman like this. You got to come up with something original. You got to come up with something really appropriate.''

"I tell you for the last time. The hour has come for us to leave.''

Falco whipped his head around in a rage. "Hey, get off my back, man! I happen to be busy here, you know? I happen to be telling you something important about this bitch here.''

He dropped his lips to her breast again and licked her nipple. "Now, where was I? Oh, yeah. Like I said, you can't just shoot a woman like this. You got to come up with something that really rings forever. You understand what I'm saying? You got to put her right into eternity. Now, of course, that takes some thought. In fact I must have spent half the night thinking about it. But in the end I got it. Man, I really got it.''

Atiff moved to Falco's side, now actually laying a hand on his shoulder. ''Listen to me. If we do not soon leave, everything we have worked for will be lost. Do you grasp what I'm saying here? Everything will be lost.''

After what must have been another sixty seconds of dead silence, Falco finally rose to his feet. ''Hey, man, we're leaving,'' he said calmly. ''We're leaving right now.''

Lara was permitted to put on a cotton shift before her wrists were cuffed behind her back. Then came the blindfold, and the long walk across cool flagstones to the colonel's waiting Mercedes. Falco couldn't seem to keep his hands from stroking her shoulders and toying with her hair now and again, before shoving her into the back seat of the car.

''Hey, Colonel, I ever tell you how me and this bitch first met? Huh? I ever tell you how I found this woman?''

''I think we should be quiet now, my friend. I think this would be a good time to remain quiet and contemplate the challenges to come.''

It was still quite early, and rush-hour traffic had not yet begun to build. The draft through the vents and cracked windows once more smelled of seaweed and tar. The fog lay in thin patches along the edges of the palisades. For the first fifteen minutes, Falco remained quiet, idly fingering Lara's hair. Then suddenly rousing himself from the trance, he started speaking softly again.

"She was nothing," he murmured. "When I first met her, she was nothing. She was just this ragged little kid, with a couple of useless brothers. So what did I do? I took her in. I bought her clothes. I taught her how to act like a real lady, and then she was really something, really something special."

He traced her lips with his thumb, traced the edges of her blindfold with his fingers.

"Hey, Colonel. You ever see that movie *My Fair Lady*?"

"Please. I think this is a good time to be quiet now."

It was nearly seven o'clock when they reached the Harbor Freeway interchange, and the traffic had finally slowed to a crawl. Although quiet now, Falco still couldn't keep his hands off Lara, still couldn't keep himself from periodically hurting her.

They entered the tunnel from a secondary passage half a mile east of the mouth. Although the approaches appeared absolutely dead, more than fifty Desmodos waited inside. Most waited in silence, either seated along the damp walls or milling below the steps. There were whispers when Falco and the colonel entered, but even the whispers died when Lara appeared.

Falco was the first to speak, formally addressing his warriors from the landing above the vaulted gallery. Lara, still bound and blindfolded, knelt at his feet. Atiff remained in the shadows.

"This, my brothers, is the day we've been waiting for," Falco began, "the day when we carve our place in history. But before we begin, we have to deal with a little problem here. It's a little problem that I think some of you already know about, a little problem involving the lady. Now, I realize that she's been an inspiration to a lot of you, a queen. But that only makes this moment more meaningful. It only makes it all the more meaningful now that we've come to see her true colors."

He snapped his fingers, and Lara rose to her feet.

"Now, of course, she's still real fine on the outside, you know? She's still really something to look at on the outside. But on the inside, my brothers . . . on the inside, she's real bad."

He began to finger the hem of her dress as if appraising the fabric. Then finally glancing back to the crowd below, he stripped her in a single flourish. There was an almost intangible knot of excitement from below as sixty pairs of eyes fixed on her naked form.

Falco smiled. "Sure, I know what a lot of you are thinking right now. Hey, I been there myself. But you guys don't want to mess with this bitch until she's been purified."

He snapped his fingers again, and two boys with tattoos on their shoulders and arms leaped forward and joined Falco on the landing. He spoke rapidly to them in Spanish, pointing to a network of water pipes extending from the wall. The boys responded with nods and slowly led Lara down the steps. As they moved through the parting crowd, two dozen hands reached out to stroke her skin. But no one actually spoke to her.

The youths secured her to the pipes at an awkward angle, facedown on the cold concrete, wrists above her head and legs slightly spread. Falco knelt beside her, and removed the blindfold so she could see the razor that he held. Then once more brushing his lips across her naked shoulder, he slowly opened a six-inch gash along each forearm.

"Don't worry, baby," he whispered. "I didn't hit the artery."

She shook her head, her eyes finally moist with tears. "Please, Falco. Please don't leave me like this."

"Hey, baby, I ain't going to leave you."

"Please, Falco, *please*!"

"No, baby, I don't want you begging now. I just want you to lie here and feel it." He left her with a last gentle kiss on the lips, then slowly rose to face the anxious eyes around him.

"No one is to touch her," he said. "Do you understand? Just let her bleed."

24

The forecast had not changed: late-night and early-morning low-lying clouds along the coast, clearing by noon. The first thing Schwarz noticed, however, were the gulls... at least a dozen squawking gulls, circling above.

"What do you make of that?" he asked as he walked with the others across the TraveLodge parking lot to the van.

Lyons glanced up to the agitated flock above. "Those," he replied, "are sea gulls."

"Exactly," Gadgets agreed. "They're sea gulls. So what are they doing twenty miles inland?"

"Maybe they like the food better here," Blancanales replied.

"Or maybe it's a sign," Gadgets whispered. "Maybe it's some kind of damn sign."

It was just after nine on a warm, gray morning; Able Team knew they'd be sweltering by noon. They drove erratically, blending with the streams of commuters trying to make their way across the city. All around, frustrated motorists remained locked in a trance as they concentrated on pavement and chrome, while their knuckles gradually grew white around the steering wheels.

"Can you imagine doing this every day of your life?" Blancanales asked. "Enough to drive you totally around the bend."

"Yeah," Lyons said. "It's a whole lot more restful crawling through rat-infested tunnels looking for a bunch of maniacs."

"We won't have to look for them," Gadgets said softly.

"Huh?" Blancanales grunted.

"I said we won't have to look for the Desmodos. They'll find us."

"How do you know?" Lyons asked, dead serious now.

"Because I feel them," Gadgets replied. "I feel them everywhere."

His eyes, however, were once more fixed on circling gulls in the distance.

"WHAT SORT OF BIRDS are those?" Atiff asked.

Falco glanced up at the flock of gulls. "How should I know? What am I? Some sort of birdman, or something?"

Atiff frowned in disapproval, and shook his head. "Actually, my friend, you look more like a terrorist. Why don't you calm down?"

It was half past nine, and the traffic had all but slowed to a stop in front of the office complex where Falco and Atiff had parked to watch the ebb and flow into City Hall. In an effort not to attract suspicion, Atiff had a briefcase and had purchased a newspaper. His blazer, tie and flannel slacks also suggested that he was an ordinary citizen, possibly a law clerk or even an attorney. Falco, however, wore a pair of jeans, a T-shirt and a black leather jacket.

"Listen," Falco spit, "you play it your way, I'll play it mine. Got it?"

"Yes, but that's the whole point, my friend. We are no longer playing. Today it is for real. Now, either you control yourself, or I shall be forced to place you under my control. Do you understand?"

Falco looked at him, then slowly withdrew the straight razor from his pocket. "Go screw yourself, Colonel."

Atiff made no attempt to defend himself. He didn't even bother to move back out of arm's reach.

"If you kill me," he said, "my comrades will follow you to hell just to cut your heart from your chest."

Falco held the colonel's gaze for a moment, then returned the razor to his back pocket. "Okay, man. Just so long as we understand each other."

Checking first to make sure the other Desmodos were in place, they finally joined the teeming throng of pedestrians on the sidewalk. They continued across the street at a casual pace, then stopped on the lawn of City Hall.

"Signal your people," Atiff ordered.

Falco extended an arm in a broad arc, and within minutes at least a dozen Desmodos materialized out of the surrounding crowds. Another two dozen lingered on the opposite corners and watched from the steps of a bank and clustered around a snack truck half a block to the south. Although they drew a few curious glances, no one took more than a passing interest until a boy named Panther unzipped a canvas bag and withdrew a Silkworm and launcher.

Then a number of things happened all at once.

A young man in gray flannel shouted something to a companion.

An elderly woman screamed, and threw herself to the grass.

Two more women scurried behind a row of parked cars.

A passing security guard struggled to draw his weapon, but was tackled by three razor-wielding Desmodos. The first cut open his left eye and sent him screaming to his knees. The second cut severed a tendon in his neck, and the guard's head suddenly dropped like a withered flower. The third cut slashed his throat, and sent at least a pint of blood pumping to the lawn.

Several screams followed from witnesses, but by that time Falco had lowered his arm.

Then came the white flash, then an oddly muffled thump, then at last the fireball spraying fragments of bricks and glass across the pavement.

SIXTEEN MEN AND WOMEN suffered the initial effects of the blast: five attorneys from a public defender's unit, half a dozen paralegals, three secretaries and a couple of security guards. They were conscious of the light and what might have been a solid wave of air. Some, gazing at the critical wall, were also conscious of flame and an odd notion of collapsing space, as if the foyer had somehow imploded. Then came the choking concussion, with the impact of a massive club or a wall of boiling water.

Those still conscious at that point were probably next aware of the debris, the shards of brick and glass that shredded their flesh and smashed their bones. Then at last there were the screams, although most of the first sixteen could not possibly have heard them.

There was nothing in City Hall security manuals on how to respond to a rocket attack. Of the two guards still left standing in the foyer, one threw himself to the tiles, while the other sat down in the corner. Of the half a dozen civilians still alive, two or three simply wandered in a daze, while the others continued to scream in agony.

WHISPERS OF A DRAFT through the maze of ventilation shafts, the plop-plop of dripping water and the occasional squeal of hungry rats echoed through the Desmodos' tunnel. Now and again there was also the crackling static of the shortwave radios attached to Able Team's packs.

"Looks like we missed the party," Blancanales said as he peered into the empty gloom.

Schwarz shook his head. "No, there's something going on in there. I can feel it."

Lyons started to protest, but catching a glimpse of Gadgets's eyes, he finally said nothing.

They moved in a ragged line, cutting the gloom with Mag-Lites attached to their weapons. The Politician still carried the awesome over-under combination, Lyons still packed the MK-7 and Gadgets the Atchisson. Each man also packed two M-26 grenades and their slightly modified .45s.

They had reached a sort of circular cavern, possibly designed as a turnabout. Beyond branched two tunnels, one going north, the other south. Schwarz projected his lights down the first until it faded into utter blackness, then turned the light on the second with the same results.

Blancanales turned to Lyons. "Now what, Great White Leader?"

Lyons glanced into the blackness to his left, then into the blackness on his right. "Good question."

"Why don't we split up?" Schwarz said. "You guys go south. I'll go north."

Lyons took another minute to survey the diverging tunnels, then finally shrugged. "All right. But at the first indication of trouble, you get on that radio. Understand?"

Schwarz nodded, but said nothing.

Alone now, he moved at a slightly slower pace, continually spraying the ceilings and walls with the beam from his Mag-Lite. Here and there he paused to examine some sign of recent habitation—cigarette butts, crushed beer cans, spent cartridges—but generally he just kept moving. Once or twice, he found himself thinking of the time he'd already spent in those tunnels, but for the most part his mind was clear, alert, ready for almost anything.

Except maybe a simple song lazily sung in the heart of the darkness.

Gadgets switched off the Mag-Lite, and moved to the wall. He took another fifteen steps, running his hand along the slimy wall for direction. Releasing the safety on the Atchisson, he took another eight or nine steps forward, and crouched in the deepest shadows below the pipes.

At first he saw nothing beyond the hint of a form apparently suspended in the air. Then by degrees, closing the distance an inch at a time, he began to discern the outline of a boy slowly rocking back and forth on his haunches.

He rose, keeping his eyes fixed on the boy's hands, straining his ears for the sound of a cocking weapon.

But the boy wasn't even close to squeezing the trigger of the AK-47 that lay across his knees.

Gadgets took another step forward, but still didn't lower the Atchisson. "Where's your brothers, pal?"

The boy's reactions were very slow; he merely grinned, nodding. "They gone, man. They gone to torch this city into nothing."

"What about you?"

The boy grinned again, this time with a sleepy shrug. "Me? Me, I'm just sitting here singing my song and flying high. Not that I won't be kicking ass soon, but first I got to just sit here a while, just sit here and watch that lady fade away."

Gadgets slowly shifted his eyes to what looked like a pale wisp of smoke gently shivering in a breeze. Then he began to discern a second figure closer to the wall.

"Pretty radical, huh?" The boy smiled. "Pretty radical, ain't it?"

But it wasn't until Schwarz had switched on the Mag-Lite and trained the beam on Lara's form that he even began to grasp just how far out it was. Although he couldn't tell if she was still breathing, a great deal of her blood lay in shimmering pools and her eyes stared blankly at nothing. Her lips were slightly parted. Her hair was damp with perspiration.

"Why haven't you tried to help her?" Schwarz asked, feeling the rage rising up from the pit of his stomach, feeling his own blood starting to pound in his ears. "Why?"

"I don't know." The boy shrugged. "I guess I just didn't feel like it."

"Yeah, I can understand that," Schwarz said as he laid the Atchisson aside. "I can definitely understand that," he said, and pulling a rope and gag from his pocket, he tied the boy up.

Gadgets quickly tore off strips from his field jacket, and knelt beside Lara to apply the tourniquets.

Her pulse was weak, but steady, and when he untied her bonds, she looked at him.

"You're going to be all right," he whispered as he drew his coat around her shoulders, and gathered her into his arms. It was impossible to tell if she heard him.

Gadgets had just picked her up when Lyons and Blancanales appeared.

"She alive?" Lyons asked.

"Yeah," Gadgets breathed, "she's alive."

"Then we'd better get going."

Using the same crumbling staircase Falco and Atiff had used less than an hour before, the three men emerged into the daylight a hundred yards from the tunnel's mouth. Almost immediately their attention was drawn to the dense cloud of black smoke billowing above Bunker Hill, to the circling choppers and to the shriek of sirens that shattered the morning.

"What the hell is that?" Blancanales asked.

Lyons shook his head, and glanced at his wristwatch. "Probably City Hall."

"Then what are we waiting for?"

Lyons turned to Schwarz, who was still holding Lara in his arms.

"Gadgets?"

"Just call an ambulance, and tell them to bring lots of blood. I'll catch up with you later."

After another moment's hesitation, Lyons nodded. "All right, old buddy, we'll see you in a while."

It took Lyons and Blancanales less than a minute to sprint the hundred yards to their van, start the engine and plow on out of there.

25

The crowds had already lined the sidewalks on Hill Street; traffic had slowed to a snail's pace. In the end, Lyons had to jump the curb in order to drive the van to the blood-soaked pavement in front of City Hall, where Hector Florio, with a dozen uniformed cops, was crouching behind a barricade of black-and-whites.

"What have we got?" Lyons asked.

"What do you think?" Florio replied. "The Desmodos hit the place with another goddamn rocket."

"How many down?"

"Fifteen and still counting."

"Maybe you'd better get some of these people out of here."

Florio glanced over his shoulder to the growing crowds across the street. "Maybe I should also pray for a cloud of locusts, and a flood."

An obviously frantic detective scrambled up from behind a fender. His knuckles were white around the barrel of his pump gun. There were spots of blood on his shirt.

"I just patched into building security, sir," he said. "The first two floors are gone."

"Any idea how many we're facing?" Florio asked.

The detective shook his head. "Thirty, maybe more. And they're armed to the teeth."

"Civilians?"

"At least fifty on the upper floors."

"What does SWAT say?" Lyons asked.

But before the detective could respond, Florio answered for him. "SWAT says, 'Help!'" he said with a bitter smile. "SWAT says 'Call in freaking Superman.'"

"Maybe they'll settle for Ironman," Blancanales said. "Maybe they'll settle for Ironman and a pissed-off Politician."

There were shots from an upper-story window, and a careless cop sagged to the pavement amid a tiny explosion of blood. In response, a number of officers trained their weapon on the window and squeezed off pointless shots.

A second detective had scrambled out from between the black-and-whites, this one appearing more frightened than the first.

"Sir," he said, panting. "Apparently they've got the mayor in there, and at least half the city council."

"Any dialogue?"

The detective shook his head. "No, sir, not yet."

"Then what the hell is their game plan?"

As if in response, a high and terrified scream broke from a window.

"That," Blancanales said, "is their game plan."

FALCO'S GAME PLAN WAS exactly what it seemed: the systematic infliction of terror. Having led about two dozen Desmodos up to the seventh floor where the mayor and seven frightened council members were moving along the corridor, he immediately set to work.

The first to fall was the representative from North Hollywood, a young and generally aggressive man named Walter W. Tang. The leader of the council members fleeing along the corridor, he initially spotted Falco from the top of the staircase. He then shouted a frantic warning to the others, and attempted to shield a young woman. Then screaming something unintelligible, he sought cover in the doorway of an adjacent office. But by that time, Falco had already unleashed a spray of bullets from his Uzi.

Six slugs caught Councillor Tang as he stumbled for the door, six slugs from the left shoulder blade to the small of the back. The impact seemed to bend him like a bow, while six corresponding splotches of blood appeared on the tiles in front of him. As the councillor turned and sank to his knees, a second quick burst caught him in the face and actually lifted the top of his head off.

There were screams from the other horrified council members, including the representative from the Seventh District. In an effort to restore some semblance of order, the mayor calmly suggested that they all return to the council chamber... which was exactly where Falco wanted them.

Twelve men and women were under Falco's control in the council chamber: the mayor and the six remaining councillors, two clerks, a stenographer, a bailiff and a secretary named Kim Song. Falco's attention was focused on the mayor.

The mayor was a portly man, with pleasant features and close-cropped graying hair. As a former

LAPD officer, he had long maintained a reputation of staying cool under fire, and the current situation was no exception. Boldly and defiantly returning Falco's gaze, he calmly asked the Desmodo leader who he was and what he wanted.

Falco, however, was in no mood to be questioned, and he simply told the mayor to shut his fat mouth.

The next to speak was the bailiff. A former high school lineman by the name of Tommy Knowlen, he had never been one to shrink from duty, and while Falco was occupied with the mayor, Knowlen drew his .38 revolver and sighted down the barrel to the base of Falco's skull.

"Freeze," Knowlen shouted. "Freeze, or I'll nail your ass right here and now."

At least nine Desmodos responded with cocked weapons leveled at Knowlen. But having committed himself to the role of a hero, Knowlen was in no position to turn back now.

"I swear to God," he shouted. "You tell your punks to lay down their weapons, or I'll blow you apart."

Falco slowly turned to face Knowlen and grinned. "Now, what are you going to do with that little peashooter, huh?" he asked.

Although Knowlen was wavering, visibly shaking, he still kept his revolver fixed on Falco's head.

"Just tell them to lay down their weapons," he said. "Just do it."

Falco shook his head. "Let me tell you a secret, man. All I got to do is snap my fingers, and you'll be dead before you can even pull the trigger. You understand what I'm saying? One little snap of my fingers, and you'll be dead before you can even blink your eyes. So why don't you put the .38 down on the table, man? Why don't you put it down, and save the Dirty Harry stuff for your girlfriend? What you say, man? Save it for another day, huh?''

Knowlen hesitated for a moment, first glancing at the mayor, then at the Desmodos around him. Finally lowering the revolver, he dropped it on the table.

"Now, don't that feel better?" Falco asked. "Don't that feel a whole lot better?''

But although Falco was still smiling, something definitely looked wrong with Falco's eyes now, something definitely wrong with the way he continued to look at Knowlen. Then, finally, slowly, he nodded to a slender Desmodo in the corner and snapped his fingers.

The Desmodo let loose with a long burst that caught Knowlen in the kidneys. The bailiff lurched forward, eyes wide with disbelief, mouth already starting to foam with blood. For a moment he stood there, left hand quivering like a leaf in the wind, lifeless eyes still fixed on Falco's fingers, lips trembling as if trying to form a word.

"Next?" Falco said.

"MAYBE I SHOULD GET on the bullhorn and talk to them," Florio said.

"And tell them what?" Lyons replied. "That they're surrounded?"

They were still crouched behind the black-and-whites, still essentially pinned down by sporadic sniper fire from above. Although there had been no more fatalities, at least two officers had been badly cut when the windshields of their units had exploded.

"Well, what do *you* suggest we do?" Florio asked.

Lyons peered over the bullet-riddled fender at the shattered doors and rubble-strewn entrance. "I think," he said, "that it's probably time to pay them a little visit."

"If I send a team in there, Falco's going to start dumping bodies out the window faster than we can count 'em."

"I'm not talking about sending in a team, Hector. I'm just talking about a little probe."

"But even if you make it past the second floor, how do you expect to—"

"Hector." Lyons shook his head. "Why don't you just let me worry about all that, okay?"

ALTHOUGH IT WAS NOW fairly quiet in the council chambers, it was a brittle silence. The six city officials remained frozen in their chairs. The clerks, the stenographer and the secretary had squeezed themselves in a corner. The mayor stood on the podium. The Desmodos watched, menacing, from along the walls, some almost appearing bored. Falco moved between the tables, inspecting the frightened faces.

"Now what should we do for an encore?" he said. "I guess that's what you're all wondering right now, huh? What's that crazy greaser going to do next?"

He paused before a woman from one of the westside districts, an attorney who was rumored to have been in bed with Western Petroleum.

"Well, the fact is," he said, smiling and running his fingers through her hair, "I don't really know what we're going to do next. I figured we just play it by ear.''

He moved on, pausing beside the stenographer, a slightly graying woman wearing an excess of rouge. But after toying with a pendant around her neck, he only sneered.

Then he saw the young Oriental woman.

She was seated on the linoleum, her legs folded beneath her trim, black skirt. With her hair in bangs across her forehead and neatly trimmed along her shoulders, she could easily have passed for sixteen or seventeen. Falco was also intrigued with her body, which was slender and boyish.

He told her to stand up and approach him.

She glanced at the mayor with frightened eyes, then delicately rose to her feet and stepped into the center of the chamber. Falco responded with a smile, and slowly proceeded to examine her. He placed a finger under her chin and turned her head to the right and the left. He circled behind her, and ran his knuckle along her spine. He lifted her hair aside, and lightly kissed her on the neck.

"Hey, what's your name, baby?" he asked softly. "Huh? What's your name?"

Her lips moved, but nothing came out.

"Couldn't quite hear you, baby. So how about you tell me again, huh? What's your name?"

"Kim," she whispered, tears now forming in her eyes.

"Huh? Got to speak up, baby."

"Kim Song."

"Kim Song? Well, that's a good name. That's a real good name. Nothing wrong with that name. Tell me something," he whispered, caressing her cheek. "How did a beautiful woman like you get mixed up in all this political shit? Huh? Woman like you should be home with her man, not sitting around here with this bunch of poodles."

"Please," she whispered. "Please don't hurt me."

Suddenly from the corner, the councillor from the Sixth District rose from his seat. A former UCLA track and field star named Jack Rigg, he was an imposing figure, with broad shoulders and enormous hands. His voice boomed out across the chamber, and the ferocity in his eyes startled Falco for a moment.

"Look here, punk. If you want money or some sort of political response, we are willing to negotiate. But you have absolutely no right to torment this woman and I demand that you stop immediately."

Falco peered over the woman's shoulder with an easy smile. "Uh, say that again, dude?"

"You heard me. I demand that you stop tormenting that woman."

Falco nodded, stroking his chin. "Yeah, that's what I thought you said."

He casually snapped his fingers again, and the chamber was suddenly filled with the crack of more gunfire.

Councillor Rigg looked as if he had been hit with fifty thousand volts, suddenly going rigid and rising to his toes. The blood seemed to explode out of his stomach, splattering several of his colleagues. Then, hit by a second and a third burst, he went skidding across the linoleum.

"Now, where were we?" Falco said, smiling.

I-BEAMS HUNG from gaping holes in the ceiling and walls. Large chunks of concrete lay scattered on the floor among the human debris. A mutilated woman was draped over a railing. Although she'd obviously been injured in the initial blast, someone had cut her throat, too.

"Looks like they really did a number here," Blancanales whispered as he and Lyons picked their way through the rubble to the staircase.

"Problem is," Lyons replied, "I've got a feeling that this little number's still going on."

There were two more bodies along the staircase leading to the first floor. Farther along the corridor, a young man in a cheap suit lay amid scattered papers. Although his face looked composed, someone had literally gutted him.

Around the corner, a narrow stretch of linoleum led to clerical offices. Blancanales had taken the lead, and moving quietly on the balls of his feet, he suddenly saw a flash of brown dart out ahead and vanish.

"Bad guy?" he whispered to Lyons, who had seen it too.

Lyons shook his head. "Maybe, maybe not."

"Well, only one way to find out, right?" Blancanales said as he slid into an alcove beside a drinking fountain.

He released the safety of the Remington, stuck four fingers beyond the alcove and started counting. One, one thousand. Two, one thousand. Three, one thousand. Four, one thousand. A split second later, Lyons sprayed two quick bursts into the plaster at the end of the hall, and Blancanales made his move. He took a long leap, then sprang off the opposite wall. When he drew in sight of the crouching Desmodo, he let loose a blast to the ceiling and screamed, "Freeze."

But whether from instinct or a death wish, the Desmodo simply lowered his AK-47. Blancanales waited another second, then couldn't wait any longer. His first shot opened the kid's belly, spraying blood and bits of tissue on the tiles. His second shot obliterated the jaw and left the boy shivering on the floor.

"You tell me." He sighed as Lyons joined him beside the body. "What the hell is driving them?"

Lyons regarded the huddled and bloody mess below—a sixteen-year-old punk in Reeboks and Levi's, with a red bandanna around his head and nothing else to show for his death.

"I think we'll find the answer to that one," Lyons said, "when we take a look at Falco."

FALCO STOOD beside Kim Song, holding the razor in his right hand. He was about to remove the buttons from her blouse.

"What's the matter?" he leered. "Aren't you boys enjoying this?"

He turned to the councillor from the Second District, a distinguished-looking elderly man with white hair and a thin, severe mouth.

"Hey, Pop," Falco said. "What's your name?"

The councillor replied with an indignant glare. "My name is Anderson," he said.

"Well okay, Andy. How about you and I play a little game now, huh? How about you and I show these poodles just how much we like this lady here? What do you say? You want to play that kind of game?" Then lifting his razor to the trembling girl's throat, he said,

"Hey, I'm not fooling around here, man. Now, get over here!"

The councillor rose from his chair stiffly, and approached Falco. His hands were clenched in fists at his side. His eyes were fixed on the far wall. Kim briefly glanced at him, shifting her eyes like a frightened rabbit.

"Okay, Pop, now this is how we play," Falco said. "First we're going to satisfy all your secret fantasies. And I know you got some secret little fantasies. So why don't we start by having you take a real close look at her, okay? Go on. You don't have to be ashamed. You got the perfect excuse. 'Cause if you don't take a real good look at her, I'm probably going to carve you like a turkey. So go on, look at her!"

Anderson shifted his eyes until they rested on the girl's tear-streaked face.

"Now, touch her, Pop. Go on, touch her."

But although the councillor managed to lift his arm, he still couldn't seem to unclench his fist.

"Oh, I get it." Falco smiled. "This is what they call honor, right? Like you'd rather die than lose your honor, huh? Well, that's cool. But I got to tell you, Pop, dying ain't much fun. So how about we try it again, huh? Now all I want you to do is touch her. You understand?"

He withdrew the razor from Kim's neck, and laid it against Anderson's.

"Now, touch her," he whispered. "Touch her!"

Although it seemed to take forever, the councillor finally extended his hand to Kim's breast.

"Now, that wasn't so bad, was it?" Falco grinned. "In fact, I bet you even liked it, right?" Then slowly drawing the razor along the councillor's neck so that a thin line of blood stained his collar, he said, "Now, you go sit down, Andy, and be a good boy."

He returned his attention to the girl, bringing the razor up against her throat. Then suddenly flicking it away, he left a tiny speck of blood.

"Now, that didn't hurt, did it?" he breathed. "Well, did it?"

She winced, but still remained silent, trembling like a terrified bird.

"What's wrong, baby? You don't like it?" he slurred.

"Please," she whispered.

He smiled, dabbing away the speck of blood with his finger. "Please, what? Huh, baby?"

"Please don't hurt me."

He glanced back over his shoulder at the Desmodos lining the walls. "Hey, she says she don't want to be hurt no more. You guys hear that? This bitch says she don't want to be hurt no more. You think she means it or what? Huh?"

But by now even Falco's own warriors had grown silent, watching with impassive faces, some of which betrayed traces of disgust.

Obviously unconcerned about what his men might or might not have been thinking, however, Falco turned his gaze back to the woman.

"Well, I'll tell you something, baby," Falco continued. "I never met a bitch who didn't like a little pain now and again, 'cause it brings 'em back to basics. You understand what I'm talking about? We get born with pain, and we die with pain. And when we feel it in between, then we know exactly who we are. So you got to flow with it. You got to feel it and just start flowing with it.''

He felt her shivering under his touch again. ''Now, I want you to flow with it this time, baby. I want you to *flow* with it.''

She shut her eyes, finally unable to keep herself from sobbing.

He moved the razor's edge to the corner of her eye, while resting his palm on her hip. ''You're scared of dying, aren't you? You're scared that maybe this is going to be the day you meet the great Kahuna.'' He very gently drew the razor's edge across the jugular vein. ''Well, I got some news for you, baby, it's just a little kiss away. It's all just a little kiss away.''

But before he could bring the razor back to her throat, bring it down in a long arcing stroke from the shoulder, everything seemed to stop.

''Enough!'' Atiff shouted from the doorway, stepping forward with the barrel of an Uzi resting on his forearm. ''I think this has gone far enough.''

''HOW FAR DO YOU PLAN to take this?'' Blancanales asked.

Lyons peered out from behind the bullet-shattered wall, and gazed down the long corridor to where Atiff had posted four Desmodos at the front of the staircase.

''As far as we have to,'' Lyons said. ''Why?''

Three or four 9 mm rounds tore off another chunk of plaster above them.

''Just asking.'' Blancanales said.

They had reached the second floor by now, and another rank of deserted clerical offices. Among the debris along the corridor were fragments of blown windows, bits of blasted tiles and a lot more blood.

"All right," Lyons whispered. "Let's get going."

They moved at a cautious pace, half-crouching along the wall. In addition to his MK-7, Lyons now carried a grenade.

There were more shots from the bottom of the stairwell, and Lyons dived into an office on the left while Blancanales slid through the door on the right.

"Now what, fearless leader?" Blancanales murmured.

But Lyons had already begun to move, rolling out of the office door and springing forward with a spray of lead from his parapistol. Although his first slugs merely ripped more plaster, his second burst obviously caught some flesh as a piercing shriek rose and then faded to a whimper.

"Cover me," Lyons whispered. Then, advancing with another burst, he slid into a janitor's closet.

A girl, maybe eighteen or nineteen, lay amid a mess of paper towel rolls, jugs of industrial detergent and damp mops. Her ankles had been chained, and her wrists cuffed to the broom rack. Her underwear had been used as a blindfold. Although her body was covered with bruises and what looked like cigarette burns, she didn't appear to be too badly hurt.

Lyons withdrew the gag from her mouth, removed the cuffs and wrapped a raincoat around her that he found hanging on the door.

"You all right?" he asked.

She nodded, then shook her head and began to cry.

Lyons clenched his jaw, but said nothing. Carefully removing the chain from her ankles, he told her to wait where she was until the shooting stopped.

"Then I want you to get the hell out of here. You understand? Just get the hell downstairs," he said.

Although there were still occasional shots from the staircase, the last burst from Lyons's MK-7 had obviously given the Desmodos there something to think about.

He peered around the closet door, until he caught sight of Blancanales. After they exchanged hand signals, he moved out again. He kept low, slinking along the wall like a shadow. When Blancanales began squeezing out rounds from his AR-15, Lyons increased his pace but stayed in a crouch until he neared the staircase.

He inserted a fresh magazine containing ten rounds of NATO specification ammunition into the roller-fed side of his parapistol. He glanced back to Blancanales, then inched forward for another glimpse of the staircase. He counted three heads peeking over a barricade of tables, chairs and a massive oak door blown from its hinges. Then he laid down the MK-7 and withdrew an M-26 fragmentation grenade.

"You, out there!" he shouted. "Lay down your weapons now!"

Nothing.

"I repeat. Lay down your weapons and—"

"Eat shit, and die!" screamed a voice from the staircase. Another dozen 9 mm rounds powdered the plaster less than a foot from Lyons's head.

Lyons rolled back against the wall, and slipped the index finger of his left hand into the ring attached to the grenade's firing pin. He shut his eyes with a tired breath, recalling the girl in the closet, the carnage on the ground floor and finally the cuts on Schwarz's arm. After calculating distance and trajectory, he pulled the pin with his right hand. Then he counted off two more seconds. With a last searing image in his mind of what the Desmodos had done to Gadgets, Lyons hurled the grenade.

The blast was deafening, an almost palpable echo that rolled off the linoleum in a shattering wave. Then there was nothing except the ringing silence.

Lyons approached slowly, flanked by the equally cautious Blancanales. The breeze through recently blown windows rustled papers all around them. What had sounded like someone moaning, turned out to be just a gently swinging door.

"Talk about urban strife," Blancanales whispered as they drew in sight of the bodies. The first two Desmodos, approximately eighteen years old, had been blown over the barricade and lay sprawled on the staircase above. The third, of indeterminate age, had been virtually shredded to the bone. Among the debris all around were fragments of whiskey bottles and bags of crack. There was also a lot of cash: twenty-, fifty- and hundred-dollar bills.

"Pretty much tells the whole story, doesn't it?" Blancanales said. "Dope and money. Money and dope."

Lyons leaned over a heap of splintered tables, and gazed up the staircase. "Looks that way," he said.

"So how do we play it?"

"One floor at a time."

"TERRORISM IS NOT barbarism, my friend. Terrorism is a precise science."

Although Falco had not laid down his razor, he had finally stepped away from Kim Song. Nothing else, however, had changed. The walls were still lined with the two dozen wary Desmodos. The mayor still stood fixed behind the podium. The remainder of the council members were still rigid with fear.

Colonel Atiff continued speaking softly to Falco. "Naturally you despise these people, and naturally you wish to see them humiliated. But their final humiliation will only be achieved through our victory. For that reason we must control our emotions and begin the next phase of the operation."

Falco glanced over his shoulder at the girl, now clutching her arms around herself and weeping. Then he turned his gaze back to the colonel. "The Desmodos are still mine," he finally said, seething. "Got that? The Desmodos are still *mine*!"

Atiff laid a calming hand on Falco's sweat-drenched back where only three or four minutes before he had contemplated pumping in a dozen rounds. But ultimately Falco was right. The Desmodos were still his.

"And that is why we must act as a team, my friend. That is why we must act as a synchronized machine if we hope to achieve our goals today." Atiff glanced at a clock above the mayor's podium. "Now, very soon we will begin to broadcast our demands from the radio facilities upstairs. But until those demands are met, we must remain vigilant, continually on the lookout for imperialist treachery. Because even as we speak they are coming, slowly working their way past the bodies of your loyal brothers in order to destroy our dreams.''

Falco glanced at the girl again, then to the double doors. Although there were still echoes of gunfire from the lower floors, apparently the explosion of what he assumed to have been a grenade had ended his troop's effective resistance.

"I ain't afraid to die," Falco whispered.

Atiff nodded, his hand continuing to rest on Falco's back. "Of course, you are not afraid to die. But there is a difference between dying victoriously and dying in failure. So let us begin marching toward victory. Let us begin marching toward victory together.''

The remaining council members were ordered to rise and move to the door. The two clerks and the stenographer were handcuffed to a table. Falco stationed himself behind Kim Song. Atiff slipped a pair of plastic handcuffs on the mayor, and gently nudged the man off the podium. Four Desmodos, picked at random, were instructed to cover the hallway. The massive oak doors were slowly inched apart.

"SHOW TIME," Blancanales whispered.

He and Lyons lay crouched at the foot of the staircase. Between the stairs and the council chamber at least seven more Desmodos lay behind a barricade of steel and fiberboard furniture. Four massive filing cabinets had also been dragged into the corridor in order to form a crude bunker. Eighteen feet beyond the bunker were the council chamber doors. Then there was another empty stretch of linoleum and finally the elevator leading to the radio facility below the city hall roof.

Although Lyons had withdrawn another grenade, he had laid it aside after an initial reconnoiter. He had also switched his MK-7 from full automatic to semi-auto, and instructed Blancanales to do the same with the AR-15.

"What's the matter?" Blancanales grinned. "Odds aren't steep enough for you?"

Lyons returned the grin, while nodding toward the council chamber doors. "I just kind of get the feeling that Florio wouldn't be too happy if we nailed the mayor by mistake."

Then for a while they waited, occasionally marking the sound of a cocking weapon, but mostly just absorbing the silence. Finally, noting the click of a lock and those slowly opening doors, Blancanales repeated his whisper. "Show time."

The hand-cuffed mayor, with Atiff following closely behind him, emerged first. Next, the four remaining councillors were gently prodded into the hall. Finally, clutching Kim Song, Falco appeared.

Blancanales reacted first, inching the barrel of his AR-15 over the edge of the step. Next, praying that the hostages were still capable of logical reactions, Lyons shouted, "Hit the floor!"

Eight shots cracked out from the barricade, another six or seven from the colonel's Uzi. But as the four councillors and the girl dived for the linoleum, Blancanales squeezed the trigger.

Falco screamed, clutching his shoulder and spinning with the impact. A second burst from the colonel's Uzi slammed into a kneeling councillor, and parted his skull.

"You shoot again, and they *all* die!" Atiff screamed. "You understand? They all die!"

But even if Lyons and Blancanales had wanted to shoot, they couldn't have possibly survived the exposure, because following another scream in Spanish, the remaining Desmodos opened up with everything they had.

Bullets, glancing off the tiles, screamed along the staircase. A fist-size chunk of plaster landed on Lyons's back. Smaller chips peppered his cheek with tiny cuts. Blancanales had managed to squeeze off a couple more rounds, but mainly to show them that he was still alive and kicking.

"Looks like this is where we start attacking in another direction," he shouted.

He didn't know whether Lyons even heard him above the roar of withering fire.

Then just as suddenly as it had started, the firing stopped. There were sounds of magazines and empty shells hitting the floor, but nothing else.

Lyons edged forward to the top step, but didn't actually peer out until he had the grenade in his hand. Then very slowly raising his head, he gazed across the littered linoleum.

Nothing. Not a whisper, not a breath, nothing.

He slid back down the stairs, picked up the chunk of plaster that had bruised his back and hurled it like a grenade into the Desmodo barricade.

Still nothing.

He picked up Blancanales's conversion, eased up the muzzle of the Remington and wasted at least four hundred dollars' worth of city property... but still received no reply. Finally, presenting the most obvious target imaginable, he started along the corridor.

The councillor whom Atiff had just shot lay huddled amid heaps of correspondence blown from one of the filing cabinets. There were at least a dozen memos clearly bearing the mayor's signature, several more signed by various councillors. Also scattered across the linoleum were spent shells and fragments of crack.

"Don't you just hate it when they run away," Blancanales said, gazing at the littered corridor.

Lyons, however, ignored the remark. "Maybe you'd better get on the radio to Florio."

"And tell him what?"

Lyons took a deep breath, then shook his head. "Tell him that we are unable to pursue at this time without endangering the lives of the mayor and the other hostages."

"Anything else?"

Lyons glanced down at the council member, at the widening stain of blood on his chest and the missing section of his skull.

Finally he said, "And tell him to get us some stun grenades, so we can try to save some of these people."

When the message had been radioed down to Florio, Lyons and Blancanales picked up their gear and proceeded down the corridor. Among the debris the Desmodos had left behind were more than sixty rounds of 9 mm ammunition and another fully functional Squad Rifle with laser sights and a flash suppressor. In the council chamber they found the clerks and the stenographer still handcuffed to a table. The bodies of the dead were sprawled among the chairs.

But what intrigued Lyons the most, held his gaze like a magnet for at least sixty seconds, was a line of blood that he had a hunch was Falco's—a twelve-foot trail from the center of the hall to the elevator doors.

26

Florio had not had time even to digest Lyons's status report before the limousine appeared. It came from the southeast corner of the city hall block, a sleek and enormous Cadillac parting the crowd behind six motorcycle cops. Although the windows were tinted, the outline of the solitary passenger was faintly discernible—a big-shouldered man with a massive head.

"Who the hell is that?" Florio asked.

The young detective by Florio's side responded with a sheepish grin. "Kinda looks like it might be the doctor, sir."

"Doctor? What doctor?"

"You know, sir. *The* Doctor."

"Oh, shit."

"You want me to bring him here, sir?"

Florio glanced back to the blasted foyer, then up to the blown windows along the fourth and fifth floors.

"No, Henderson. I don't want you to bring him here. I want you to shoot him."

Someone had given North a yellow hard hat, although it would have proved about as effective as a shower cap if hit with a 9 mm slug. He also wore a SWAT team vest beneath his academic tweeds. When he finally managed to waddle between the black-and-whites to where Florio was kneeling, he was sweating like a pig.

"I just want you to know that this happens to be a command performance, Captain. I did not request to be here. I was ordered."

Florio let his sunglasses slip down his nose for a better look at the man. "Ordered, Doctor?"

"By the President," said North. "And I'll have you know that he is not at all pleased with the performance of your department today, not at all pleased."

By this time, there were between twenty and thirty patrol cars surrounding City Hall, at least sixty officers on the front line. Although sporadic shots were still directed from the building to the street, there had been only minor injuries from flying glass and fragments of brick.

"Perhaps you had better fill me in," North said.

Florio shook his head with a thin smile, and nodded to the wreckage behind him. "That," he said, "is City Hall. Up there are more than twenty perpetrators with automatic weapons and God knows what else. They blew the hell out of the first floor with a Chinese missile and are presently holding members of the city's council as hostages. They also, I am sorry to say, have our fair city's mayor." He leveled his gaze back at the doctor. "Any questions?"

North removed a handkerchief from his breast pocket, and dabbed at his sweating face. "Where are the hostages being held?"

"Broadcast room."

"Have there been demands?"

"Not exactly."

"What's that supposed to mean?"

"It means that they haven't had to make demands. If they want something, they take it."

North squinted over the fender of the patrol car, peering across the scorched lawn, then up to those ranks of shattered windows.

"Well, Doctor?" Florio glared at the other man. "What's your prescription?"

North ducked back down behind the fender. "Take me to a telephone, and patch me through to the broadcast room."

IT WAS HOT in the broadcast room. Even after Falco had smashed a window with another enraged burst from his Uzi, the air remained stagnant, oppressive. His shoulder was still bleeding. The pain had grown tolerable after a few hits of China white, but the blood continued to seep through the dressing. For a while he had tried to will the wound to close, to concentrate his energy on the ragged hole and actually *will* the flesh together again. Then sliding into a China white glide, he began to realize that the bleeding was good, that it was a necessary part of the purification he must endure before achieving his destiny.

On a slightly parallel track, Atiff, too, had begun to see his destiny in terms of an ebb and flow—specifically, the ebb and flow of electrical waves that would carry his message to the world outside. Unfortunately, however, he couldn't seem to get the transmitter to work. In fact, he couldn't even figure out how to turn it on.

As for the others, the three remaining councillors simply sat on the floor and stared off into space. The

mayor kept his eyes on Falco, or the rank of Desmodos watching from the wall. Kim Song continued to
tremble in a corner.

Then the phone rang…and kept on ringing at least
a dozen times before Atiff finally picked it up.

NORTH TOOK THE TELEPHONE but held it at arm's
length as if he expected it to explode. It was extremely
warm inside the back of the truck that now served as
the LAPD command post. The six or seven officers
and SWAT team members pressing close to watch the
doctor didn't make him feel any better, either.

"Okay." Florio sighed. "You're on."

North took a deep breath. "This is Dr. North," he
said sternly.

"And what in hell do you want?" Atiff asked
coolly.

"To talk."

"About what? This oppressive weather, which I am
sure has left us all a little out of sorts?"

At least half the perspiring officers in the truck responded with thin smiles.

"We want to help you," North continued. "We are
genuinely concerned about your problems and we wish
to help."

"Oh, this is excellent," Atiff replied. "Because I
was just now thinking how nice it would be if someone could help me. You see, I am having a slight
problem with the machinery up here, a slight problem
with this radio transmission device. Now, do you think
there is someone who could help me? Hmm? Would
that be too much to ask?"

North glanced at Florio. Florio glanced at the SWAT commander, who responded with a curt nod.

"Yes, there is someone here who you can help with that problem. But first I must be informed as to why you need a radio transmitter."

"Why, Doctor? Why to broadcast my demands, of course. Surely you must know that this is the standard operating procedure of all fanatic madmen like myself. We must broadcast our demands."

"And what, may I ask, are your demands?"

Although Atiff was silent for at least twenty seconds, it was easy enough to imagine his leering grin. "Tell me how to activate this infernal machine and you'll hear my demands soon enough," he said.

There was another exchange of glances and nods among North, Florio and the SWAT commander. Then finally mouthing the words, "I know what I'm doing," North returned to the telephone.

"As much as I'd like to hear your demands," North continued, "I'm really not in a position to grant you broadcast time. Now, if you want to discuss the—"

"Doctor," Atiff said calmly, "are you presently in a position to view the window where I am looking out?"

North gazed up through the truck's open door along with Florio and the others. "Yes, Colonel. I can see the window."

"Then I invite you to witness this little testimony to my determination."

Although the councillor's scream could not be heard inside the van, it was obvious that he was still alive when he was shoved out the window . . . tottering for a moment on the ledge as if attempting to regain his balance, then crashing to the pavement below.

"Nice going, Doctor," Florio said.

FIRST THERE HAD BEEN a softly fading scream. Then whirling to face the rank of shattered windows in the room immediately below the broadcast room, Lyons had briefly caught a glimpse of a falling shadow. Then it was very quiet. Indeed, apart from the sputtering air conditioner, there was only the undulating static from the walkie-talkie.

"Scratch the Third District," Blancanales said. "Only four more to go."

Lyons looked at him. "What are you talking about?"

"They just dropped one of the hostages. That means they've got four hostages left."

"So?"

"A couple of dozen Desmodos, Falco and Atiff. And the only thing that's keeping us from kicking their butts are two councillors, a lady and the mayor."

Lyons shook his head with an exhausted sigh. "I kind of get the feeling, Pol, that we're not in a position to keep that kind of scorecard. Know what I mean?"

"So what are we in a position to do?"

Lyons reached for the walkie-talkie. "I'll show you."

WITH THE LATEST DEATH of the councillor, the streets below were once again filled with pandemonium. Camera crews from all the network and local television stations had clustered around the perimeter of the police lines. The escaping hostages had been herded into waiting ambulances. Street vendors, capitalizing on the crowds, had begun to offer a variety of snacks: doughnuts, pretzels and hot dogs on a stick.

"I have a right to know what you're planning," North said. "I have an obligation to the President."

Florio looked at North, then laid down the walkie-talkie.

"Okay, Doctor. I'll tell you what I'm planning. I've got two very capable men up there, and I am about to provide them with the cover they need to storm that damn broadcast room before anyone else takes a fall. Now, does that answer your question?"

North pressed his handkerchief to his forehead, and squinted out to the glaring rumble on the lawns. Two members of the SWAT team had just sprinted through the blasted doors. Among their equipment were at least twenty pounds of ammunition and what looked like sixty feet of scaling rope.

"I suppose you realize that you're probably endangering the mayor's life with these adolescent heroics," North said.

Florio ignored the man, and signaled to his fire team crouched behind the patrol cars.

"You're also probably endangering the lives of countless other citizens," North added. "And naturally I will have to inform the President of the fact that this entire tactical farce is actually being directed by two clearly unstable and unauthorized killers."

Again, however, Florio ignored the man, while signaling to a sniping team deployed behind an LAPD van.

"And just for the record," North continued, "I should also like to add that I've already consulted my attorney regarding those ridiculous and entirely unfounded charges concerning my relationship with the Center for Middle East Studies...which, I might add, happens to be an extremely reputable organization that has served as a consultant for some of the foremost—"

"Doctor," Florio finally interrupted, "if you don't shut your mouth, I just may be forced to take Mr. Lyons's advice."

"What the hell are you talking about, Captain?"

Florio nodded to a window high above where Lyons might or might not have been watching. "Lyons just told me to shoot you, Doctor, and I kind of think he was serious."

THE TWO SWAT TEAM members laid the equipment on the council chamber table: coils of nylon rope, grapnels, pitons, air-powered launchers, safety belts, sixty rounds of assorted ammunition, two M-18 smoke grenades, two M-26 white phosphorus grenades and a number of stun grenades. The stun grenades, designed to blind and immobilize an enemy temporarily with a tremendous flash of light and sound, were cylindrical tubes with firing mechanisms that were designed to be activated by an upward flip of the thumb. Although Able Team had used these weapons with great success in the past, they had never encountered this particular design.

"I'm instructed to inform you, sir, that support fire will commence only on your signal," the taller of the two SWAT team members said.

Lyons nodded, and began to inspect the equipment.

"I'm also instructed to inform you that Captain Florio will disavow any knowledge of this operation if it goes sour."

Blancanales turned from the window, and grinned. "Don't worry," he said. "If this operation goes sour, even *I* will disavow any knowledge of it."

The two SWAT team members returned the grin, but they also seemed glad to leave.

"So what do you think?" Lyons asked when he and Blancanales were alone again.

Blancanales shook his head, gazing down from the window. "I'm a rock climber, okay? Give me a sixty-maybe seventy-foot face with good contour, and I'm as happy as a kid in a candy store. Give me a six-story drop and the possibility of some creep shooting at me, and I'm not so happy."

Lyons picked up the air-powered launcher, then ran his hand along the rope.

"Well, look at it this way," he said. "We take the elevator and we're definitely dead the moment the doors open. We take the stairway, and we're bound to run into Desmodo action before we hit the broadcast room. We swing in through the window, then maybe we've got a chance at catching them with their pants down. Besides, it's too nice a day to stay inside."

Still looking down at the bloody concrete below, however, Blancanales only managed a weak smile.

"THE FOLLOWING is a message from the oppressed peoples of the world," the colonel read from a tattered piece of paper. "The mayor of your fair city is currently our prisoner, as are two members of your city council. The body lying in front of this building is further evidence of our determination. We will now present a list of our demands.''

The colonel paused at this point, fumbling with another tattered piece of paper. He had spent more than two years planning for this moment, and almost an hour simply trying to figure out how to activate the radio transmitter and adjust the mike. But now that it had begun, he was surprised at how calm he felt, how entirely ready to either live or die . . . depending upon the will of Allah.

"At this very moment, there are twenty-seven political prisoners in the Musadim Prison in Jaffa, Israel. They are being unlawfully held, without charges and without bail, by the Israeli oppressors. We have attempted to secure their release through peaceful measures, but those attempts have come to nothing. Thus on behalf of the World Revolutionary Movement, I demand the immediate release of these prisoners. Within three hours of this broadcast, these prisoners are to be en route to the land of their choice. Their safe conduct out of the state of Israel is to be guaranteed by the Israeli government. Once they are safe and out of reach of Israeli officials, we will arrange for the release of the hostages. If, after three hours, the release of these prisoners has not occurred, we will have no choice but to conduct another execution.''

FLORIO TOOK the walkie-talkie away from the radio and spoke into it.

"Did you copy that?"

"Yeah," Lyons said. "I copy."

"So what do you make of it?"

"Simple. They know the Israelis on their own won't budge an inch on this kind of prank, but they figure they might just knuckle under if Washington puts the heat on them. And what better way to get the President out of bed than to threaten to knock off the mayor of a major American city?"

"So what do you want to do?"

Lyons glanced at Blancanales, who was leaning from the window preparing the ropes.

"I want to move out, and I want you to keep your people the hell away from us. You copy?"

"Yeah," replied Florio. "I copy."

"And one more thing. Pol and I are going to stay out of sight of the broadcast room windows. Do not, I repeat, do not let your men fire unless we signal from the west end of the building. You copy?"

"I copy."

"Oh, and Hector?"

"Yeah?"

"I kind of have a feeling that Gadgets may be showing up pretty soon."

"And if he does, you want me to—?"

"Just stand aside and let him work."

"Copy."

"HEY, YOU GUYS FEEL the earth shake?" Falco grinned.

He was still seated on the linoleum, facing the mayor, Kim Song and the two surviving council members. Although Atiff had ordered six of the Desmodos to construct and man another barricade in the corridor outside the broadcast room, the bulk of Falco's nervous warriors were still seated against the far walls. Some of them kept their eyes fixed on Falco, some on the hostages, some on the restless profile of Atiff in the sound booth.

"Soon as I heard that message," Falco continued, "it was like the whole earth just started trembling. I mean it. It was really something. You deliver that message, man, and it's like the whole planet just stops and listens. 'Cause that thing had some power, man. I mean it had real power. Even—what's his name?— Martin Luther King never had that kind of power. I'm telling you it was like...well, like the voice of God, man. It was like the voice of—"

"Shut up," Atiff said quietly. "Just shut up."

The heat had grown almost unbearable by now, like a weight that seemed to press down on everyone. Only Atiff, essentially a desert warrior, still appeared cool.

"From this point forward, I will tolerate only absolute obedience," Atiff said. "Is that clear? Only absolute obedience. Those who do not comply will be shot. I repeat, those who do not comply will be shot." He glanced at Falco. "And there will be no exceptions."

Having hit himself with another rail of China white, however, Falco took no offense, but merely grinned again. "Hey, Colonel," he said, "why don't you lighten up a little. We're all friends here, okay? We're all just like one big happy family. So just lighten up."

Atiff did not reply, but returned to the broadcast booth. At his departure the Desmodos seemed to relax.

Falco's wound still bothered him. Although the bleeding had subsided, it still hadn't completely stopped. The pain was like a white-hot disk beneath his shoulder blade unless he deadened it with narcotics.

Falco looked to his left at the girl. Her head now rested on her shoulder. Her eyes were shut. Her left hand had slipped to the floor.

"Pssssst, baby," Falco whispered. "Hey, Kim. I'm talking to you."

She opened her eyes, but did not move her head. Before she could respond, however, the mayor cut in. "Look, why don't you just leave her alone?"

Falco picked up the Uzi, and held it at arm's length so that the muzzle pointed directly into the mayor's nose.

"Hey, was I talking to you, man?"

"Just leave her alone," the mayor said sternly.

Falco smiled, but kept the Uzi in place, inches in front of the mayor's left eye. "Oh, I get it," he said. "This is where the hero of the story sticks out his neck for the lady in distress. Yeah, this is where the brave hero puts his life on the line to save the lady's honor. Well, that's cool. That's real cool. Except I don't think she wants you to save her right now."

Falco lowered the Uzi, and turned to Kim. "Talk to me, baby."

The girl shuddered slightly, drawing her legs beneath her.

Falco reached out and clasped both hands around her ankle, beginning to pull her toward him, to actually slide her across the linoleum.

She responded with a whimper, but otherwise did not try to fight him. Yet finally looking into his eyes, watching the pupils grow larger and larger as he pulled her closer, she suddenly saw him wince with pain.

"Shit!" he screamed, releasing her ankle and clutching his wounded shoulder. He sagged back to the wall, groping for the little bag of China white, before glancing at the fresh blood soaking through his T-shirt once again.

27

It almost felt like a carnival. Although the crowds had finally been cleared from the streets immediately around City Hall, at least two hundred spectators still milled about along the adjoining blocks. Vendors continued to sell snacks. Amateur photographers continued to prowl the perimeter, hoping for that fifty-thousand-dollar shot.

The SWAT commander spoke softly on the walkie-talkie, while signaling to a team of snipers behind the black-and-whites, then laid it down and turned to Florio. "Apparently your men have moved to the east ledge," he said. "Meanwhile, there's no sign of any movement in the broadcast window."

"And nothing more on the radio?" Florio asked.

"Only static."

The commander ran a hand through his steel-gray hair. "You want a little advice ... off the record?" he asked.

Florio shrugged with a sigh. "Why not?"

"Unless you send in some support, your friends up there don't have much of a chance."

"Yeah, well I can't play it that way," Florio responded.

"Okay, suit yourself. But I'm telling you that sooner or later those boys are going to need some inside help, even if it's just one man flanking from the stairs."

Florio shrugged again. "Maybe you're right, but I'm still not in a position to authorize anyone going in there except—"

"Me," Gadgets said as he slid to the rear of the truck.

Although still covered with Lara Cardinales's blood, Schwarz could not have looked more at ease: the Atchisson casually slung over his left shoulder, his aviator sunglasses resting on the top of his head, a can of Diet Coke in his left hand.

No one questioned his arrival. "Your friends are about here," the commander said as he jabbed a finger on a blueprint of City Hall. "The only other access to the broadcast room is along this staircase, here." Another finger jabbed the paper. "Now, of course, you can always take the elevator...assuming that the Desmodos have turned it back on, which I doubt. Or you can swing down on a cable like your buddies...which I wouldn't recommend."

Gadgets finished his drink, crushed the can and tossed it in a wastebasket.

"What's this area?" he asked, pointing at the blueprint.

"Crawl space," the commander replied.

"You mean a ventilation shaft?"

"That's right. A ventilation shaft. But if you're thinking about using it to try and come in on top of them, you're out of your mind."

"I know," Gadgets said. "I'm completely out of my mind."

THERE WERE DOZENS of pigeons on hand to watch as Lyons and Blancanales stepped out onto the window ledge. Most were gray and mangy looking, grown fat from scavenging in the parks below. They had clustered beneath the eaves and along the edge of the roof where Blancanales had anchored the ropes. Their eyes seemed filled with a mixture of defiance and curiosity. More than once Lyons had to nudge them aside with the toe of his shoe, praying that their murmuring protests would not arouse suspicion.

"Now, isn't this fun?" Blancanales whispered. "Aren't you just having the time of your life?"

Lyons gazed down to the empty pavement eight floors below, then up to the nylon ropes that kept snagging on unseen objects.

"Yeah." He gave a hollow laugh. "I'm having the time of my life."

The two Able Team commandos continued to move at a snail's pace. Two steps forward along the eight-inch ledge, one step back to disentangle the rope from the ornamental masonry that adorned the roof of City Hall. The mounting breeze was also beginning to cause problems.

They paused where a portion of the ledge had crumbled away in the last earthquake. They were now only about twenty or thirty feet from the window of the broadcast room.

"Question," Lyons said. "What happens if one of those yo-yos down there in the crowd happens to spot us, and then gets it in his head to warn Atiff, or shout something?''

Blancanales hesitated a moment, and looked down at the teeming throngs below, then back along the ledge to the window.

"Answer," he said. "We go down a lot faster than we came up."

SCHWARZ MOVED FAST. He took the first five flights at a near sprint, then paused only three minutes on the sixth floor to catch his breath. Here and there were the bodies of clerks and secretaries, but he hardly even bothered to look. In the council chamber, he found what Lyons and Blancanales had found: bodies amid debris of bloody plaster and splintered furniture.

He had to stand on the chair to dislodge the grate from the ventilation shaft, then had to muster all his strength to drag himself into the crawl space. It was a good deal warmer than he had anticipated, and the dust was virtually intolerable. But at least there were no rats.

He traversed a good fifty feet before he heard the voices, soft and indistinct murmurings like conversations from a dream. Using the Mag-Lite, he checked a crude sketch he had drawn in the command truck, then continued crawling forward, hesitating only when he reached the grate above the broadcast room. A voice echoed up through the darkness.

"HEY, COLONEL, ain't it about time to throw another one out the window?''

Atiff glazed out of the broadcast booth to where Falco still sat slouched against the wall. Although no more than an hour had passed since the colonel had read his demands, he, too, was growing restless. He didn't like the wait. He didn't like the heat. And he especially didn't like Falco's outbursts.

"Let me tell you how I see it," Falco continued. "We gave these guys three hours, right? Three hours to have your pals released from jail. Okay, but what happens in the meantime? I'll tell you what happens in the meantime. They call in all kinds of guys to kick our butts."

Although this speech drew a few quick glances from the mayor and the Desmodos along the far wall, no one even bothered responding until Falco picked up his Uzi again.

"Hey, I'm serious about this, man. I think we should toss that little bitch out the window just to keep them on their toes."

But by then Atiff had withdrawn a Browning 9 mm semiautomatic pistol. "The girl stays where she is," he said.

"No, she don't." Falco spit. "The girl goes. She goes right out the window like a bird with a broken wing."

He rose to his feet and moved over to Kim Song.

"Sit down!" Atiff commanded. "Do you hear me? I said sit down!" he repeated as he slipped off the safety of the Browning.

But Falco had also released his safety. Leveling his Uzi at Atiff, he grabbed the girl by the wrist and yanked her to her feet.

"Falco," Atiff called. "Let her go. Do you hear me? Let her go!"

Falco turned to face the colonel, his left arm encircling the girl's waist, his right hand still holding the Uzi. "Hey, Colonel," he said softly, "she ain't worth it. You understand what I'm saying? She ain't worth it."

Atiff, however, just kept staring at the man. "I'm warning you, Falco. Let her go! Let her go right now!"

Then a lot of things happened at once.

Having torn off Kim's blouse, Falco had slid his hand up to her breast. She, in turn, tried to twist out of his arms. Atiff shouted Falco's name again, and fired four shots in the ceiling. Falco, releasing the girl, also fired into the ceiling.

But the shots were lost in the blast and flash of Carl Lyons's stun grenade.

It was like a thousand popping flashbulbs, while the deafening crack was like a thousand cherry bombs. There were confused cries, bodies crashing into walls, and dozens of knee-jerk shots. Then swinging in from the opposite end of the window, Blancanales tossed the first smoke grenade.

Immediately long coils of blue-black smoke spewed up to form a blinding curtain. There were more wild shots from the interior, but by this time Lyons had slid through the window and had also begun firing.

He fired from the hip, spraying from left to right at the first Desmodo, a lean kid named Rudy. Blood spurted from the boy's rib cage, his eyes briefly widening in shock, then going blank as he slipped to the floor.

"Kill him!" Falco shouted as he grabbed the mayor by the neck and retreated to the door. "Kill them!"

But as another Desmodo attempted to obey, Blancanales switched to the Remington and blew a four-inch hole in the boy.

There were six or seven shots from the rear of the room where Atiff struggled with a councillor, literally grabbing the man by the collar and dragging him into the corridor. The shots were followed by those of more fleeing Desmodos.

Somebody screamed, "Don't shoot! You'll hit the mayor!"

Falco laughed hysterically from the doorway. "Yeah, man, don't shoot your mayor!"

The girl screamed next, recoiling from a bleeding Desmodo, who had lunged out of the swirling smoke and grabbed her left wrist. Lyons responded with a quick burst, three slugs to what looked like the punk's chest. The Desmodo tumbled forward, sprawling onto the girl, and knocking her to the ground under him as he did.

"They're getting away!" the remaining councillor shouted. "They're getting away with the mayor."

But as Lyons attempted to rise from the floor, he found himself looking down the barrel of another AK-47.

Two shots flashed out of the blue-black smoke. The first from Politician's conversion opened a hole in the Desmodo's neck that was almost the size of a fist. The second, from the Desmodo's AK-47, slammed into the wall inches from Lyons's face.

Blancanales released another smoke grenade. Atiff screamed another enraged order, sent a burst of fire into the plaster, then scrambled out to the corridor behind Falco, the mayor and the councillor.

"They're using our smoke to get away," Lyons shouted. But as he rose to his feet, yet another Desmodo lunged out of the swirling smoke. Ironman emptied the remainder of his clip into the reeling form, then sank down to reload.

Ten feet from the window, Blancanales had also squeezed off his last round. He withdrew another magazine and jammed it into the AR-15. But before he could even chamber the first round, he found himself facing a muscular kid and his weapon.

Blancanales shouted Lyons's name, but only because he had to shout something, had to let someone know that after all these years he was finally going to buy it. Then watching the barrel of the AK-47 swing level with his eyes, he couldn't help screaming, *"Nooooooo!"*

But when the shot finally came, it wasn't from an AK nor even from Ironman's Sterling. It was a full-blown blast from an Atchisson. It left the Desmodo momentarily wrenched like a snapping twig, blood exploding out of his chest, then hurled the corpse to the floor.

"Gadgets?" Blancanales whispered, peering through the whirling smoke at the hunched form easing down from the ventilation shaft. "Gadgets, that you?"

"Yeah," Schwarz grunted. "It's me."

A moment later, Lyons also appeared. For a minute they all simply looked at one another: Blancanales still wedged in the corner, Gadgets still planted among bodies, a dazed councillor from the Fifth District still huddled by the sound booth, the girl still

clinging to Ironman's arm…they all just looked at one
another.

"I kind of don't think this is Miller time," Lyons
finally said.

Gadgets moved toward the door to the corridor,
while Blancanales secured two wounded Desmodos
with handcuffs. Able Team worked quickly and effi-
ciently while the councillor kept whispering, "I can't
believe this is happening." Kim Song, however, was
quiet.

"Looks like they moved up to the roof," Gadgets
said. He was peering through the doorway to the corridor. Someone had left a lot of blood on the woodwork around him, and there were large splotches on
the staircase.

"Give me a head count," Lyons said.

Schwarz glanced back at the two bodies sprawled by
the window, another two staring from the corner.

"I'd say they've still got maybe fifteen or twenty up
there," he said. "Some on the roof, some probably
just below it. And of course, there are also the two
hostages."

"So we failed." Blancanales sighed. "We just up
and failed."

Lyons shook his head. "What are you talking
about? We haven't even started."

28

All Falco could do was watch. He sat with his back to the grimy wall of the passage leading from the roof. His Uzi rested on his knee, his left hand pressed to his right shoulder. Below, six or seven Desmodos were trying to construct another crude barricade along the corridor. On the roof, the colonel directed the remaining Desmodos to prepare for the last stand. The mayor and the councillor were seated on the stairwell, their wrists locked in plastic handcuffs. Now and again there were distant shots and frantic voices.

"She's still after me, you know," Falco said as the Colonel knelt down beside him. "Lara has still got it in for me."

Atiff shook his head with disgust. "You're drugged, aren't you?"

Falco responded with a lazy grin. "Hey, I been hit, man. They hit me hard."

Atiff glanced at Falco's shoulder, a mass of clotted blood and raw flesh.

"All right, my friend," he finally said. "Why don't you just sit here and keep an eye on our hostages, hmm? You think you can manage that?"

Falco grinned again, but this time the lazy edge was gone and his eyes were black and hard. "You know something, Colonel?" he said softly. "I think I'm going to enjoy watching you die."

There was more noise of gunfire from above, and what sounded like a couple of big bores slamming into the steel door that opened onto the roof. Then, following a moment's silence, a terrified youth slumped into the corridor with a bloody hand jammed under his arm.

"These assholes are shooting at us," he moaned. "They're shooting at us from the street."

"What a surprise, huh?" Falco sneered. "They're shooting at us. What an incredible surprise."

Atiff gently took the boy's wrist and examined the injured hand. The tips of two fingers had been cleanly severed.

"Tie it off at the wrist," he told the boy. "Tie it off, and you'll be as good as new."

"Hey, what about me?" Falco asked with a quiet grin. "Where do I tie my shoulder off, huh? At the neck?"

"Shut up," Atiff snapped. "Shut up, or I'll leave you here with the others."

"Leave me here, Colonel? And just where the hell do you think you're going, huh? Up in a chopper and far away? Because they ain't going to be sending no choppers. They ain't going to be sending nothing but more lead."

Another big bore slammed into the steel door above them, and another young Desmodo screamed from the roof.

"See what I mean?" Falco said.

Atiff glanced at Falco, then at the mayor and the councillor. "Can you walk?" he asked Falco.

"Sure, I can walk. I can do anything. I'm invincible, remember?"

"Then help me get these two up to the roof."

"What? Time for another statement, Colonel?"

"Just help me get them on the roof."

But after another slow smile, Falco shook his head. "I got a better idea," he said. "I got a much better idea."

"GET ON THE HORN and tell them to stop the damn shooting," Lyons ordered. "It's just going to force Atiff into tossing a hostage from the roof...or worse."

Blancanales nodded, and moved into the broadcast booth where the telephone still lay on a table.

Although most of the smoke had finally dissipated, the stench of death permeated the room. The soft moans of two wounded Desmodos came from a corner.

"Maybe we should also do something about getting the prisoners and civilians out of here," Schwarz said from his post at the door.

Lyons looked at the councillor still hunched in the corner. "How about it? You think you can escort your party out of here?"

The councillor glanced at the two Desmodos, at the leg wounds and then at their eyes. "What if they...I mean what do I do if—"

"I'll escort them down," Kim Song said.

Until that moment she had simply been watching in silence from the far end of the room. Although she had slipped on a windbreaker and wiped some of the

blood from her face, she was still a mess: arms badly
scratched from fragments of glass, an ugly bruise on
her thigh, the imprint of Falco's hand on her wrist.

"Just give me a gun," she said, "and I'll get them
downstairs."

Lyons picked up one of the AK-47s, checked the
magazine, released the safety and then cocked it. "All
you have to do is point and pull," he said to the girl.
"Anyone gives you any trouble, just point and pull."

The girl rose to her feet, nodded to the councillor to
follow, then ordered the Desmodos to get moving. As
the four went through the door and out to the staircase, Gadgets kept them covered from behind the
heaped furniture in the corridor. Blancanales picked
up the walkie-talkie to tell Florio that the civilians were
en route with prisoners. Lyons remained at the doorway, watching until he could no longer see the girl, the
councillor or the prisoners. Then he remained a little
longer, wondering if she was going to kill the boys out
of revenge.

But when the shooting started again, it wasn't from
the corridor.

"Get me Florio on the line," Lyons shouted. He
grabbed the receiver from Blancanales. "Damn it, let
me talk to Florio!"

"Carl?" Florio said, obviously speaking from the
command truck, and obviously not alone.

"Hector, you want to tell me what the hell is going
on?"

Another volley of shots rang out from the street
below, where at least a dozen SWAT snipers had been
posted.

"Well, we've kind of been superseded here."

"What?"

Lyons heard voices in the background, then what sounded like a fist slamming on a tabletop.

"It seems that some of our good friends from Washington have arrived," Florio said calmly.

"Well, you tell our good friends from Washington that their fire is doing no good at all, and that it's just going to force Atiff to play his hand a little early. Do you copy?"

"I copy, old buddy, but I kind of don't think they're going to listen."

"Why the hell not?"

"Because they have it on very good authority that the only way to handle things at this point is to keep the enemy psychologically off balance. Now, I've tried to explain that we're a little past the psychological—"

"Wait a minute, Hector. Are you telling me that North is calling the shots now?"

"Now, Carl, you've got to understand that the President has personally requested—"

"Then you tell the President that if the shooting continues, he's not only going to lose the mayor and the councillor, he's probably going to lose half a city block."

There were more voices in the background, then more sporadic shots.

"Hector, I'm not kidding about this. Atiff and the remaining Desmodos have nowhere left to go, and I mean that literally. If your boys keep taking potshots at the roof, it's only going to piss the colonel off. And believe me, that is not something we want to do. Overwhelm him, yes, but not just piss him off. Now, do you copy that or not? Hector?"

"Look, I got to go, Carl. Just sit tight. I'll get back to you."

"Hector! *Hector!*"

Lyons slammed down the phone and turned to Blancanales.

"Get your gear together," he said. "We're going up."

"Under whose authority?"

There were two or three more shots from the street below, then what sounded like some sort of Desmodo battle cry from the corridor.

"My authority," Lyons said. "We're moving out under my authority."

COLONEL ATIFF CROUCHED behind the low ledge that bordered the roof of City Hall. Beside him knelt a swarthy boy named Enrique and a somewhat paler boy called Carmen. Between them lay the dismantled components of the last Silkworm.

There were sputtering echoes of circling choppers above, but nothing immediately in sight. There were voices from bullhorns, but the colonel ignored them as well.

"Do you know what the first rule of terrorism is?" Atiff asked softly.

The swarthy Desmodo looked at him, but said nothing.

"The first rule is to kill indiscriminately, to kill without apparent logic or consideration for even women and young children. That way they can never be sure who is to die next."

He hefted up the shoulder mount, and handed it to the boy.

"You see, they think we are helpless. They think we will not risk murdering another hostage, because the hostages are our only ticket to survival. Well, in this line of reasoning they are correct. But what they have not considered, what they have not grasped at all is our determination to make our presence felt at any cost. That's why I want you to simply aim for the crowd. I don't care who dies or lives, just so long as they feel it. Do you understand? I want them to feel it."

NORTH SCANNED the rooftop from the safety of the command truck. It was odd, he thought, how quickly fortunes rise and fall. Only a couple of hours ago, he had been virtually under arrest for what had been termed an improper relationship. Now he was as good as running the show.

"It's a matter of calculated unpredictability," he had told the commander of the Terrorist Intervention Squad. "By continually altering our response pattern, we can keep them in a state of acute anxiety."

"And that's good?" the commander had asked.

"Of course, it's good."

North had then ordered the SWAT snipers to fire from the street, while he prepared himself for the next round of negotiations with the colonel.

But now, scanning the rooftops with a pair of binoculars, he suddenly began to suffer from doubt as he tried to make out what the tiny figure on the roof was holding.

"Oh, my God!" North whispered. Then he shouted over his shoulder, "Tell them to stop the shooting! Tell them to stop at once!"

But it was unlikely that anyone heard him over the blast and ensuing screaming.

There were the screams from those situated along the perimeter who actually saw the missile launched, actually saw the trailing flame and snaking path to impact. Then there were the screams from the people situated in and around the first rank of patrol cars, who actually felt the wall of hot air and crippling storm of fragments.

From North's vantage point, the effects of the blast were mainly seen in terms of the initial flash and fireball, the billowing smoke and cries of pain. He instinctively threw himself to the pavement and then started screaming with the rest of them.

"Get up, Doctor," Florio said calmly. Then lifting North's head by his hair, and shouting into his ear, he repeated, "Get up."

North gazed around him stupidly. Among the debris were pieces of bodies: a foot still encased in a running shoe, a leg still encased in gray flannel, a scorched arm still faintly smoking.

"Get up and start tending to these people!" Florio yelled.

North rose to his knees, and inspected his body for injuries. Thirty feet across the pavement, a dazed child wandered through the smoke. A woman, possibly the child's mother, had been blasted beneath one of the patrol cars.

"Look, Captain, I am hardly in a position to—"

Florio withdrew his service revolver, and jammed it against the side of North's head.

"You know, I could blow you away right now, Doctor. I could blow you away and no one would ever be the wiser. So get up, and start helping these people."

Although North finally rose to his feet, Florio still couldn't keep himself from hitting the man...a quick backhanded blow across the jaw.

"You bastard," Florio spit, and stalked off toward a telephone.

He let the phone ring in the broadcast booth at least three dozen times before he finally gave up. In a way, however, he was glad that no one from Able Team had answered. It meant they had obviously decided to move out on their own, to dispense with all the bureaucratic doublethink and to simply get on with what they did best.

He stepped out of the damaged phone booth and limped back across the scorched pavement. All around him, hysterical victims cried out for help while ambulances tried to make it through the backed-up traffic and choppers circled pointlessly in and out of the gushing smoke. Here and there a frantic voice shouted orders that no one obeyed, while television crews filmed the chaos. Eventually some of the voices were even shouting at him, but he just shrugged and kept walking.

29

A NATO round glanced off the tiles, and echoed for six or seven seconds.

"So," Falco whispered. "It begins."

He sat with his back to the concrete passage that led from the roof. The mayor and councillor lay at his feet, their wrists still handcuffed behind them. A little farther along the passage, a trio of Desmodos methodically fed 9 mm rounds into clips, and then fastened them end to end with black masking tape. Somewhat lower on the staircase, another six Desmodos waited behind stacked filing cabinets and bales of city council newsletters. There were also half a dozen gang members waiting in the utility closet and an alcove off the men's room.

A second solitary shot rang through the corridor and Falco jammed a fresh magazine into his Uzi.

"Yeah," he whispered, "it's definitely starting."

He shifted slightly to his left, then slid a little deeper into the shadow of the stairwell. He shut his eyes, took a hard breath of the rancid air and felt the pain glowing hotter in his shoulder. He turned on his side, carefully withdrew the last little bag of China white and snorted the stuff from the palm of his blood-caked hand.

"That's right, Lara baby, our last little war is definitely starting."

Although more than an hour had passed since he last felt her presence, he knew she was still very close...waiting for the chance to invade him again, to burrow into his shoulder and tear him apart with pain. Not that he couldn't help admiring her guts and the awesome extent of her hatred.

A third, fourth and fifth shot reverberated through the corridor, and someone shouted a garbled order. Then came obviously frantic footsteps, and finally Atiff appeared.

"In case you were wondering, my friend, your men have not been firing those shots," the colonel said.

Falco shrugged. "So?"

"So obviously the enemy has decided to force the issue, regardless of the risks."

Falco shrugged again. "So?"

"Exactly." Atiff smiled. "So?"

LYONS CHAMBERED another NATO specification round, sighted down the empty corridor and slowly squeezed the trigger. Then after waiting another moment in the ringing silence, he turned to Schwarz and Blancanales.

"Nothing," he said.

Blancanales sighed with a listless shrug. "What did you expect? Another little silky?"

Lyons shook his head. "I don't know. I just didn't expect them to play it so cool, that's all."

"Why not?" Schwarz said. "After all, they're holding all the cards, aren't they?"

Lyons eased the door shut, and stepped back into the room. Uncertain as to how much time would be spent here, Schwarz had dragged the bodies of the Desmodos into the soundproof broadcast booth and on leaving had shut the door...hence Florio had received no answer to his phone call.

"The way I see it," Lyons said, "we've got two choices. We can either sit here and let them kill hostages in their sweet time, or we can go for broke and maybe pull those hostages out of there. Either way, the waiting's over."

Schwarz nodded, but then said, "You're talking about the mayor up there, pal."

"I know that, but I don't think he's got much of a chance either way. Atiff's never going to let him go, and that's just the way it is. The councillor's just plain dead meat."

"Yeah," Blancanales added, "but if we try to rush them head-on, eventually there's going to come a point where Atiff will put a pistol to the mayor's head and say, 'Stop, or he dies.' What do we do then?"

Lyons shook his head. "I'm not sure, but I know we can't just sit here and wait for the shots...or another silky to be fired into the streets."

Gadgets moved to the window, and looked down at the aftermath of the slaughter below—the hysterical crowds, the bodies, the charred patrol cars.

"Maybe we should think about hitting them from a second vector," he said at last.

"You mean like taking a chopper to the roof?" Lyons asked.

Gadgets reached out the window, and took hold of the nylon rope Lyons had used to climb from the floor below.

"Actually, I was thinking about something a little more subtle."

Blancanales also moved to the window, and gave the rope a tug.

"You know these things are anchored to the roof, buddy," he said.

Gadgets shrugged. "So?"

"So, the enemy happens to now control the roof. And if I'm not mistaken, Falco just loves to cut things with his razor."

"Well, he hasn't cut it yet, has he?"

"Maybe that's because he's waiting for some jerk like you to start climbing."

Gadgets stepped away from the window, and turned to Lyons. "Look, I'm not saying it's going to be a walk in the park," he said. "But if you and Pol can keep them busy in the staircase, I think I can probably make it up there on the rope, and catch 'em from the rear. Hell, it's better than a head-on assault with no surprises, isn't it?"

"Yeah," Lyons breathed, "It's better."

THE CHINA WHITE WAS a double-edged sword, Falco thought. On the one hand, it helped to control the pain in his shoulder; on the other, it unlocked the door of that tiny cell in his brain where Lara was waiting.

"You feel her?" he whispered.

Atiff shifted his gaze from the corridor, and into Falco's eyes . . . those red-veined and hollow eyes.

"What are you talking about?" he asked.

Falco tapped a finger to his forehead, then glanced at the water-stained ceiling.

"Her!"

They were still seated in the narrow passage between the main corridor and the roof. Now and again there were nervous whispers from the stairwell where the Desmodos still crouched behind the filing cabinets and reams of city stationery. There were also the sounds of magazines sliding into place, and fingernails tapping on the barrels of AK-47s. The shooting, however, had stopped.

"I think it's going to start again very soon," Atiff whispered after another long silence.

Falco nodded with a dreamy smile, then glanced up to the ceiling again. "Yeah, very soon."

Suddenly Atiff shot out a hand, and took hold of Falco's right wrist. He found himself gazing into ravaged eyes; it was like staring into fifty feet of murky water.

"Listen to me, my friend, you must pull yourself together now before it starts. Do you understand?"

Once more Falco merely smiled. "You hear that, baby?" he whispered. "The colonel here wants me to get it together. He wants you to leave me alone, so I can get it together and die in glory for all the oppressed people of the world. Now are you going to be a good girl and let us die in glory? Are you?"

The colonel released Falco's wrist, slumped back to the wall and shook his head.

"I suppose you realize that I can't help you anymore," he said at last. "I simply can't help you anymore."

Falco lowered his gaze from the ceiling, fixing on the colonel's eyes with a sudden and almost frightening clarity.

"Hey, I got news for you, man," he said softly. "You never helped me in the first place. In fact, you never helped anybody. All that talk about freeing your pals from that jail, that was just a lot of crap, wasn't it? You knew from the start that no one was going to go free. You knew from the start that it was going to end just like this... waiting to die in another stinking hole. So don't talk to me about how you're going to help me rule this city, because the only things that rule here are the rats."

Then for a long time they just continued to sit, while the colonel watched the corridor below and Falco stared at the ceiling.

LYONS AND BLANCANALES moved out slowly along the corridor. It was darker here than on the lower floors, and the air smelled faintly of stale coffee, cigarettes and burned electrical circuits. Here and there were traces of blood, possibly Falco's, possibly that of one of the other Desmodos hit by the Remington.

"How are you fixed for stunners?" Lyons asked.

Blancanales patted the three stun grenades clipped to his breast pocket.

"What you see is what you get," he said.

Lyons was carrying two similar grenades. "All right, we'll use what we've got as a first strike, then switch to fragmentation if they're still holding out."

"I suppose you realize that the colonel's probably running the show now," Blancanales said.

"So?"

"So, I kind of get the feeling that he knows what he's doing, that he's got his people broken into fire teams and separated for defense."

"Yeah, in that case we'll just have to take them out one at a time, won't we?"

They paused at the base of a short flight of steps leading to the upper chambers. There were more traces of blood here, and spray-painted signatures on the wall. From about sixty feet beyond the steps came the faint sounds of someone nervously toying with a selector switch, constantly flipping from semiauto to full auto and then back again.

"Don't you wish there was another way to do this?" Blancanales whispered.

"What do you have in mind?" Lyons asked.

Blancanales glanced up to the ceiling at the grate of the ventilation shaft. "I'm just thinking that if it worked for Gadgets, no reason it can't work again."

Lyons also glanced up to the grate. "You're going to find it pretty cramped up there. Anything goes wrong, and you're not going to have a whole lot of room to move around."

"Yeah," Blancanales said, "but then neither does Gadgets."

GADGETS HAD NOTHING but space, limitless space as far as he could see. Below, of course, lay the street and farther out were brown hills adjacent to the freeway pass, but above was only space.

He was moving slowly now, hand over hand up the nylon rope. The pigeons watched from the ledge, but thankfully remained silent. His arms, still raw from Falco's razor, ached with every inch, but it wasn't anything he couldn't bear...particularly when he thought about what they had done to Lara.

He paused a moment, resting in the harness, and envisioned her face. He pressed his cheek against the cool stone, shut his eyes and saw her even more distinctly...her face against a field of white, her eyes clear and moist, her lips moving slightly as if to whisper something to him.

She's with me, he suddenly thought without quite knowing why. She's lying in that hospital bed, but at the same time she's right here with me.

He took a deep breath to clear his head of the strange thought, to force himself back to hard reality. He started moving again, feeling the pain in his arms, but also feeling a new sense of strength.

BLANCANALES WAS suddenly conscious of a presence. Lyons had boosted him into the ventilation shaft, he had started the long crawl through the narrow blackness, and then suddenly he was conscious of a presence.

He stopped, kneeling on what must have been more than fifteen years' accumulation of dust.

There was definitely someone out there...also kneeling, also waiting.

He released the safety on his Remington, muffling the click with the palm of his hand. He lifted the weapon, then started forward again.

Six feet. Five feet. Four feet.

Then he heard the sound of someone or something retreating.

He paused again, sliding his left hand along the barrel until it came in contact with the Mag-Lite.

Then, shifting on his knees and switching on the light, he lunged for the dark shape in front of him.

There was a muffled cry as his shoulder impacted with a yielding body, then another cry as he brought his elbow into a chin. Finally, throwing his weight into what he thought was the stomach, he jammed the Mag-Lite into the terrified face of an elderly black man.

"Don't shoot me, brother! Don't shoot me!"

Blancanales clamped his hand over the man's mouth, jammed the muzzle of the conversion into his neck.

"Keep your voice down," he whispered. "Just keep your damn voice down." Then sliding his hand away, but leaving the weapon in place, he said, "Now tell me who you are."

"Hamilton. Arthur J."

He was a wizened little man in overalls. He smelled faintly of cleaning fluid and chewing gum.

"What are you doing here?" Blancanales asked.

"What do you think I'm doing here. I be . . ."

Blancanales clamped his hand over the man's mouth again. "Keep your voice down!"

"I'm hiding. That's what I'm doing. I'm hiding from them animals down there. See, I'm the janitor, right? And I hear this shooting and screaming, so I climb up in here to hide. Now, that's what I'm doing up here, okay?"

Blancanales eased the conversion aside, lowered the beam of the Mag-Lite, and slid his weight off the man.

"That's one hell of a story," Blancanales whispered.

"Well, it's the God's truth," Hamilton replied.

"So how long have you been hiding up here?"

The old man held up his wristwatch to the faint glow of the Mag-Lite.

"Best I can tell, it'll be going on three hours now. Three long hours sitting in the dark, while them animals tramp around down there."

"And nobody's been up here looking for you?"

"Ain't too many people even know about these shafts, much less willing to crawl around them."

There were sounds of shifting footsteps below, and what sounded like another magazine jamming into an M-16.

"Hear that?" the old man whispered. "That's them right now. That's them stalking around, looking for some other poor body to shoot."

"Where's that sound coming from?" Blancanales asked, dimming the Mag-Lite again.

"Oh, maybe about sixty feet along," Hamilton breathed.

"And there's a grate through there?"

The old man nodded, then must have realized that Blancanales could not see his face.

"Sure there's a grate," he said, "but I wouldn't recommend you going through it."

"Why not?"

"'Cause that will put you almost right down on top of them."

"Yeah," Blancanales said. "Well, that sounds like just about where I want to be . . . on top of them."

As Blancanales slid on past, he heard the old man whisper, "Hey, you never told me what *you're* doing here."

Blancanales smiled. "Just passing through."

LYONS CROUCHED beside the corridor wall, just about fifteen feet below Blancanales. He withdrew a stun grenade and peered down the corridor to the second wall of filing cabinets that had been dragged from surrounding offices. Sometimes you've just got to go for broke, he thought. He quickly tried to calculate the distance, then glanced at his watch. Sometimes you've got no choice at all, except to go for broke.

And swinging out from the corner of the wall, he hurled the stun grenade.

He shut his eyes against the flash, pressed himself against the wall to help deaden the noise. Then springing out with his MK-7 on full automatic again, he let loose with half the magazine.

Two Desmodos, blinded and confused by the sudden blast of the stun grenade, had risen above the barricade. Lyons only caught a fleeting glimpse of them before his stream of NATO specification rounds cut them back down, opening their chests and leaving the boys slumped across the filing cabinets. But as he rushed forward, literally charging the barricade, a third Desmodo suddenly appeared.

He was a tall kid, with pinched features. He wore sunglasses, which, Lyons figured, accounted for his rapid recovery from the effects of the stun grenade. He shouldered an M-16, and even as Lyons sank to a combat stance and swung his MK-7 into play, he knew that he was too late, that the kid was already squeezing the trigger.

But even as all this was registering in Lyons's mind, he saw the ceiling above him explode, the fragments of steel mesh fly apart as Blancanales's conversion blasted from above.

The Desmodo looked as if he'd been struck with a sledgehammer, virtually pounded into the linoleum. Blood and bone joined the spray of plaster as the kid was tossed to the wall.

A second shot from Blancanales's conversion caught another Desmodo still staggering from the stun grenade, caught him in the back and sent him skidding across the floor on his knees.

"Hey, man, don't shoot!" a fifth Desmodo screamed. "Don't shoot!" he repeated just before two 9 mm slugs tore into the back of his head, ripping his jaw apart.

Lyons rolled for cover behind the filing cabinets, looked up to the ceiling and saw the dim outline of Blancanales still hunched in the ventilation shaft.

"They're in there," Lyons whispered, pointing to an alcove fifty feet farther along the corridor.

Blancanales nodded. But as he lowered the conversion through the blown grate, he was met by at least ten more rounds of 9 mm slugs, slamming into the plaster around him.

"You were right," he whispered to Lyons below. "There's not a whole lot of room up here."

Lyons withdrew another stun grenade, but suddenly recalling the sunglasses peering over the M-16, he replaced the stunner with a fragmentation type.

"Going for the touchdown?" Blancanales whispered.

Lyons glanced up again at the grinning face through what remained of the grate.

"You got a better idea?"

"Not really."

"That's what I thought."

Lyons pulled the pin, briefly calculated the trajectory and then tossed the grenade.

Two shots cracked from the alcove the moment the grenade left Lyons's hand. If there was a third shot, it was lost in the ensuing blast. Two bodies flew out of the alcove, arms and legs trailing behind half-naked torsos. A third Desmodo staggered to the wall, his hands clutching his intestines.

Lyons leaped over the wall of filing cabinets, as Blancanales jumped to the floor.

"Hey, don't shoot, man! Don't shoot!" came the plea from beneath the mass of bodies.

Lyons lowered the MK-7, but told Blancanales to keep him covered. Then he started forward. Among the debris were portions of two hands and scorched fingers.

The Desmodo was lying beneath two pulverized bodies that must have saved him from the worst of the blast. As Lyons approached, the boy pleaded again not to be shot, then slumped into a daze.

Lyons dragged him free of the carnage and propped him against the wall. Then withdrawing his .45, he pressed it into the boy's neck. "Straight, simple answers," he said softly.

The boy nodded, "Just don't shoot man, okay? Just don't shoot."

"Where are the rest of your buddies?"

The boy flicked his eyes along the corridor ahead of them to the last few steps before the passage to the roof.

"How many of them?"

The boy shook his head. "I don't know, man. Maybe fifteen."

"What about Falco?"

"I don't know. I haven't seen him for a while."

"And the hostages?"

"I haven't seen them, either."

Lyons glanced back to Blancanales, and motioned him into the alcove. Then grabbing the boy's arms, he secured his wrists with a pair of plastic handcuffs.

"He tell you anything?" Blancanales asked as he crouched beside Lyons.

Lyons shrugged, still watching the dazed boy. "He told me what he knew."

"Which is?"

"It's still not Miller time."

"THEY'RE USING GRENADES," Falco said softly. "That's the explosion. Grenades."

Atiff shifted his boot against the mayor's back, and glanced down the darkened passage to the steps below. "Yes, my friend," he said. "I think you are right. They are using grenades."

They were still seated just inside the door to the roof. Although the passage was now filled with threads of smoke and suspended dirt, they might have been miles away from the killing . . . except, of course, for the echo of those grenades.

"How long do you think my people can hold out against grenades?" Falco asked. "Huh? How long?"

Atiff shrugged. "It doesn't really matter. We have already made our statement, so it doesn't really matter how much longer your Desmodos survive."

Atiff nudged the mayor with the toe of his boot, but the mayor hardly responded. He nudged the councillor, but still received little more than a frightened shiver.

"Besides," he said, smiling, "it is not yet time to play these last little aces. Tactically speaking, that is, it is not yet time to play these little aces."

Falco looked at him, his lips curling into a sneer. "Hey, screw your tactics, man. Those guys are chewing my people to pieces. Now either you do something, or I'll do something. Because I ain't going to just sit here and let them eat my boys. You understand? I just ain't going to let it happen."

A full minute passed before Atiff responded. Then slowly turning his head until his eyes met Falco's eyes, he smiled. "You know, my friend, if I didn't know you better, I would be most impressed with these sentiments. Yes, I would be most impressed with this sudden loyalty to your brothers. Unfortunately, however, I happen to know you far too well to believe it."

Falco met the colonel's gaze for a moment, then finally dragged himself to his feet and lifted his Uzi.

"Tell me something, man. How come I shouldn't just blow you away right here and now? Huh? How come I shouldn't just wipe your face all over the floor?"

"Because in the final analysis you are just like me. You would rather live to fight another day than die on that stinking roof."

Falco lowered his Uzi, but still remained standing, his eyes still clearly furious. "Yeah, well I ain't going to let them chew up my boys. I just ain't going to let that happen." Then, staggering a few feet down the passage, he called for a boy named Lucky to bring up another Silkworm.

LYONS HEARD the scrape of a sole in the ventilation shaft and lifted his parapistol. The weapon was now loaded with subsonic jacketed hollowpoints specifically designed to penetrate soft tissue and reach the vital organs. Given proper angle of fire, however, Lyons was certain that his 147-grain JHPs would also penetrate the thin plaster and reach the Desmodo above him.

"Wait a minute," Blancanales whispered as his hand closed around Lyons's weapon. "I think I know who's up there."

They were crouched in the last little alcove before the Desmodo's final line of defense. Fragments of blood and clothing from the last grenade had splattered the tiles around them, but for the moment it was quiet again.

Blancanales lifted his conversion, and gently tapped the muzzle against the ceiling. Once, twice, three times.

"Hey, Hamilton, you up there?"

"What do you want?" came the whispered reply through the scorched plaster.

"Get the hell out of here."

"What?"

"I said get the hell out of here. Go back the other way, and stay put."

"What?"

Blancanales shook his head, and offered Lyons a thin smile. "Maybe you had the right idea the first time. Maybe you should just shoot him."

Lyons lowered his para pistol. "Who is he?"

"Janitor."

Lyons sighed, and turned back to face the long and rubble-strewn corridor ahead. "Great. That's just great."

Although there were no lights along the corridor and the stairwell was particularly dark, Lyons had counted at least three heads above the barricades of furniture. Beyond lay that second flight of steps below the roof, and probably another six or seven Desmodos clustered around Falco and Atiff.

"Last stand?" Blancanales asked, also peering around the edge of the alcove and down the corridor.

"Could be," Lyons replied.

"What happens if they bring the hostages out, put a gun to their heads and tell us to throw down our weapons? I mean, you want to still try to take them out?"

"Ask me that when it happens," Lyons said. "Right now we're just playing assault on the Alamo."

Lyons hefted another stun grenade, but then noting the outline of a figure moving further along in the passage, he once more decided upon a fragmentation type.

"Long ball," Blancanales whispered. "You sure you've got the arm?"

Lyons took another peek around the corner of the alcove, then quickly calculated the trajectory as imposed by the height of the ceiling.

"As a matter of fact," he said with a grin, "I'm not at all sure I've got that kind of arm."

Blancanales took a look down the corridor. "Well, I can't make any promises," he said, "but I can give it a try." He then withdrew a second fragmentation grenade, braced his back against the wall and tested the throw. "Here goes nothing," he said.

He had to expose his head and left shoulder in order to throw the grenade, and at least four rounds from an M-16 shattered the tiles around him. Fragments, like tiny needles, created pinpoints of blood on his arm while a larger wedge of plaster opened up a cut above his left eye.

But even before the shooting had stopped, his grenade exploded, throwing out some fifteen hundred bits of steel into a ten-yard killing ground.

At least two Desmodos immediately screamed, with fragments embedded in their chests. But when Lyons sprang out of the alcove, spraying still more rounds of JHP, he was nearly cut down in his tracks.

He skidded back into the shelter of the alcove as another volley from an M-16 tore away the tiles from the walls. Blancanales watched him with a vague smile, and a palm pressed to the cut above his eye.

"I told you that was a long hall," he said.

Lyons shook his head, examining a two-inch gash on his elbow where a piece of tile had caught him. "All right." He sighed. "Let's try it again."

He withdrew his last fragmentation grenade, and slid down on his belly. "If we can't get it over them, maybe we can slide it under," he whispered. Then gazing along the fifty feet of linoleum until he sighted the barricade, Ironman slowly drew back his arm.

And then froze.

"Silky!" he shouted, reaching for the MK-7 and staring at the outline of another shoulder-launched missile slowly rising from behind the barricade.

"Silky!" he shouted again, rolling into firing position and squeezing the trigger.

But even as his bullets slammed into the launcher's chest and the body arched back with the impact, the devastating Chinese missile tore out of its jacket.

Pucker and submit, they had called it in Nam. Throw yourself into the ground and don't even think about what's flying around an inch above your head. Lie down, kiss the ground and surrender to the reserves of adrenaline you didn't even know existed....

All of which was going through Blancanales's mind as he heard that Silkworm tearing through the corridor, plowing into the ceiling and exploding.

He also thought about the old janitor probably still crouching in the ventilation shaft. Regardless of the outcome, he was glad Ironman had at least managed to paste the punk who launched the damn missile.

Then as the blast began reverberating through the walls, rising to a terrific *whump* that threw out chunks of plaster the size of watermelons, he couldn't help wondering whether the ceiling would actually hold.

The ceiling collapsed in stages, first along the corridor adjacent to the alcove, then closer to the Desmodo barricade. From where Falco and Atiff lay, pressed against the door to the roof, it almost looked as if the entire floor would go... leaving dozens of mangled bodies strewn among water pipes, electrical cables and insulation sheets.

As it happened, however, only about four or five Desmodos fell beneath the collapsing debris. The rest died in the hail of bullets from Blancanales's conversion, and Lyons's .45.

"Go!" Lyons shouted. "Go! Go! Go!"

He scrambled from the rubble, not even bothering to locate his parapistol, but simply withdrawing the .45 and firing from the hip. Blancanales followed two steps behind, also firing from the hip.

Their first shots caught a Desmodo mid-stride along the passage to the roof. The double impact of a .45 slug and the steel shot from Blancanales's Remington snapped his spine like a stick and lifted him head over heels into the air. Their second shots caught a Desmodo rising from a heap of plaster dust and tiles.

Three Desmodos managed to squeeze off shots in response to Lyons and Blancanales's assault. But diving into a roll, his compact body pouncing like a cat, Blancanales came up firing and nailed all three in rapid succession.

FALCO LAID HIS RAZOR against the councillor's neck, and gazed up through the half-open door to the roof.

"You want to live or die?" he whispered.

All around him his warriors lay moaning with fractured bones, bullet wounds and open arteries. There were also at least two corpses that had taken blasts from the over-under conversion.

"Just get him moving," Atiff shouted. "Just get him through that door and onto the roof. Do you understand? We've got to get them onto the roof."

Atiff had pressed himself to the wall, the barrel of his Browning jammed into the mayor's gut. Although fragments of flying porcelain had opened cuts on his back and scalp, leaving his shirt wet with blood, the wounds were only superficial.

"Now!" Atiff shouted. "Move now!"

They broke from the shadows, Falco more or less dragging the stunned councillor, Atiff prodding the mayor. When they reached the last few feet before the door, Falco sprayed a dozen rounds into the churning dust and shouted for the survivors to follow him.

But by then there were only three: two lean brothers known as Chi-chi and Cha-chi, and a twelve-year-old Asian kid called Fong. The rest—more than a dozen lost Desmodos with names like Ricki, El Chemo, Julio and Toad—were either dead or dying.

Falco sprayed another five or six rounds as he shoved the councillor through the door to the roof, then fired again to cover the colonel's exit before dashing to cover himself.

30

Schwarz pressed himself against the stone and gazed down to the pavement below. For more than ten minutes now, he had been poised on the ledge waiting for an opportunity to haul himself onto the roof. The explosion had very nearly blown him away. Three tense Desmodos had almost caught him dangling and helpless. But when he crawled within seven feet of the rooftop, he heard the unforgettable tones of Falco's voice.

"Oh, I get it," Falco said. "This is where we sacrifice ourselves for oppressed people all the world over. This is where we die gloriously for the cause."

"Shut up," Atiff said. "Shut up and tell your people to station themselves for an assault."

As far as Gadgets could surmise, Falco and Atiff were crouched behind an electrical shed at the far east corner of the roof. He had heard three, possibly four, Desmodos moving closer to the ledge. Then hauling himself a little higher, he had also heard the hostages.

He tried to calculate the odds. Assuming that he was able to hoist himself onto the roof without being spotted, he supposed that he had a fairly good chance of nailing at least a couple of them before the others knew what was happening. Then assuming he could find a little cover, he might even be able to paste a couple more.

But probably not without fatally endangering the hostages.

Gadgets braced himself in the safety harness, and unslung his Atchisson. It was a trade-off. If he held the weapon, he could not climb. If he climbed, he could not defend himself. He experimented with wrapping the strap around his left arm, but it was useless, too confining.

He glanced up to a chopper circling in the distance, and wondered if there wasn't some way he could signal the pilot and arrange a tactical diversion.

He shifted his gaze back to the ledge and found himself staring into the eyes of another curious pigeon.

He briefly shut his eyes again, and found himself fixing on another sad vision of Lara Cardinales. Don't worry, we'll get him, he said over and over to himself.

THE M-26 SERIES GRENADE that Lyons tossed onto the roof had a five-second fuse. After pulling the pin, however, Lyons had waited for the count of two before actually releasing the device. Then, although he had intentionally thrown it low, skidding it across the roof's surface, the twelve-year-old Asian kid named Fong was still able to catch it.

He caught it with his left hand, while diving from the wall. Then pressing it into his chest and rolling onto his stomach, he curled into a tragic ball.

The blast lifted him at least a foot into the air, spraying flesh and bone another six or seven feet. A second Desmodo watching from beside him was immediately drenched in the blood, while even Falco and Atiff were covered with spots. The armed response was almost instantaneous.

The two surviving Desmodos immediately opened up with their M-16s on full auto, splintering the door with a dozen rounds between them. Falco had also begun to fire by then, letting loose with almost an entire magazine.

But Atiff, still crouched behind the electrical shed with his Browning at the mayor's skull and his left foot jammed into the councillor's groin, merely waited.

"Able Team!" he shouted when the firing stopped. "Able Team, do you hear me?"

Lyons, pressed against the wall just inside the door, shouted back, "Yeah, we hear you."

"I am Colonel Atiff of the World Revolutionary Movement, and I am presently holding a 9 mm pistol to the head of the mayor of Los Angeles. Also in immediate range of my pistol is the city council representative from the Fifth District. Now, do you wish to pursue this battle with arms, or do you wish to talk?"

Lyons exchanged glances with Blancanales, shrugged with a grim smile and then withdrew a last fragmentation grenade.

"We want to talk," Lyons shouted.

Atiff glanced at Falco, nodded with a sly smile, then turned his head back to the door. "A wise choice," he shouted.

Atiff rose to his feet, dragging the mayor with him and pressing the Browning into the mayor's neck. "Say something," he whispered. "Say something to them."

The mayor hesitated, shivering as the breeze blew over his sweat-drenched clothing.

"Anything will do," Atiff whispered. "Now speak."

"You in there," the mayor shouted. "These men are not bluffing."

Blancanales smiled at Lyons, then inched a little closer to the bullet-shattered door. "What a surprise," he whispered. "They're not bluffing."

"Now these are our demands," Atiff shouted. "First you will contact your superiors and inform them that we require a helicopter and qualified pilot to transport us to the international airport. Then we require an aircraft and qualified pilot to transport us to an overseas destination. Is that clear?"

Lyons shook his head, exchanged the fragmentation grenade for a stun grenade and smiled again. "Yes, Colonel, that's clear."

"Finally, as a token of your sincerity through these negotiations, we demand that you immediately throw down your weapons and step out onto the roof with your hands firmly placed upon your head. Is that also clear?"

Blancanales inched back from the door, and inserted a fresh clip into his Remington. "Remember when I was asking you what we do if . . ." He grinned.

"Yeah," Lyons whispered. "I remember."

"Well?"

"Colonel," Lyons shouted, "we have no means of immediately communicating with our superiors. Unless we are permitted to use a telephone or descend to the streets, we cannot relay your demands. I repeat, we

cannot relay your demands." Then, turning to Blancanales, he said, "Let's see him field that one."

But Atiff was already smiling again, already smiling at the stupidity of the American mentality.

"We shall discuss these problems when you have
stepped out onto the roof. Is that clear? We shall re-
solve these problems together when you have thrown
down your weapons and presented yourselves."

Another silent exchange of glances in the darkened
doorway, while Lyons continued to finger the stun
grenade and Blancanales eased his hand along the
double barrel of the conversion.

"I will say it again. Lay down your weapons, and
step out onto the roof with your hands firmly placed
upon your heads.

"Sounds like he's serious," Blancanales finally
whispered. "Sounds like he's real serious."

And as if to underscore the point, Falco suddenly
shouted, "Right now! Get out here right now, or I
start cutting off ears. You hear me? Right now, or I
start cutting off ears!"

Once again, Blancanales exchanged a quick glance
with Lyons, while Lyons shook his head.

"You tell me," Lyons whispered. "Throw the
stunner and rush 'em?"

"Risky," Blancanales replied. "Real risky."

"So's not doing anything."

Then came an aching scream and frantic plea, "Oh,
my God, no. Oh God, please not that!"

FALCO EASED the razor's edge along the back of the
councillor's ear. His left arm, locked around the man's

neck, held him steady. His lips, whispering into the ear he was severing, were only an inch or two away.

"Now this ain't going to hurt nearly as much as you think, not unless you start jumping around."

"Oh God, no!"

A thin line of blood sprang from the cut skin, and drenched the councillor's collar.

"Hey, I hardly even scratched you," Falco whispered. He slid the blade another quarter of an inch along the ear, this time deep enough to hit the cartilage.

The councillor screamed again.

But Falco just kept cutting...until Gadgets squeezed the trigger.

GADGETS SHOT HIGH, because given the Atchisson's spread there was no other way to avoid hitting the councillor. He was still braced in the safety harness, with only one leg over the ledge of the roof. Then as Falco whirled, and the councillor spun free, Gadgets shot again for the legs.

Three pellets entered Falco's legs, two above the left knee, one below the right. He stumbled with the shock of it, but still managed to level his Uzi and fire. The slugs exploded off the ledge where Gadgets hung, spraying sharp chips of stone and dust into the Able Team warrior's face. He swung back blinded, then slowly sank down out of sight again.

"Kill him!" Falco screamed to the two Desmodos stationed along the wall. "Kill him!"

But before they could respond to their leader's order, Lyons had already tossed the stun grenade.

A lot of things went through Ironman's mind as he lifted his .45 and sighted down the barrel: that the stunner was probably a little less effective in daylight, that Blancanales probably should have been making this shot with the AR-15, that although Falco's Uzi posed the most immediate danger, there was really no alternative but to go for Atiff.

Lyons fired from a wide stance, the classic position with the left hand supporting the right wrist. He fired with a full breath in his lungs and a conscious command to relax, to relax and trust his instincts. Then even as Falco began to level his Uzi and Atiff screamed, "Shoot and they die!" Lyons pulled the trigger.

The big slug struck Atiff above the bridge of his nose. The shot was so close to the mayor's head that he jerked as if he'd taken the impact. But the moment Atiff began to crumple, the mayor had enough presence of mind to roll behind the electrical shed for cover.

About a dozen blind shots followed Lyons back into the doorway: four or five from Falco's Uzi, another six or seven from a stunned Desmodo. Blancanales tried to return the fire, but splintering fragments of wood and plaster drove him back into the shadows.

Falco screamed again, "Kill them! Kill them!" then dived behind the councillor.

But by now Gadgets had once more hauled himself up to the edge of the roof, and leveled his Atchisson.

He fired without thinking, aiming for the first Desmodo's back, and pulverizing a square foot of flesh. He caught the second Desmodo in horrified mid-turn, caught him square in the face. Finally, leveling the

Atchisson at Falco, he still couldn't see clear of the hostage.

"Do it," Falco said calmly. Then, glancing over his shoulder at Blancanales and Lyons in the doorway, he repeated the order, "Go ahead and do it."

He rose to his feet very slowly, the Uzi jammed in hard beneath the councillor's chin. Then, stepping to the edge of the roof and more or less facing all of them, he yelled, "Come on, let's see if you can kill me before I can squeeze the trigger."

Gadgets slipped a leg over the ledge, slid out of the safety harness and withdrew his .45. He held the weapon at arm's length: back straight, left hand supporting the right, weight evenly distributed on both feet. Twenty feet to Gadgets's right, stood Lyons and Blancanales, their weapons also trained on those portions of Falco's body not shielded by the councillor.

But none of them squeezed a trigger.

"Hey, I know what you're all thinking," Falco said. "You're thinking that even if you could blow me away before my little finger jerks, you're thinking that the impact's going to knock me right over the edge...and that I'll take this guy with me. Am I right? Huh? That what you guys are thinking? You shoot me. I go flying. And it's bye-bye Señor Councillor."

"Well, I got news for you, guys. That's exactly what's going to happen. Even if you blow my head off so I can't jerk my finger, this arm of mine is going to stay locked around this councillor's neck until we both hit the pavement down there. Splat."

"Why don't you just put down the Uzi," Lyons said. "Just put it down, and call it a day."

Falco probably did not even hear Ironman, because by now his eyes were entirely fixed on Gadgets.

"I know you, don't I?" he whispered. "I know you."

"Yeah," Schwarz said. "You know me."

Then for a moment they simply looked at each other, faced off from nine paces, while Gadgets continued staring down the barrel of his .45.

"Okay," Falco whispered. "Okay, baby, take it easy. Take it easy." Then suddenly he winced with a shooting pain in his shoulder and a spasm that jerked his whole arm.

Lyons fired the instant the Uzi slipped past the councillor's throat. He fired for Falco's head, praying that the impact wouldn't throw him off the edge. Gadgets dived a split second later, simultaneously grabbing the waistband of the councillor's trousers, and firing point-blank into Falco's ribs. The double explosions sent a long mist of blood into the air, and left Falco wide-eyed and slack-jawed.

But he still wasn't dead.

He seemed to waver for a long time before finally falling. His gaze was fixed on the sky above. His arms were extended forward as if to embrace someone just out of reach. His lips might have been trying to form a name. Then slowly lifting his arms like the hovering gulls above, he silently toppled backward to the pavement far below.

CLOSE TO ONE HUNDRED spectators were on hand to witness Falco's death. Although obviously only a fraction of those actually saw it—the body tremendously arched as if powered by flight, the trailing hair and stiff arms—they all heard the impact.

He landed on the pavement, about eight feet beyond the curb. His arms and legs were still spread. His eyes were still wide and determined. The body was still there when Able Team descended to the streets, still there when Lyons confronted Dr. North.

North was seated in the rear of his limousine when Lyons approached. The tinted windows were rolled up, the doors were locked. After repeatedly rapping his knuckles on the windshield, Lyons finally had to smash the glass and literally drag the doctor out.

"You satisfied, Doctor?" Lyons asked softly.

They were standing about fifteen feet from where the Silkworm had struck. Although the dead and wounded had been removed there was still a lot of debris in the street.

"So how about it, Doc? You satisfied, or not?"

North gazed stupidly at the carnage, then suddenly bent over and vomited. The dozen or so cops watching from the sidelines either sneered or turned away.

"You have no right to harass me," North said when he had recovered. "You simply have no right."

Lyons looked at him. "Is that so? Well, let me tell you something, Doc. I've dealt with a lot of scum in my time. In fact, you might say I got something like a Ph.D. in scumology. But in a lot of ways you might be the worst I've ever seen. And you know why? Because you're subtle about it. You make it all look real respectable. You conduct your little experiments. You write your little papers. You give your little lectures and serve on your little panels. And after a while people start believing that maybe what you're doing is okay, that maybe there's some truth to what you're saying. But you can't fool me, Doc...and you can't fool those people whose blood you're standing in."

He grabbed North's arm, not particularly hard, but firmly.

"Come with me, Doc. There's something I want to show you."

Lyons pulled the doctor at a quick pace through the line of black-and-whites until they reached Falco's body. Then shoving the doctor still closer, Lyons forced him to look.

"You see that, Doc? Huh?" He pointed to Falco's head, which had virtually been split open. "You see that?" Then finally grabbing North by the collar, he said, "Now you want to study brains? Well, study that."

North was vomiting again when Lyons left him, left him on his knees in front of Falco's body. Then although North finally shouted something about his lawyer, Lyons didn't even bother looking back.

IT WAS NEARLY NIGHTFALL before the crowds began to disperse, and some semblance of order was restored. The mayor and the councillor had been taken to the nearest hospital, but the television news teams were still on hand. So were the cops, the Feds and the hard-core curiosity seekers. A secondary command post had been established in the lobby of an attorneys' complex.

The men of Able Team sat sprawled on a bench next to Florio. Dazed citizens huddled on the floor beside the plastic palms. Odors of coffee and cigarettes mingled with the stench of fear. Somewhere not far away, an attorney was talking to a wounded victim and explaining that the city was possibly liable.

"Probably time for us to be moving on," Blancanales said.

Lyons glanced at Florio. "What do you say, old buddy, have we done enough damage to your city yet?"

Florio grinned, and clapped his hand on Lyons's shoulder. "Hey, you can give me a call any time you feel like kicking ass and destroying public property, any time at all."

"Yeah, well I'll keep that in mind." Lyons smiled and rose with the others from the bench.

"And Carl?"

"Yeah?"

"Thanks."

Outside, an odd hush had descended on the streets. Lingering spectators still watched from the corner, and cops still paced the sidewalk, but for the moment at least no one had much to say.

Even Blancanales had finally grown quiet, with his eyes fixed on the pavement, his hands jammed in the pockets of his fatigues.

"I can probably get us booked on an evening flight," Lyons finally said as they crossed the empty street to their van.

"That's fine with me," Blancanales replied. "In fact the sooner the better."

"How about it, Gadgets?" Lyons asked. "You want to just get the hell out of here?"

"Sure," Gadgets breathed. But then he suddenly stopped. "I mean, no. There's something I've got to do first. Someone I've got to see."

"Look," Blancanales said, "if it's just a matter of picking up a souvenir, I'll take you to the gift shop at the—"

Gadgets turned to face them both. "Hey, there's someone I've got to see, all right?"

When they finally returned to the van, they discovered that a rear panel had been defaced with a smear of hasty graffiti. At first glance the message appeared to be meaningless, nothing more than a few angry slashes in black spray paint. Then after a moment's consideration, Lyons finally decided that the slashes formed a word: Bad.

31

Lara lay between waking and dreaming, while a television flickered silently on the other side of the room. From the corridor came sounds she had been hearing for hours: hushed voices of doctors and nurses, the squeak of their soles on the linoleum, the occasional cry of a patient in pain and the laughter of indifferent orderlies. She had also heard the pigeons on the ledge, and the call of the circling gulls.

It was half past eight in the evening when Gadgets entered her room. The silent television still carried gray images of sprawled bodies, demolished vehicles, weeping children and bloodstained pavement. But the flickering light only enhanced her beauty. Her hair was spread against the white pillowcase. Her lips were slightly parted. Her left hand was curled beneath her chin.

"Remember me?" he whispered when she opened her eyes.

She blinked with a vaguely confused expression then gave him a weak smile. "Yes, I remember you."

He placed a small vase of roses on the nightstand.

"I don't know how long they'll last," he said.

She extended a bandaged arm and very gently touched a petal.

"Don't worry," Gadgets said. "No thorns."

She smiled again, withdrew a rose and pressed it to her lips.

"They're beautiful," she whispered. "Thank you."

"Well, I just thought—" He broke off, meeting her gaze and noting the tears forming in her eyes. "Look," he finally said, "I don't know why I'm here. I guess I just wanted—"

"No, I'm glad you came." She smiled. "Really I am."

He sank to a chair beside the bed, suddenly realizing how tired he was, how incredibly burned out.

"By the way," he said. "I talked with the cops, and they're just going to let it slide as far as you're concerned. I mean, no one will be bothering you."

She nodded again, but said nothing.

"You thought about what you're going to do now?" he asked.

She shook her head, gazing at those flickering pictures again, at images of more blood on the steps of City Hall, blown windows and shattered doors.

"What about you?" she finally asked. "What are you going to do?"

He shrugged, also gazing at those images. "I don't know. I guess just keep moving on."

"You mean out of the city?"

He nodded. "Yeah. Out of the city."

She hesitated, watching the images switch from the reality of downtown Los Angeles to the unreality of some situation comedy apartment.

Then she said, "You don't think that maybe I could..." She gave a small sigh, and shook her head. "No, I guess not."

"I don't have the kind of life I can share with anyone, Lara."

She nodded with more tears in her eyes. "I know."

Then for another long moment they simply sat in the flickering light and silence, her hand extending from the bed to meet his.

"You know, I dreamed about you," she finally said softly. "When they were operating on me, I dreamed about you."

"Yeah? What was I doing?"

"You were after him. You know, Falco. You were climbing up the side of this building, and you were after him."

He nodded, watching her profile, her eyes fixed on the blank wall beside the television.

"For a while I was kind of worried about you. I thought maybe you were going to fall, or maybe he was going to get you first. So I was trying to help you. I was trying to hurt him, so he wouldn't be able to get you. Then he and I kind of fought for a little while, but I can't remember the rest."

She sighed again, then turned and smiled. "Some dream, huh?"

"Yeah. Some dream."

"SO HOW IS SHE?" Lyons asked.

Gadgets shrugged again. "She'll be all right."

"And what about you?"

"What *about* me?"

Lyons laid a hand on Gadgets's shoulder. "Well, how are you feeling?"

Gadgets took a deep breath, and gazed out across the darkening hospital grounds. "Old," he said. "Old and tired. Now, do we have a plane to catch, or what?"

It was a cool night, with winds that carried the scent of the sea. Although the streets were filled with strolling crowds, it was somehow strangely quiet. Even along the worst streets, even within those valleys of tenements . . . all quiet.

"Kind of feels like the first Sunday after the war," Blancanales said from the rear of the van.

His eyes were fixed on passing crowds along Alvarado Street, on the children lingering in a shabby arcade, on elderly women leaning from windows and shouting from the balconies.

"Kind of feels like maybe something's really changed around here," Blancanales added.

"I wouldn't count on it," Lyons said, as he gazed out to a particularly wasted stretch of Tenth Street, where members of a gang called the Dead Boys had already painted their names over the black Desmodo signatures.

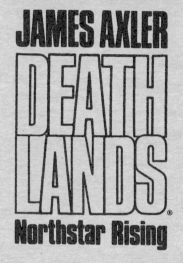

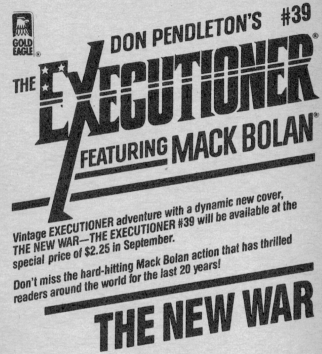